BLACK SANDS

THE SEVEN KINGDOMS

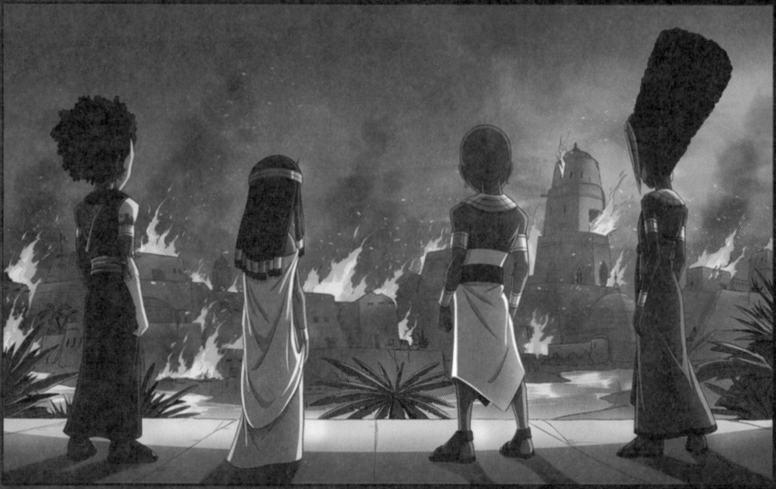

Written by Manuel Godoy and drawn by David Lenormand, Black Sands is a story about a young boy named Ausar whose life goal is to rule Kemet. This goal leads him on a journey to far off lands in the ancient world where he deals with the complicated issues involving wars and ancient gods that seek his death. He is accompanied by his kinfolk Seth, Auset, and Nehbet as they travel the world.

The world of Black Sands is deep and the original cultures of the time are all represented in this sci-fi, fantasy retelling of ancient myths.

ISBN 13: 9780999473481

Table of Content

1 - Issue 1

22 - The City of Kerma

23 - Ausar, The Bringer of Order

24 - The Queens of the North and the South

25 - Diplomacy Between Kingdoms

26 - Apedemak, the Protector of Kush

27 - Issue 2

53 - The War Between Gods and Men

54 - The Kushite Empire

55 - The Kingdom of Sumer

56 - The Dark Pharaoh

57 - The Anunnaki

58 - Issue 3

91 - The Island of Minoa

92 - Titans

93 - Memphis

94 - Spartan Society

95 - Tehuti

96 - Dedication

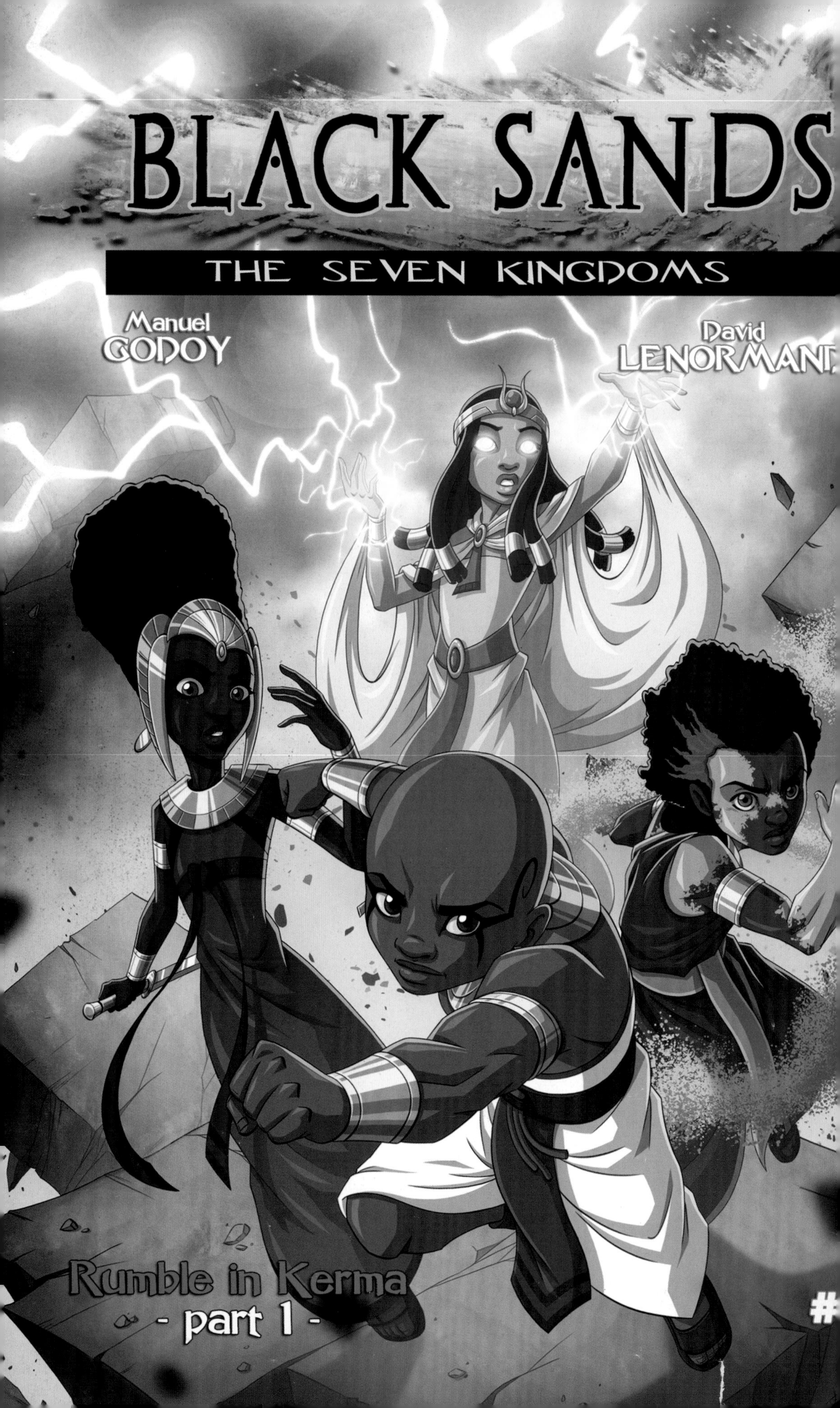
BLACK SANDS
THE SEVEN KINGDOMS
Manuel GODOY
David LENORMANT
Rumble in Kerma
- part 1 -
#

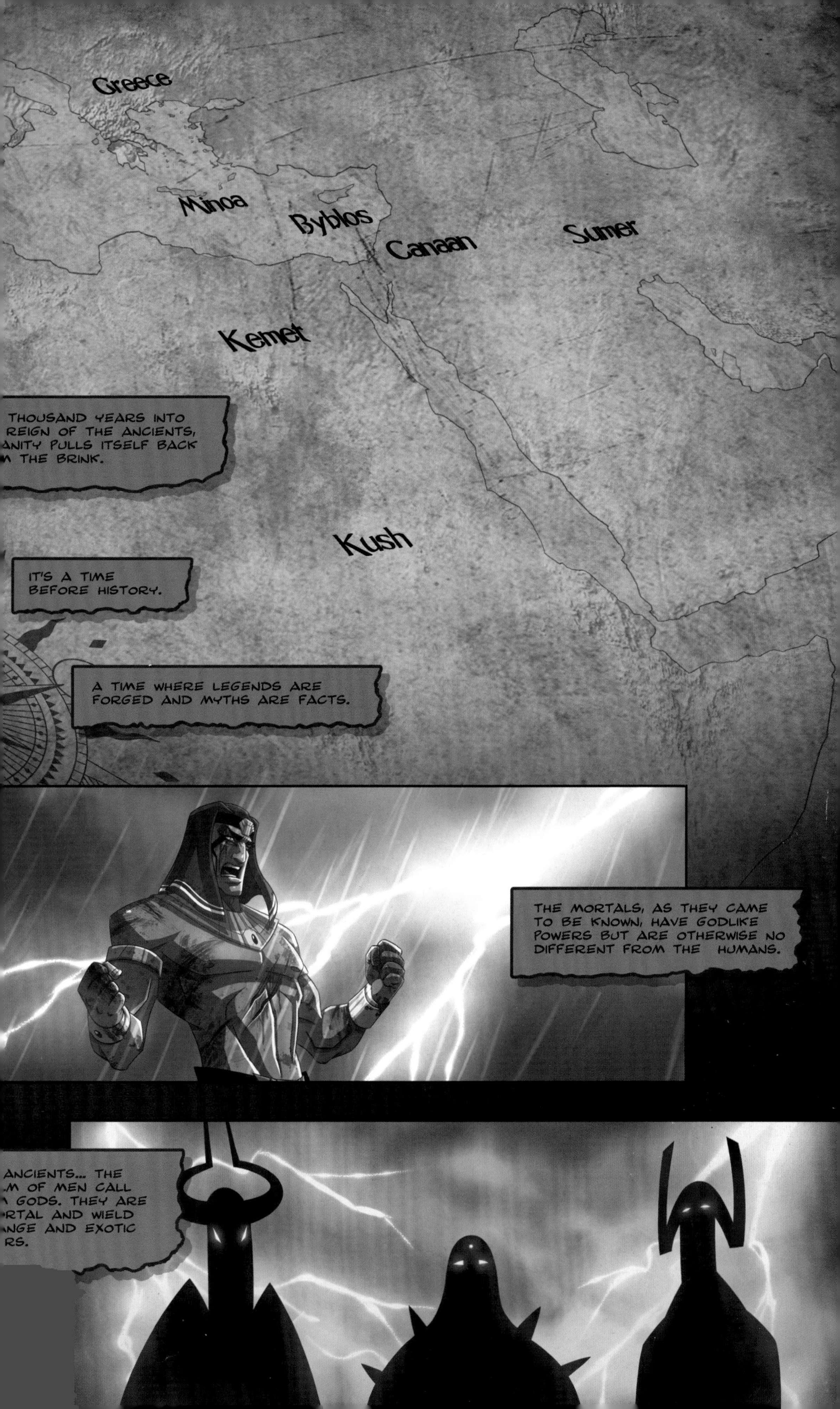
Greece
Minoa
Byblos
Canaan
Sumer
Kemet
Kush
THOUSAND YEARS INTO REIGN OF THE ANCIENTS, ANITY PULLS ITSELF BACK M THE BRINK.
IT'S A TIME BEFORE HISTORY.
A TIME WHERE LEGENDS ARE FORGED AND MYTHS ARE FACTS.
THE MORTALS, AS THEY CAME TO BE KNOWN, HAVE GODLIKE POWERS BUT ARE OTHERWISE NO DIFFERENT FROM THE HUMANS.
ANCIENTS... THE M OF MEN CALL GODS. THEY ARE RTAL AND WIELD NGE AND EXOTIC RS.

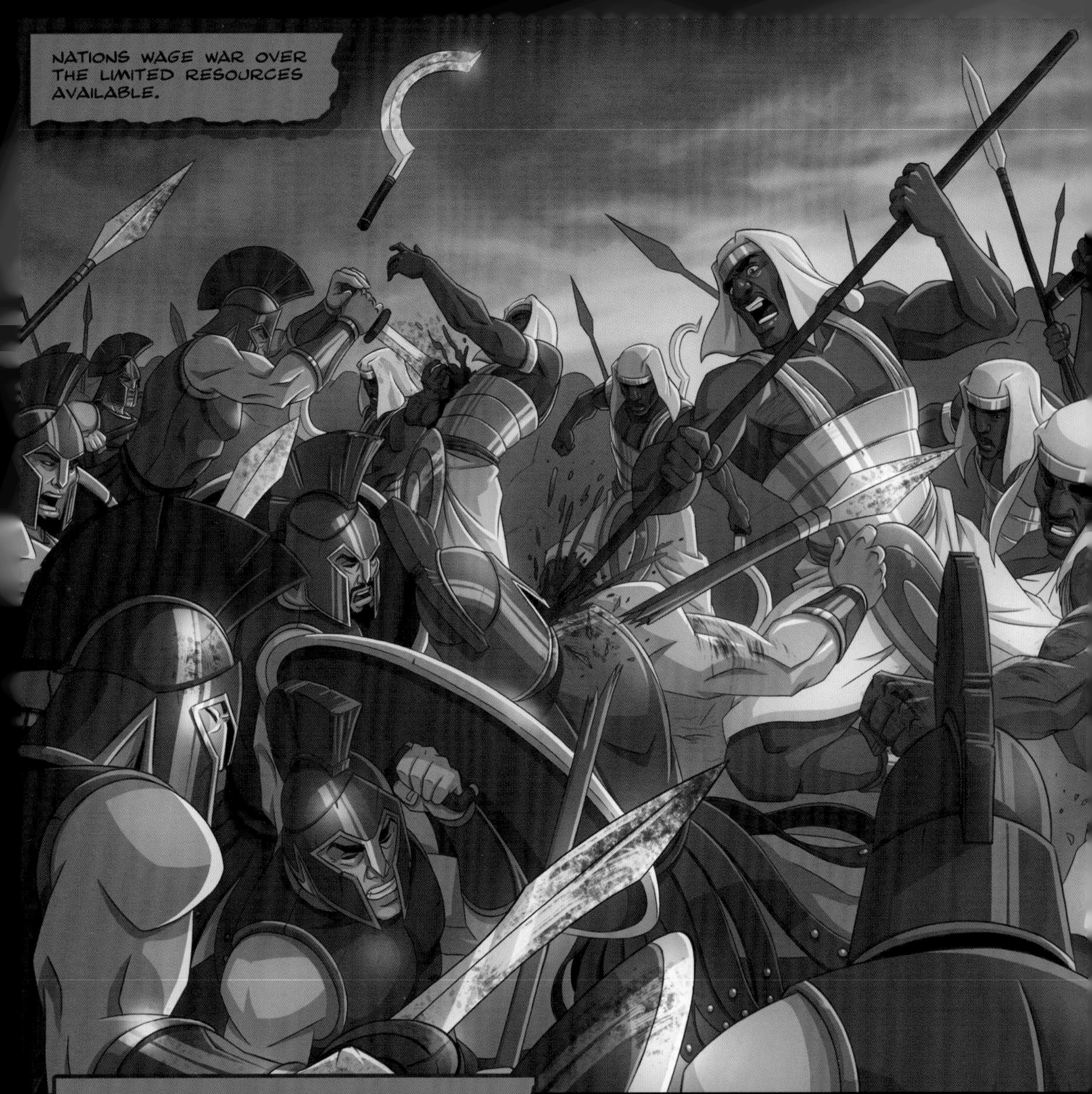
NATIONS WAGE WAR OVER THE LIMITED RESOURCES AVAILABLE.
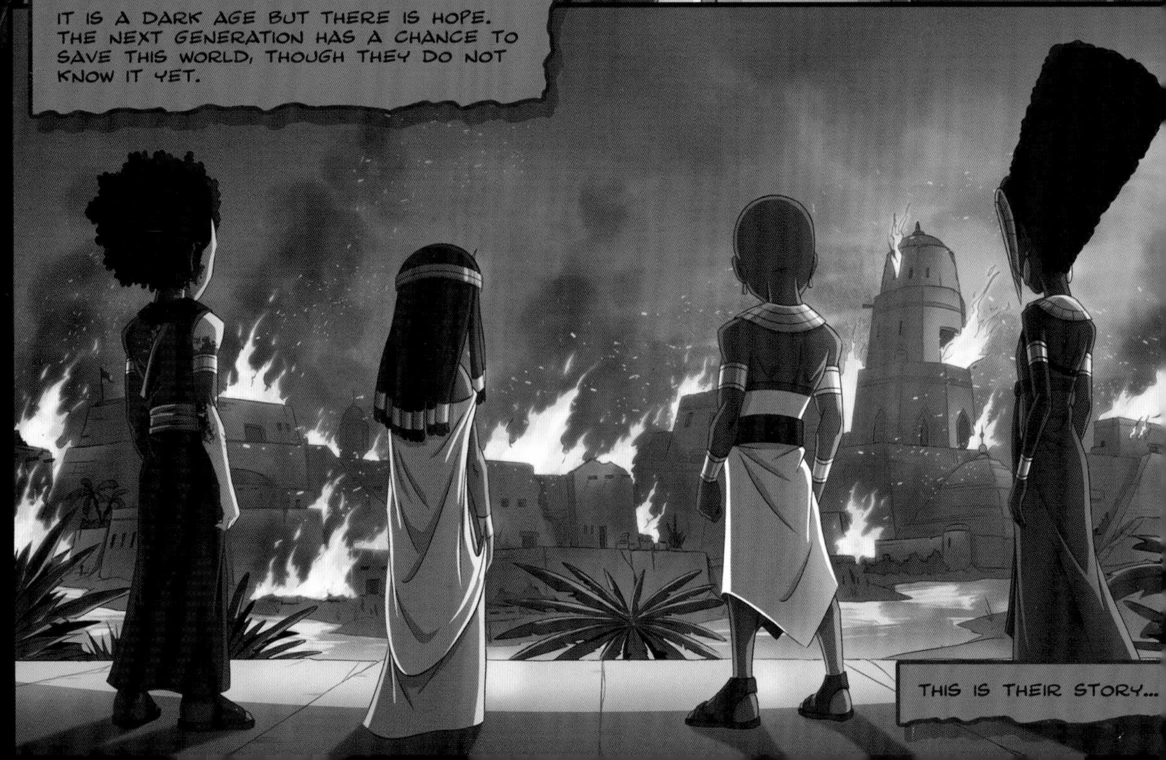
IT IS A DARK AGE BUT THERE IS HOPE. THE NEXT GENERATION HAS A CHANCE TO SAVE THIS WORLD, THOUGH THEY DO NOT KNOW IT YET.
THIS IS THEIR STORY...

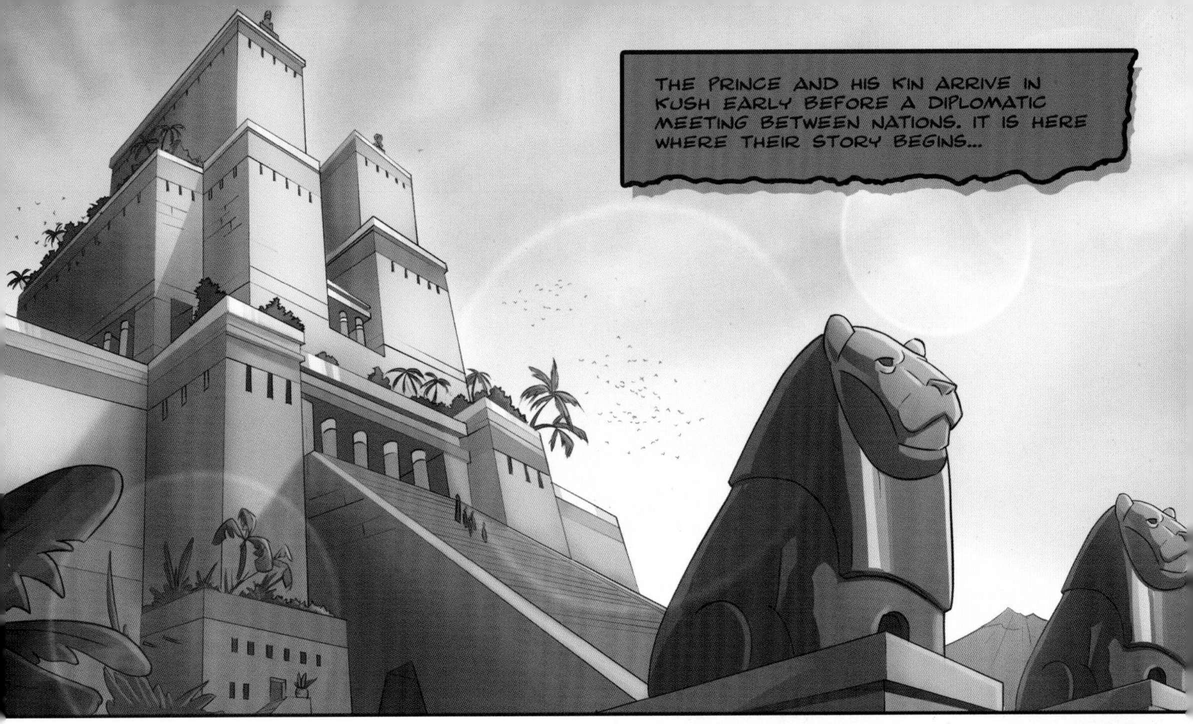
THE PRINCE AND HIS KIN ARRIVE IN KUSH EARLY BEFORE A DIPLOMATIC MEETING BETWEEN NATIONS. IT IS HERE WHERE THEIR STORY BEGINS...

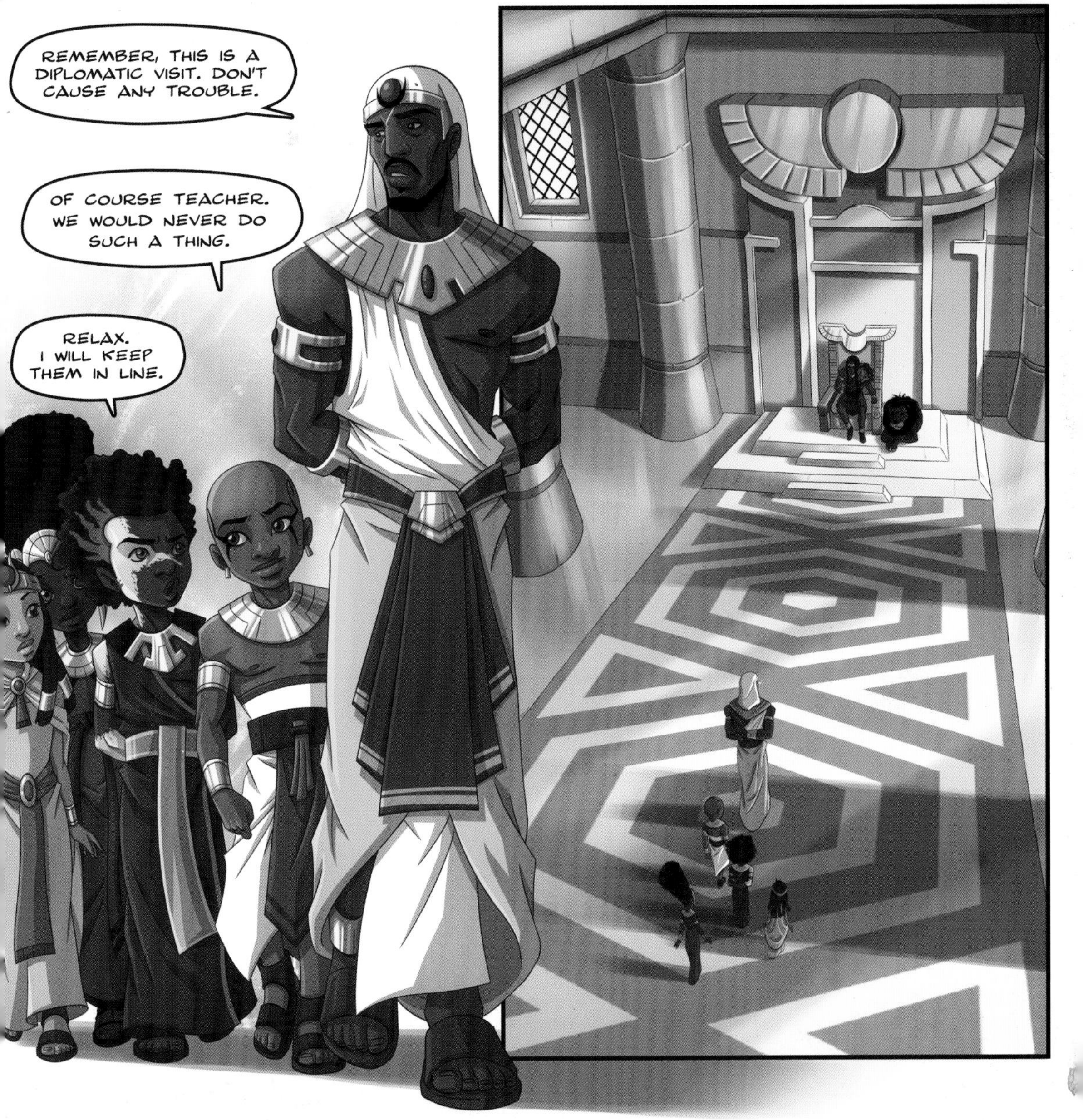
REMEMBER, THIS IS A DIPLOMATIC VISIT. DON'T CAUSE ANY TROUBLE.
OF COURSE TEACHER. WE WOULD NEVER DO SUCH A THING.
RELAX. I WILL KEEP THEM IN LINE.

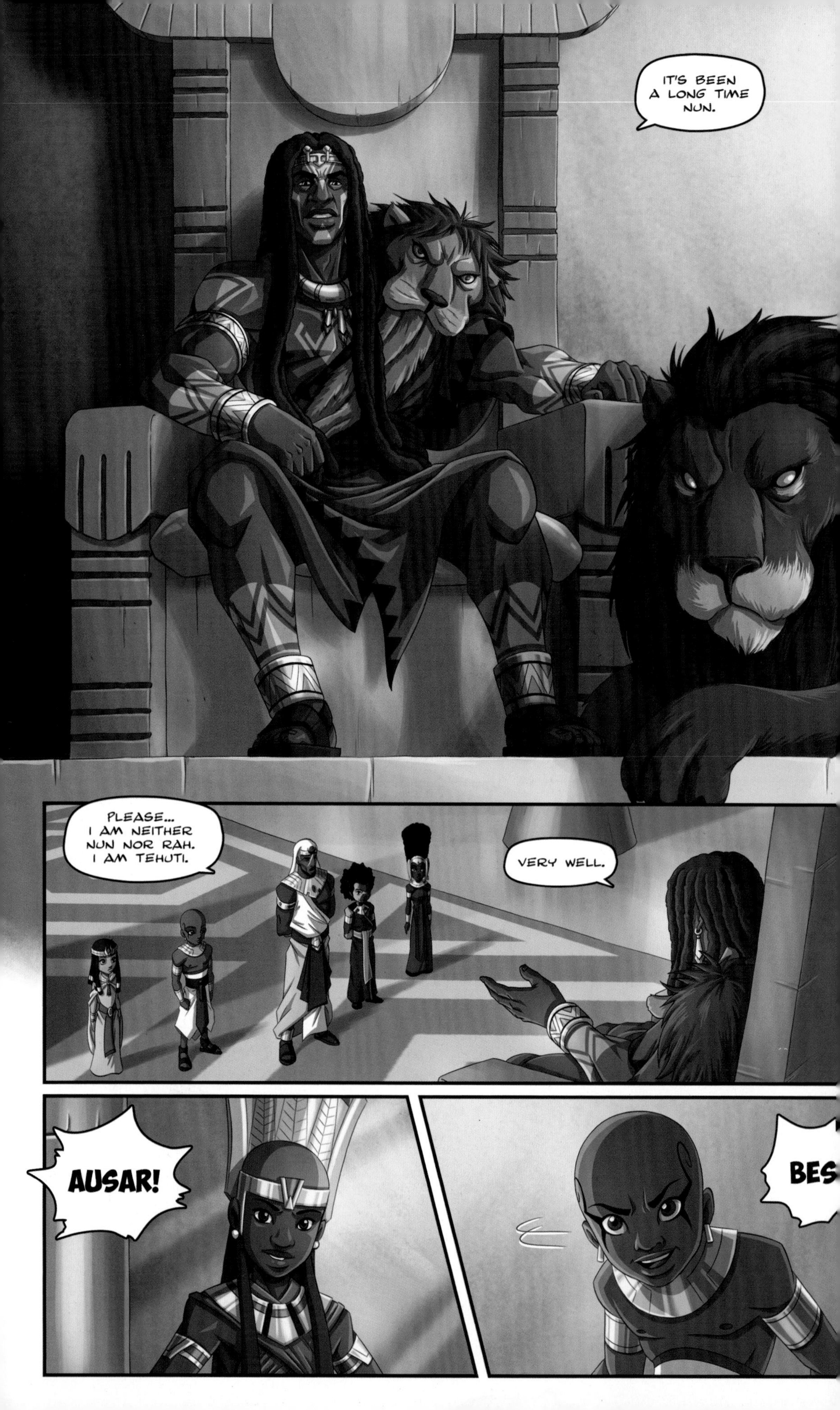
IT'S BEEN A LONG TIME NUN.
PLEASE... I AM NEITHER NUN NOR RAH. I AM TEHUTI.
VERY WELL.
AUSAR!
BES

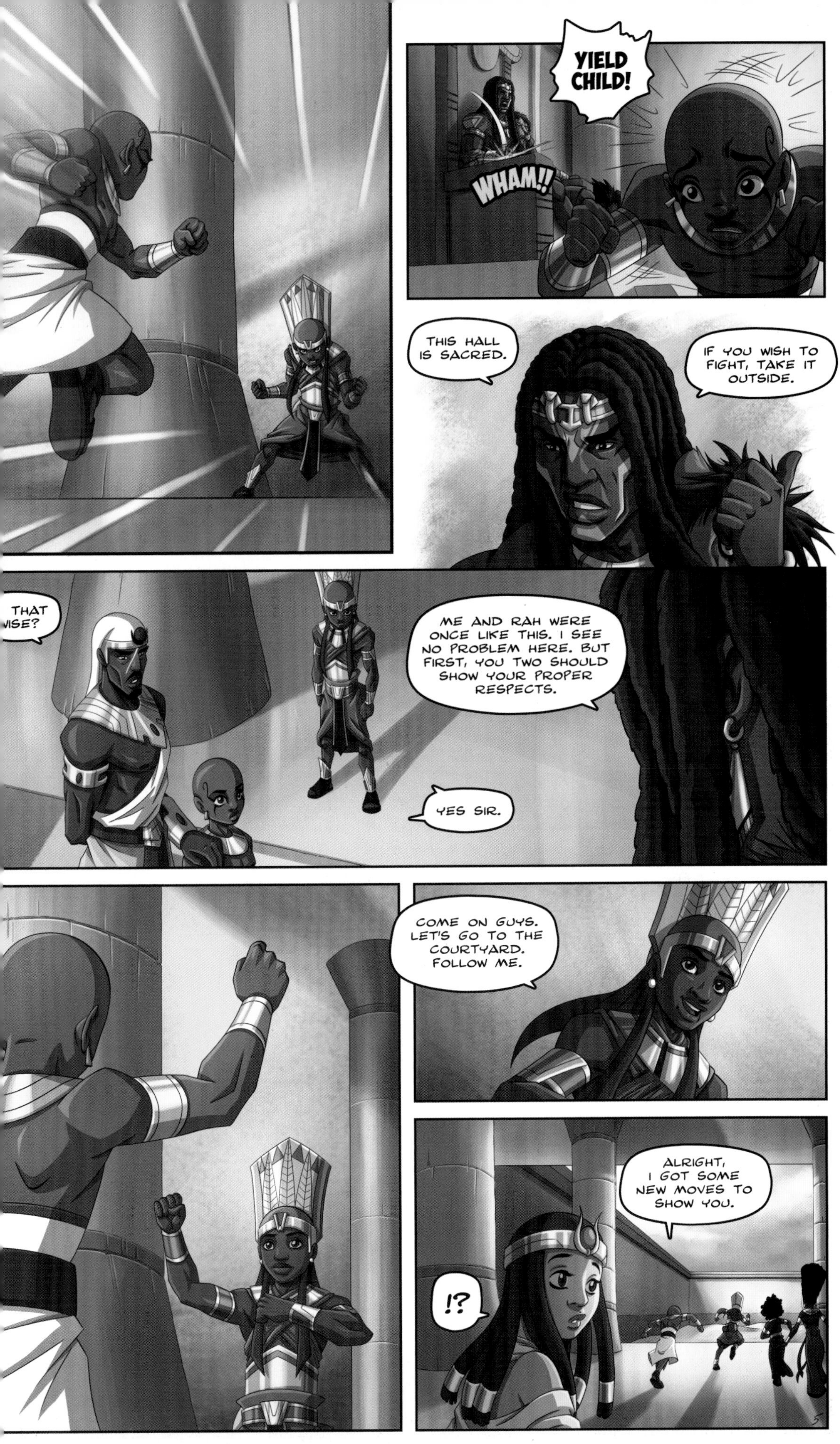
YIELD CHILD!
WHAM!!
THIS HALL IS SACRED.
IF YOU WISH TO FIGHT, TAKE IT OUTSIDE.
THAT
ME AND RAH WERE ONCE LIKE THIS. I SEE NO PROBLEM HERE. BUT FIRST, YOU TWO SHOULD SHOW YOUR PROPER RESPECTS.
YES SIR.
COME ON GUYS. LET'S GO TO THE COURTYARD. FOLLOW ME.
ALRIGHT, I GOT SOME NEW MOVES TO SHOW YOU.
!?

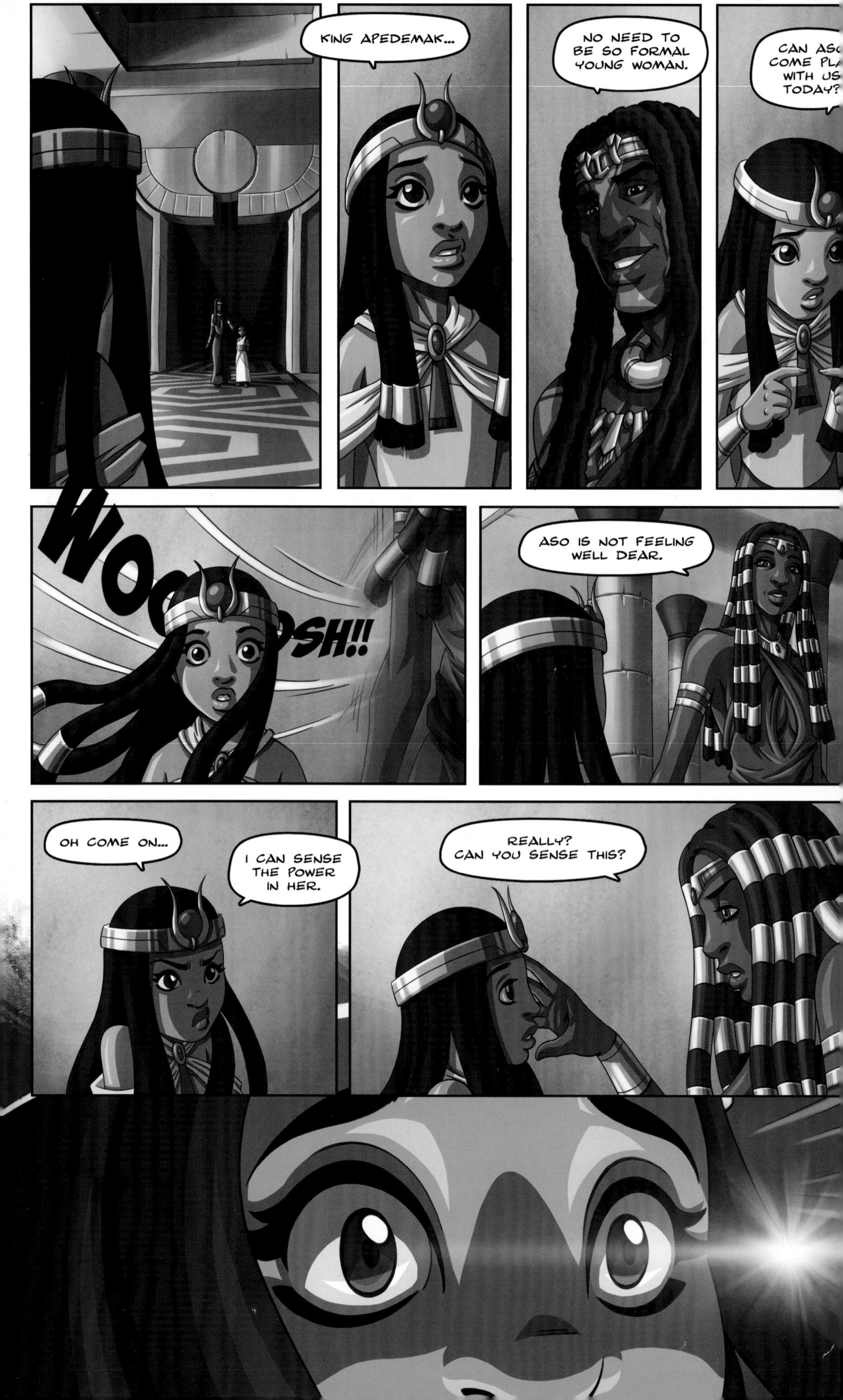

KING APEDEMAK...
NO NEED TO BE SO FORMAL YOUNG WOMAN.
CAN ASO COME PLAY WITH US TODAY?
WOOOSH!!
ASO IS NOT FEELING WELL DEAR.
OH COME ON...
I CAN SENSE THE POWER IN HER.
REALLY? CAN YOU SENSE THIS?

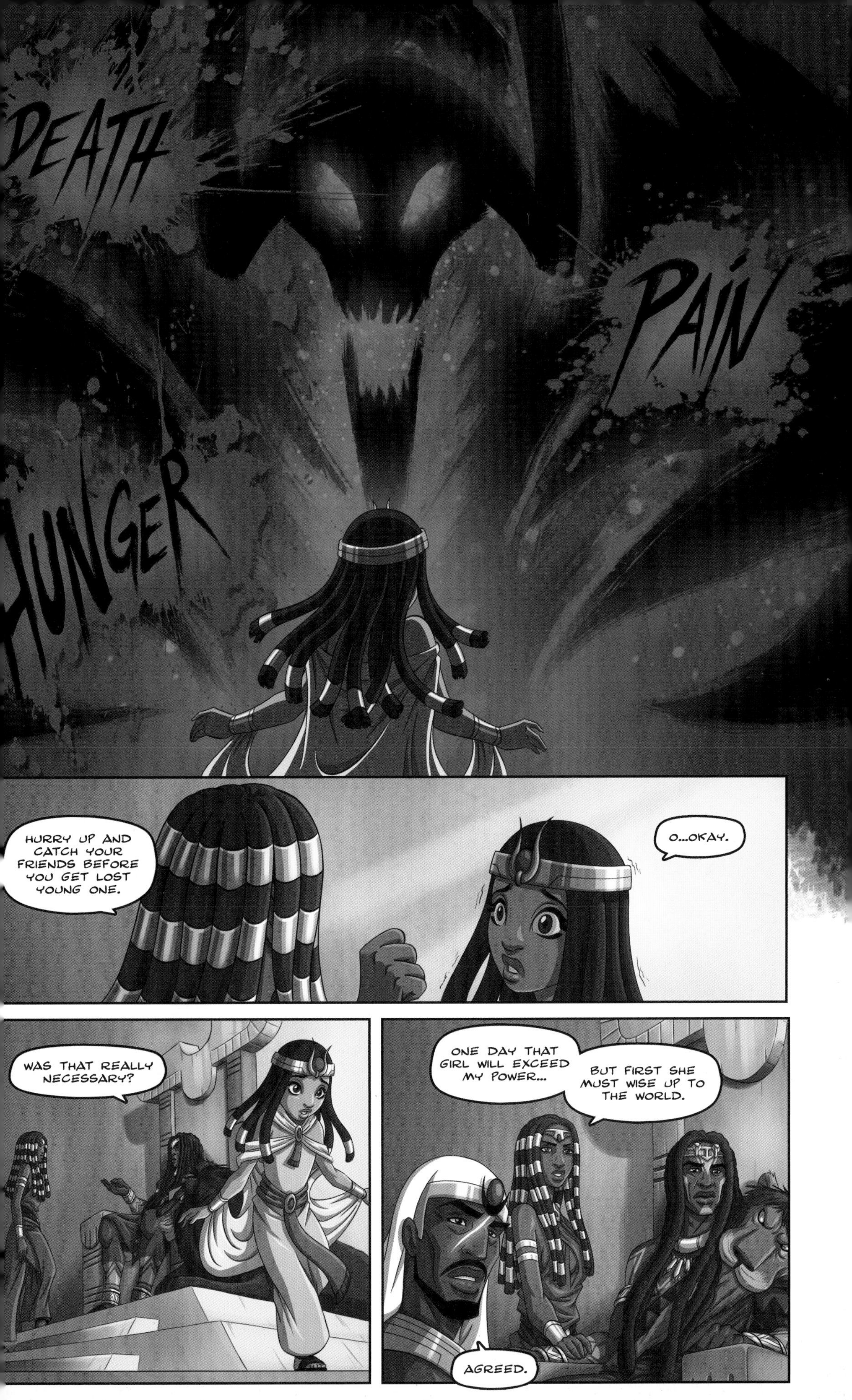
DEATH
PAIN
HUNGER
HURRY UP AND CATCH YOUR FRIENDS BEFORE YOU GET LOST YOUNG ONE.
O...OKAY.
WAS THAT REALLY NECESSARY?
ONE DAY THAT GIRL WILL EXCEED MY POWER...
BUT FIRST SHE MUST WISE UP TO THE WORLD.
AGREED.

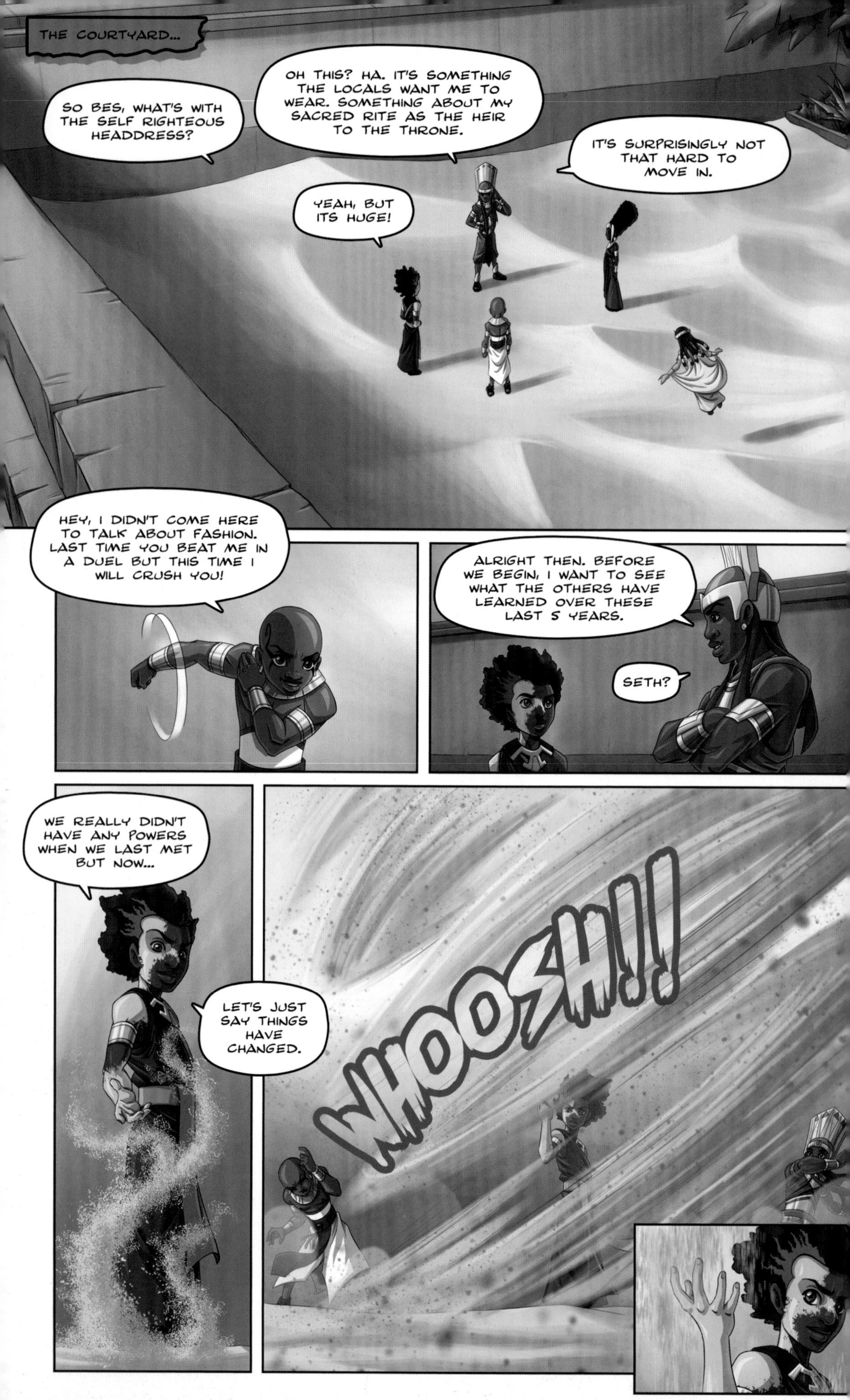
THE COURTYARD...
SO BES, WHAT'S WITH THE SELF RIGHTEOUS HEADDRESS?
OH THIS? HA. IT'S SOMETHING THE LOCALS WANT ME TO WEAR. SOMETHING ABOUT MY SACRED RITE AS THE HEIR TO THE THRONE.
IT'S SURPRISINGLY NOT THAT HARD TO MOVE IN.
YEAH, BUT ITS HUGE!
HEY, I DIDN'T COME HERE TO TALK ABOUT FASHION. LAST TIME YOU BEAT ME IN A DUEL BUT THIS TIME I WILL CRUSH YOU!
ALRIGHT THEN. BEFORE WE BEGIN, I WANT TO SEE WHAT THE OTHERS HAVE LEARNED OVER THESE LAST 5 YEARS.
SETH?
WE REALLY DIDN'T HAVE ANY POWERS WHEN WE LAST MET BUT NOW...
LET'S JUST SAY THINGS HAVE CHANGED.
WHOOSH!!

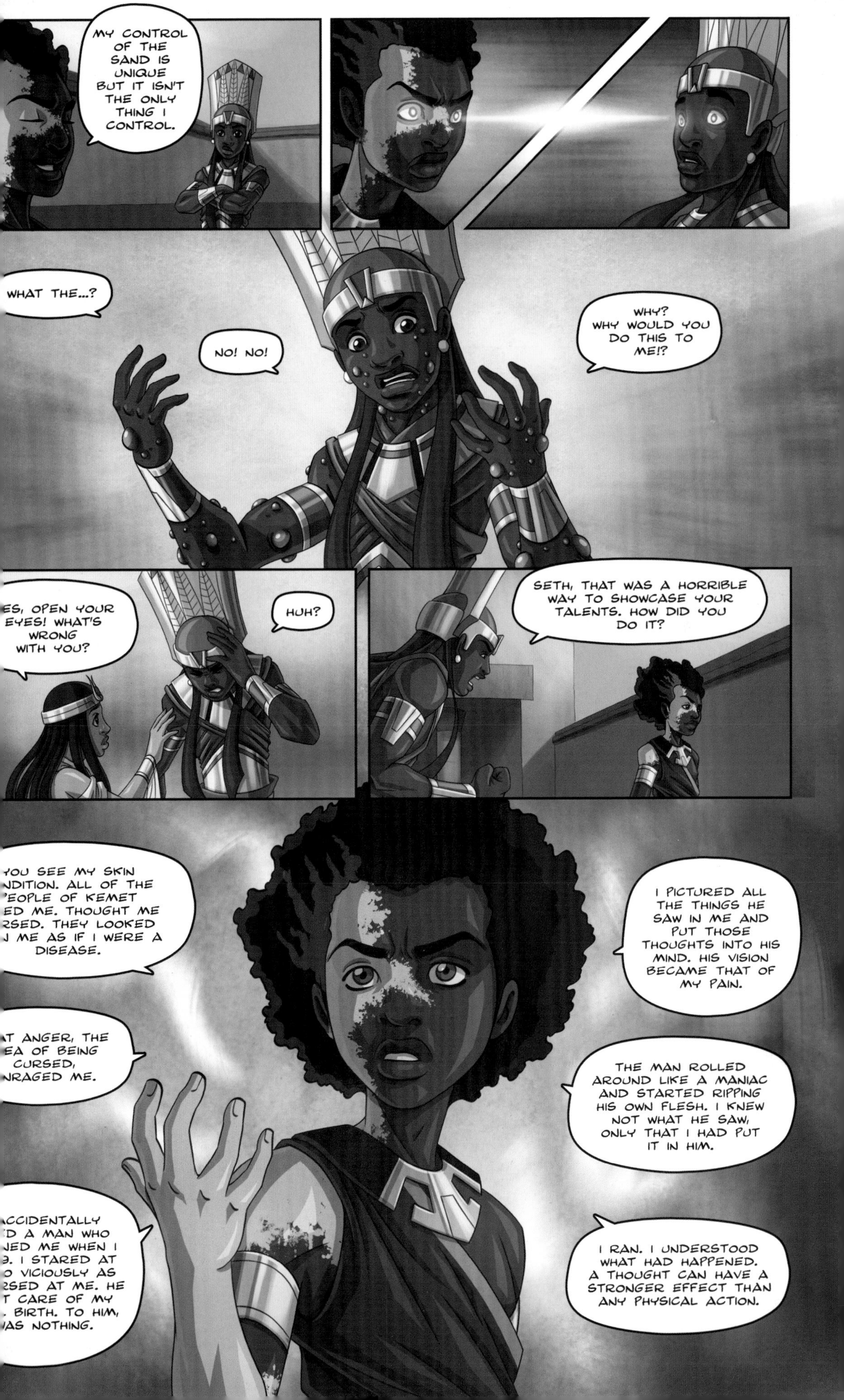
MY CONTROL OF THE SAND IS UNIQUE BUT IT ISN'T THE ONLY THING I CONTROL.
WHAT THE...?
NO! NO!
WHY? WHY WOULD YOU DO THIS TO ME!?
ES, OPEN YOUR EYES! WHAT'S WRONG WITH YOU?
HUH?
SETH, THAT WAS A HORRIBLE WAY TO SHOWCASE YOUR TALENTS. HOW DID YOU DO IT?
YOU SEE MY SKIN NDITION. ALL OF THE PEOPLE OF KEMET ED ME. THOUGHT ME RSED. THEY LOOKED N ME AS IF I WERE A DISEASE.
AT ANGER, THE EA OF BEING CURSED, NRAGED ME.
ACCIDENTALLY D A MAN WHO NED ME WHEN I 9. I STARED AT O VICIOUSLY AS RSED AT ME. HE T CARE OF MY BIRTH. TO HIM, AS NOTHING.
I PICTURED ALL THE THINGS HE SAW IN ME AND PUT THOSE THOUGHTS INTO HIS MIND. HIS VISION BECAME THAT OF MY PAIN.
THE MAN ROLLED AROUND LIKE A MANIAC AND STARTED RIPPING HIS OWN FLESH. I KNEW NOT WHAT HE SAW, ONLY THAT I HAD PUT IT IN HIM.
I RAN. I UNDERSTOOD WHAT HAD HAPPENED. A THOUGHT CAN HAVE A STRONGER EFFECT THAN ANY PHYSICAL ACTION.

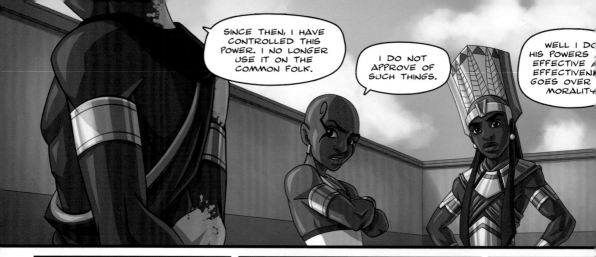

SINCE THEN, I HAVE CONTROLLED THIS POWER. I NO LONGER USE IT ON THE COMMON FOLK.

I DO NOT APPROVE OF SUCH THINGS.

WELL I DO HIS POWERS EFFECTIVE A EFFECTIVEN GOES OVER MORALITY

REALLY? NEHBET, YOU TH...

?!

WAIT, WHERE DID SHE GO?

I KNOW I JUST HEARD HER.

HEY AUSET, WHERE IS SHE?

I AM RIGHT HERE...

NEHBE

MY SPECIALTY IS DECEPTION. I SWITCHED WITH AUSET WHILE YOU WERE LISTENING TO SETH.

THERE ARE MANY WAYS MY SKILLSET HELPS ME DECEIVE BUT FOR NOW, THIS IS WHAT I AM SHOWING.

HAHA! THAT IS WHY YOU ARE MY FAVORITE WOMAN IN THE WHOLE WORLD!

OKAY IT'S MY TURN!

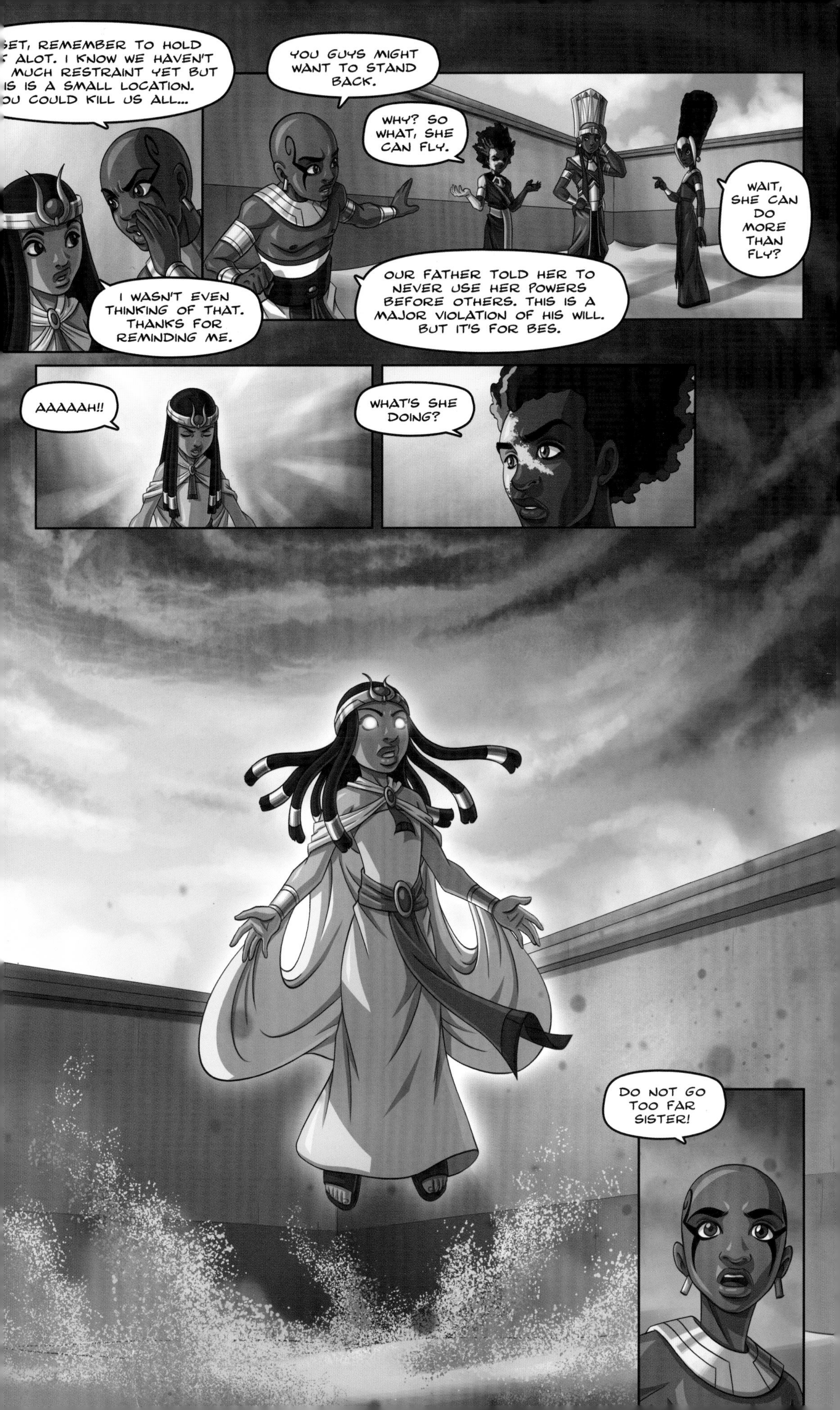

ET, REMEMBER TO HOLD ALOT. I KNOW WE HAVEN'T MUCH RESTRAINT YET BUT IS IS A SMALL LOCATION. OU COULD KILL US ALL...
I WASN'T EVEN THINKING OF THAT. THANKS FOR REMINDING ME.
YOU GUYS MIGHT WANT TO STAND BACK.
WHY? SO WHAT, SHE CAN FLY.
WAIT, SHE CAN DO MORE THAN FLY?
OUR FATHER TOLD HER TO NEVER USE HER POWERS BEFORE OTHERS. THIS IS A MAJOR VIOLATION OF HIS WILL. BUT IT'S FOR BES.
AAAAAH!!
WHAT'S SHE DOING?
DO NOT GO TOO FAR SISTER!

I CAN MANIPULATE NATURE...

CRACK!!

WOOSH!!

THAT'S WILD SIS.

SHOW T
BOYS
REALLY
THE S

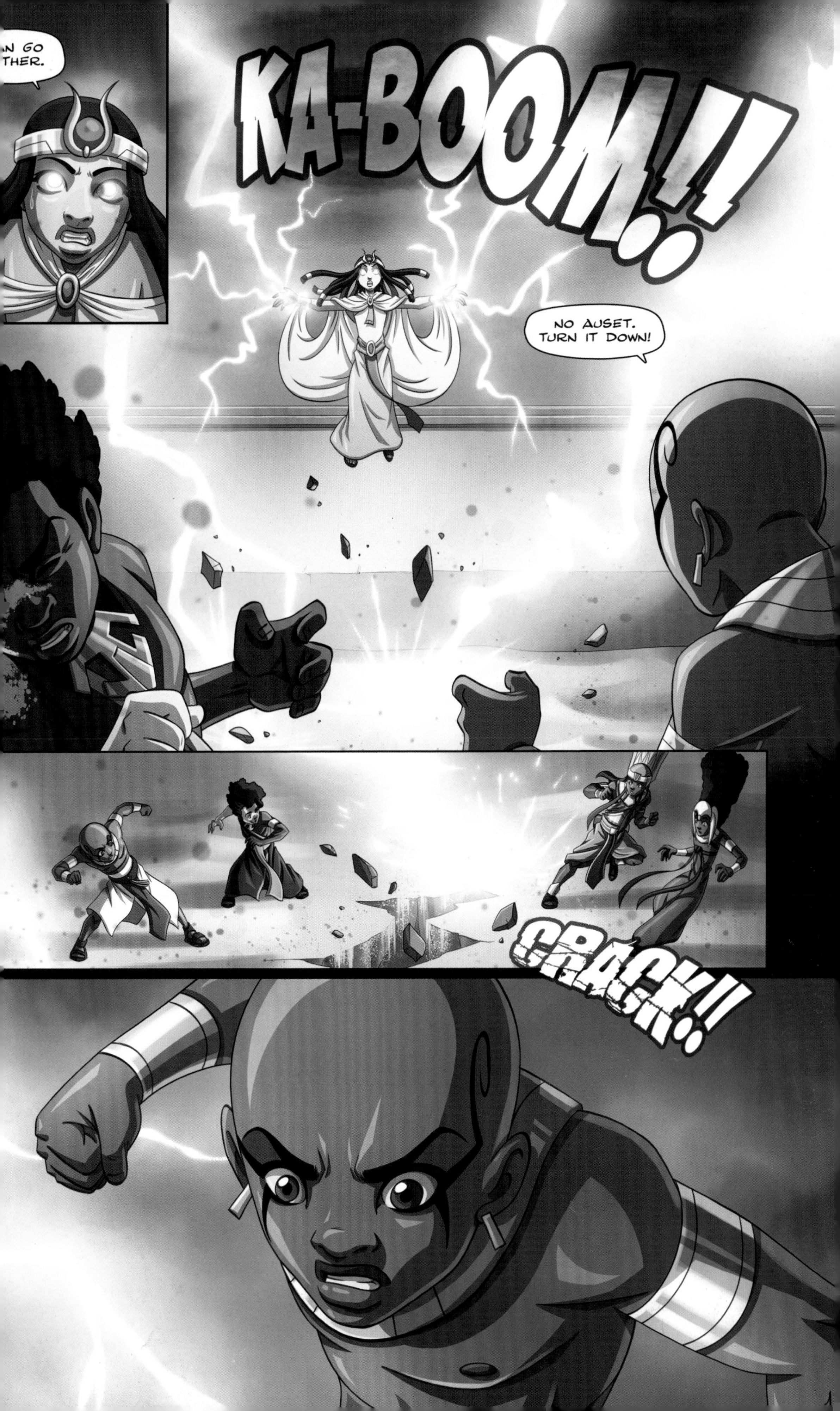

AN GO
THER.
KA-BOOM!!
NO AUSET. TURN IT DOWN!
CRACK!!

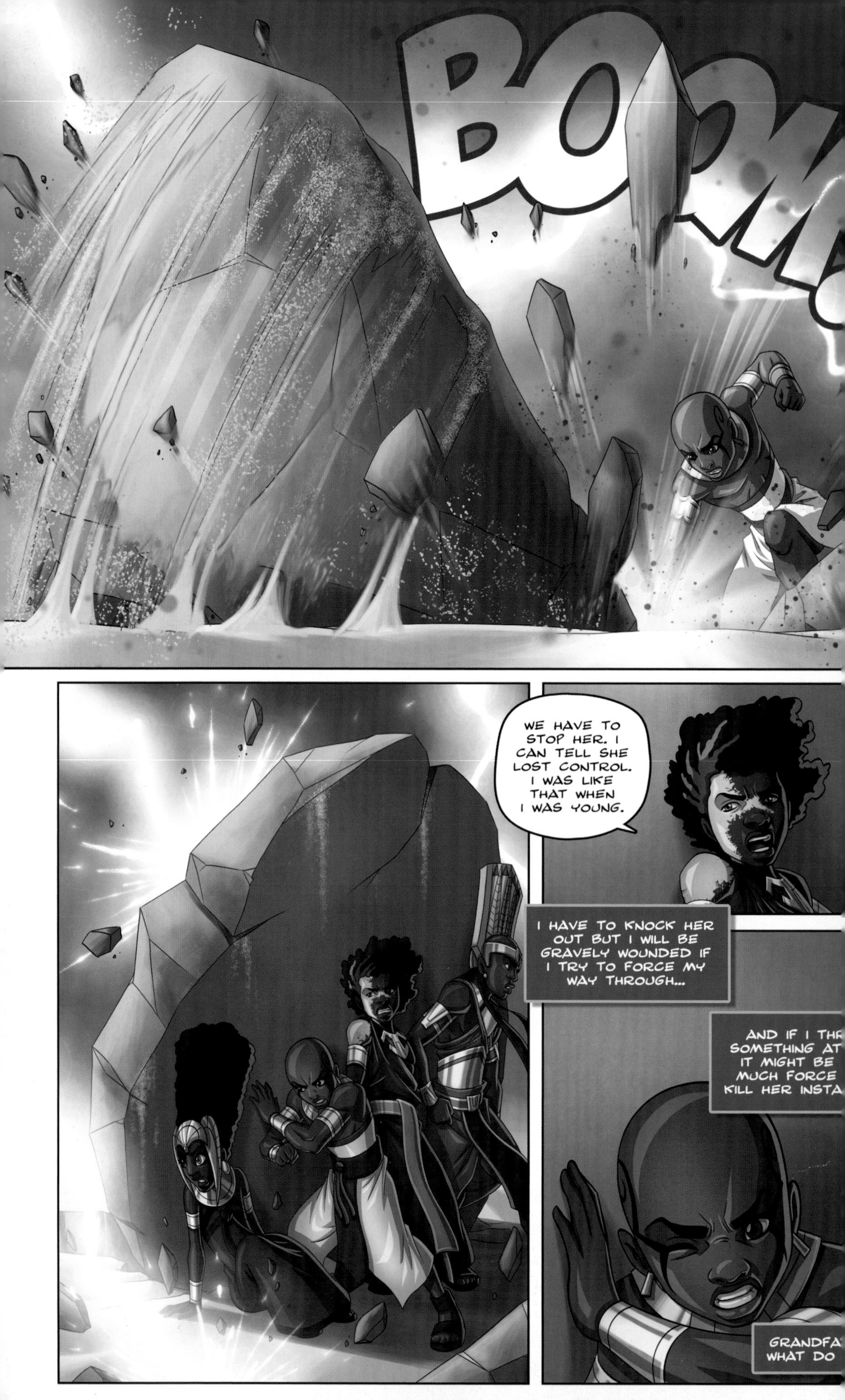
BOOM
WE HAVE TO STOP HER. I CAN TELL SHE LOST CONTROL. I WAS LIKE THAT WHEN I WAS YOUNG.
I HAVE TO KNOCK HER OUT BUT I WILL BE GRAVELY WOUNDED IF I TRY TO FORCE MY WAY THROUGH...
AND IF I THR SOMETHING AT IT MIGHT BE MUCH FORCE KILL HER INSTA
GRANDFA WHAT DO

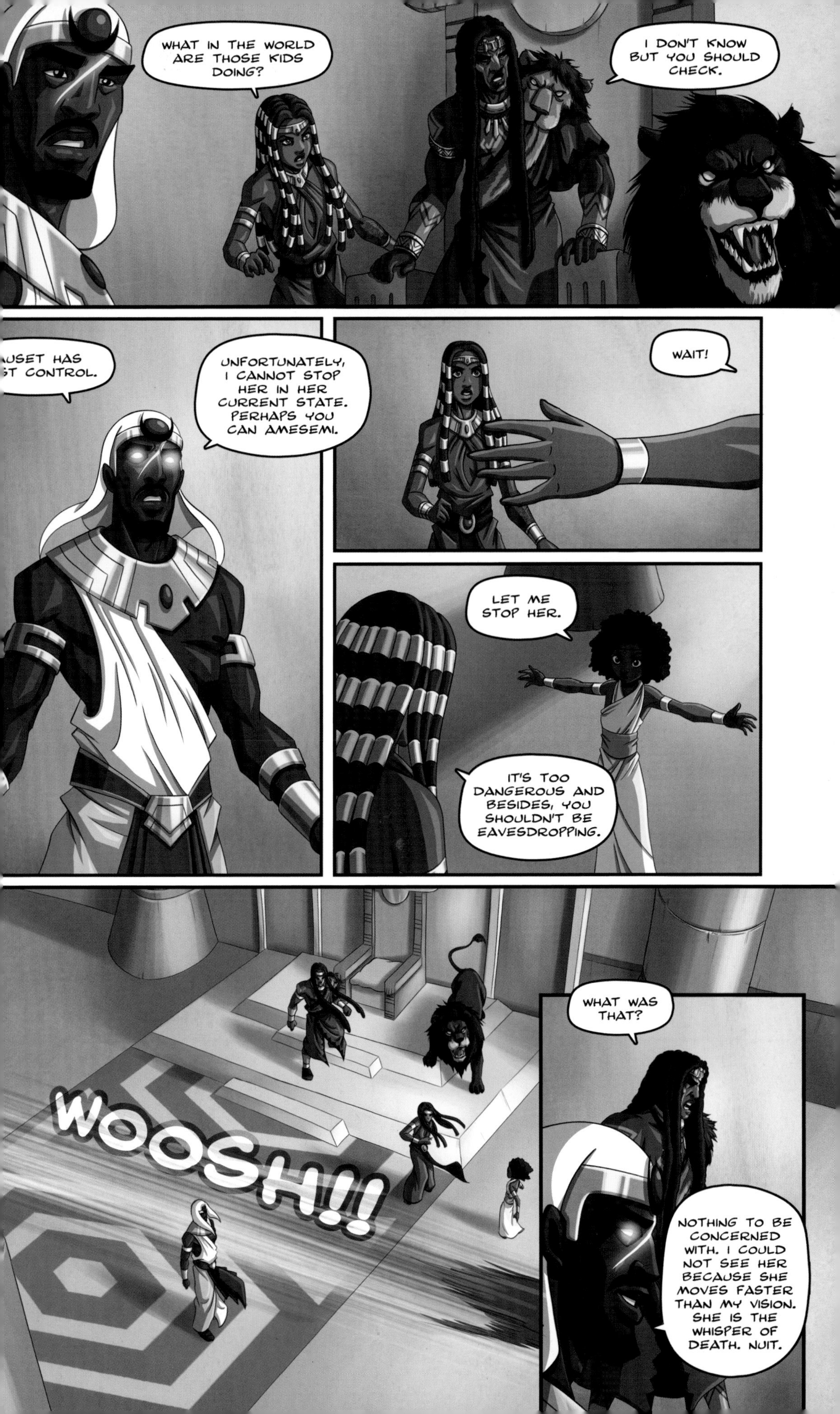
WHAT IN THE WORLD ARE THOSE KIDS DOING?
I DON'T KNOW BUT YOU SHOULD CHECK.
USET HAS ST CONTROL.
UNFORTUNATELY, I CANNOT STOP HER IN HER CURRENT STATE. PERHAPS YOU CAN AMESEMI.
WAIT!
LET ME STOP HER.
IT'S TOO DANGEROUS AND BESIDES, YOU SHOULDN'T BE EAVESDROPPING.
WOOSH!!
WHAT WAS THAT?
NOTHING TO BE CONCERNED WITH. I COULD NOT SEE HER BECAUSE SHE MOVES FASTER THAN MY VISION. SHE IS THE WHISPER OF DEATH. NUIT.

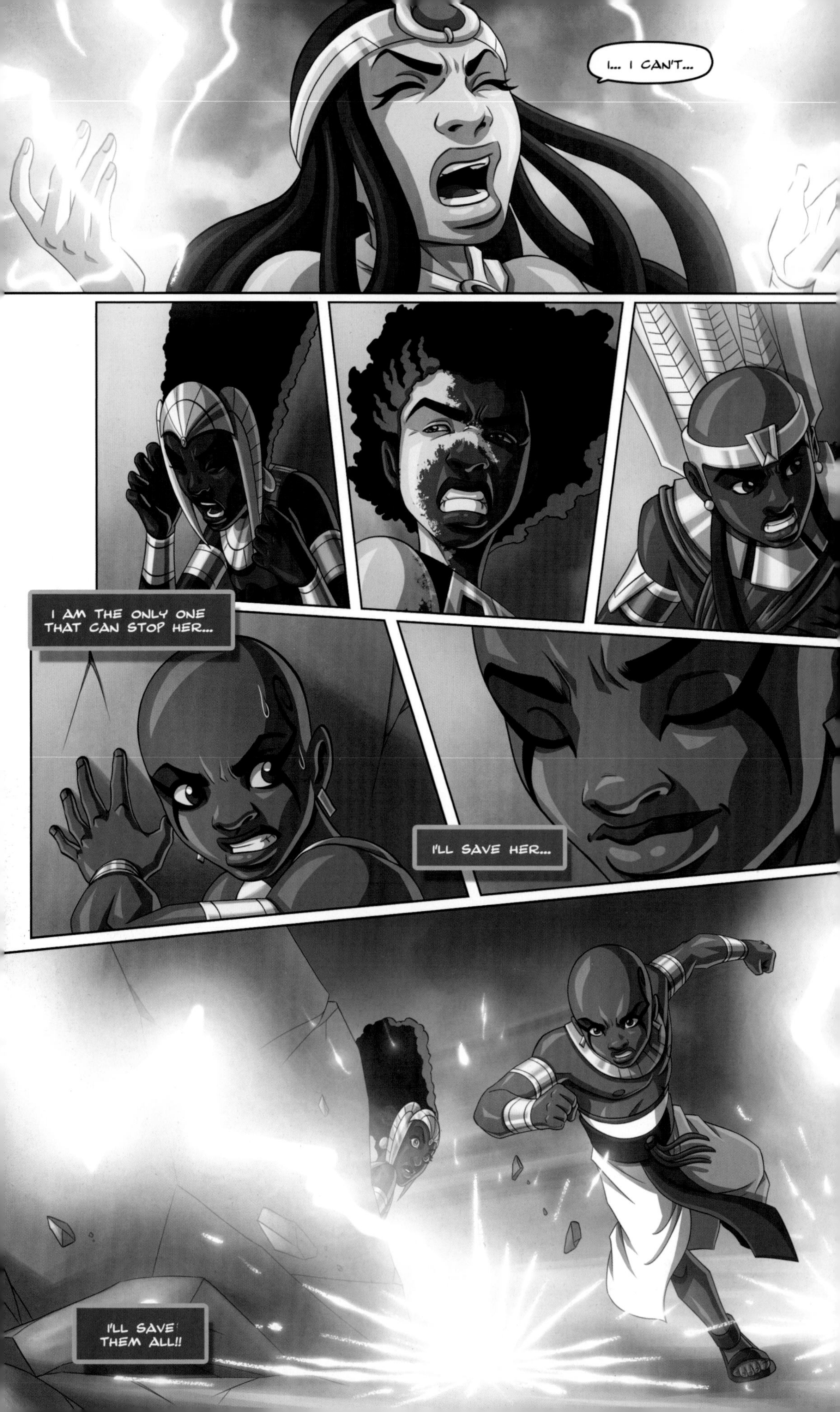
I... I CAN'T...
I AM THE ONLY ONE THAT CAN STOP HER...
I'LL SAVE HER...
I'LL SAVE THEM ALL!!

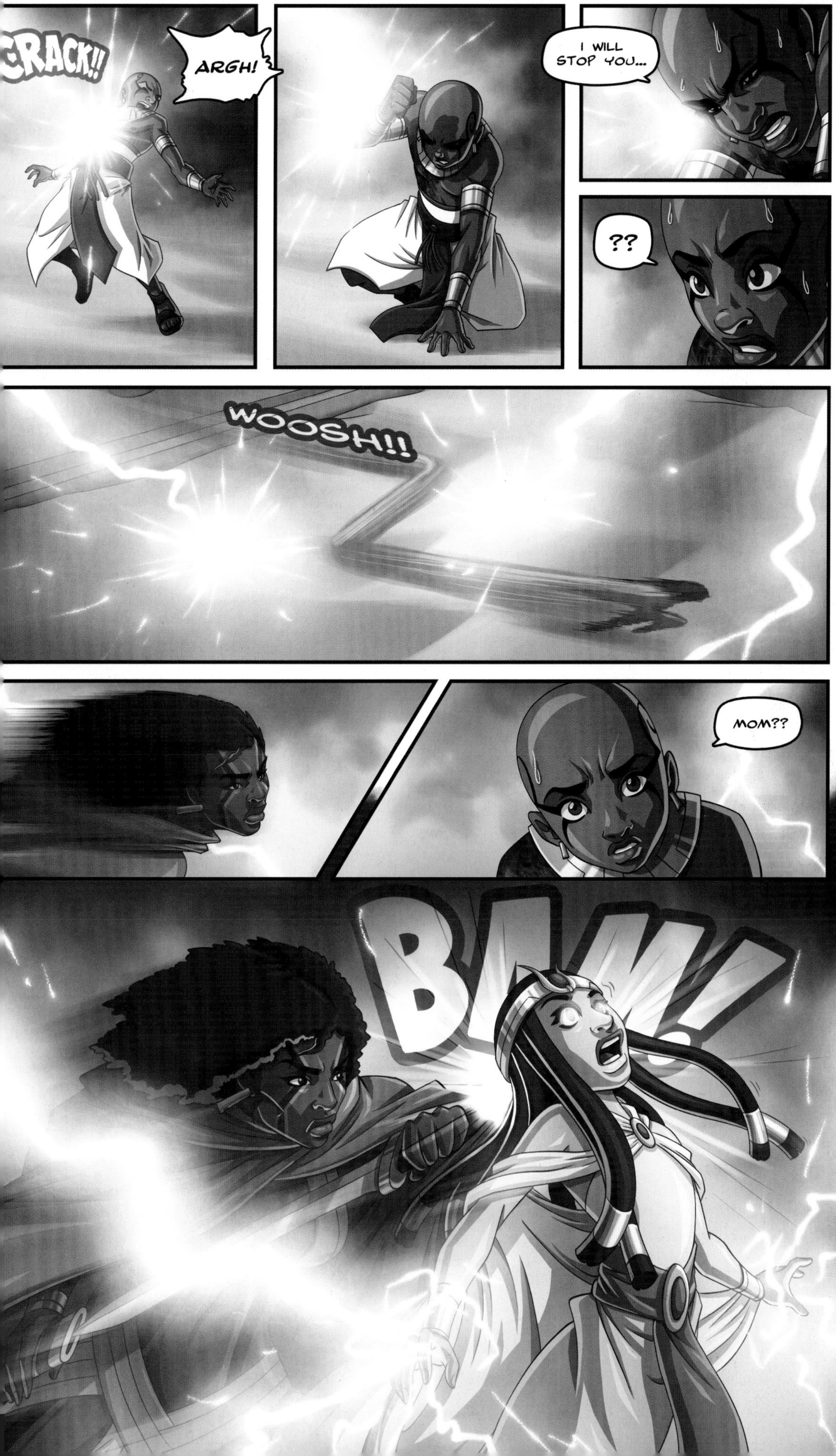
CRACK!!
ARGH!
I WILL STOP YOU...
??
WOOSH!!
MOM??
BAM!

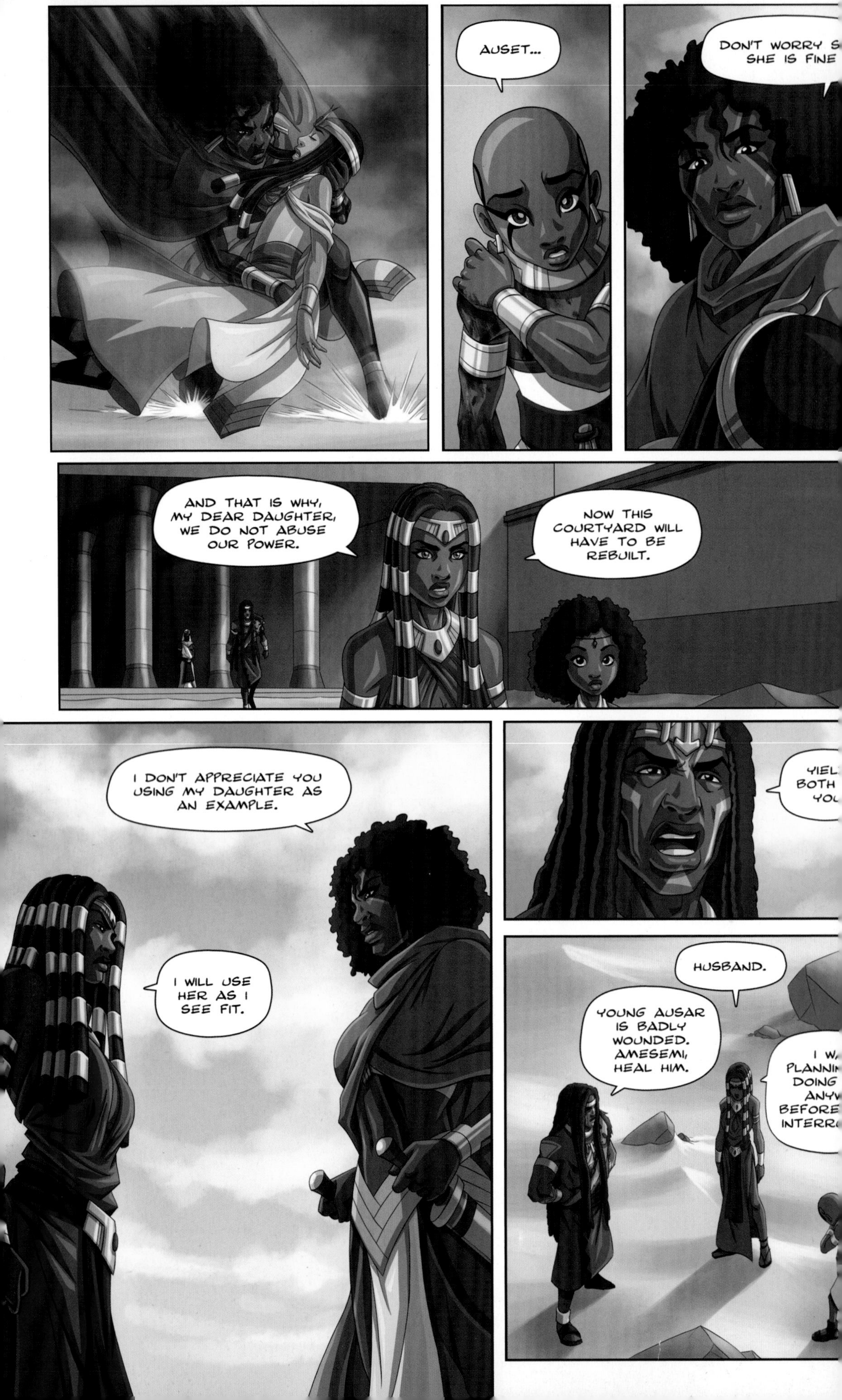
AUSET...
DON'T WORRY S
SHE IS FINE
AND THAT IS WHY, MY DEAR DAUGHTER, WE DO NOT ABUSE OUR POWER.
NOW THIS COURTYARD WILL HAVE TO BE REBUILT.
I DON'T APPRECIATE YOU USING MY DAUGHTER AS AN EXAMPLE.
I WILL USE HER AS I SEE FIT.
YIEL
BOTH
YOU
HUSBAND.
YOUNG AUSAR IS BADLY WOUNDED. AMESEMI, HEAL HIM.
I WA
PLANNIN
DOING
ANYW
BEFORE
INTERR

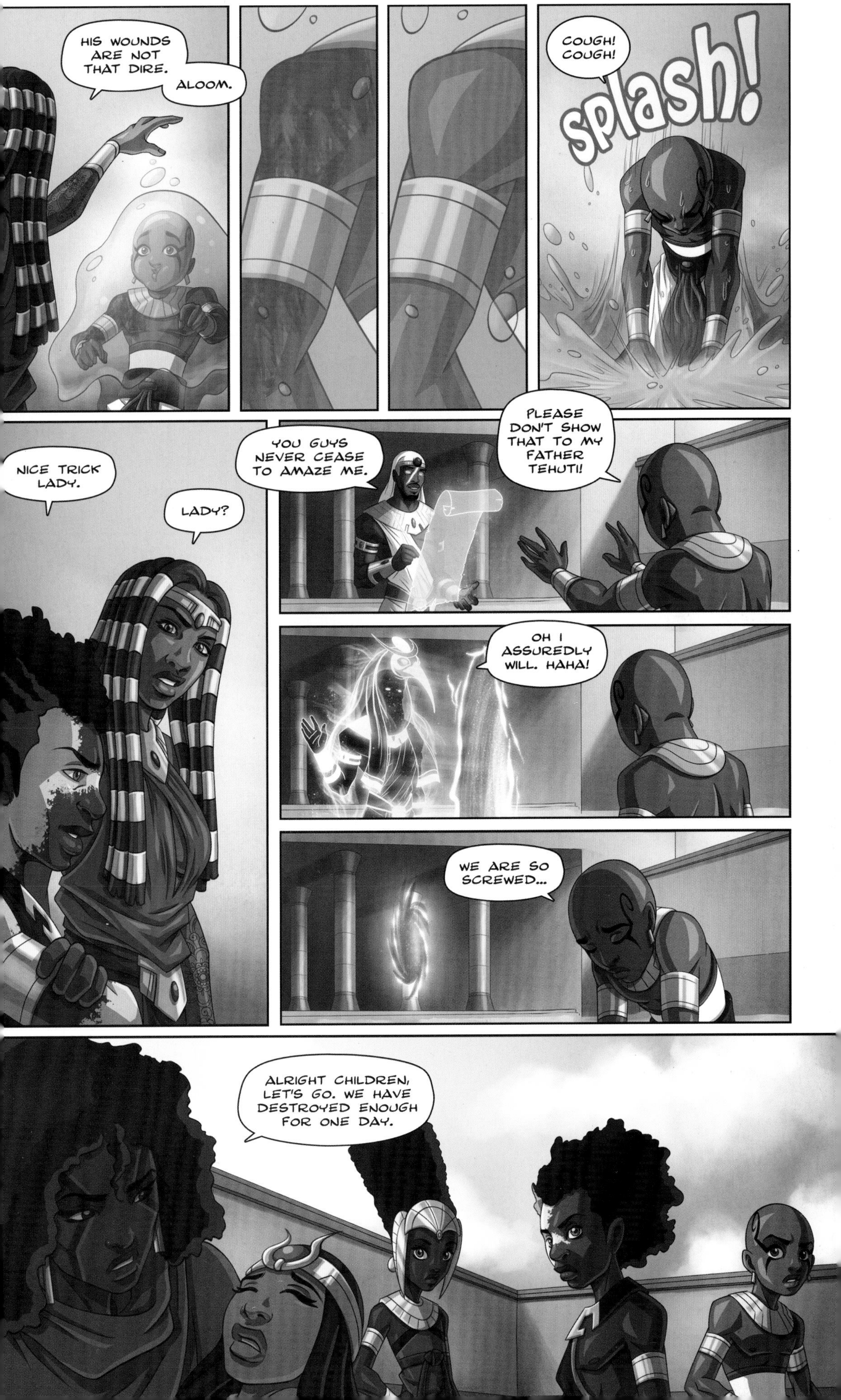
HIS WOUNDS ARE NOT THAT DIRE.
ALOOM.
COUGH! COUGH!
splash!
NICE TRICK LADY.
LADY?
YOU GUYS NEVER CEASE TO AMAZE ME.
PLEASE DON'T SHOW THAT TO MY FATHER TEHUTI!
OH I ASSUREDLY WILL. HAHA!
WE ARE SO SCREWED...
ALRIGHT CHILDREN, LET'S GO. WE HAVE DESTROYED ENOUGH FOR ONE DAY.

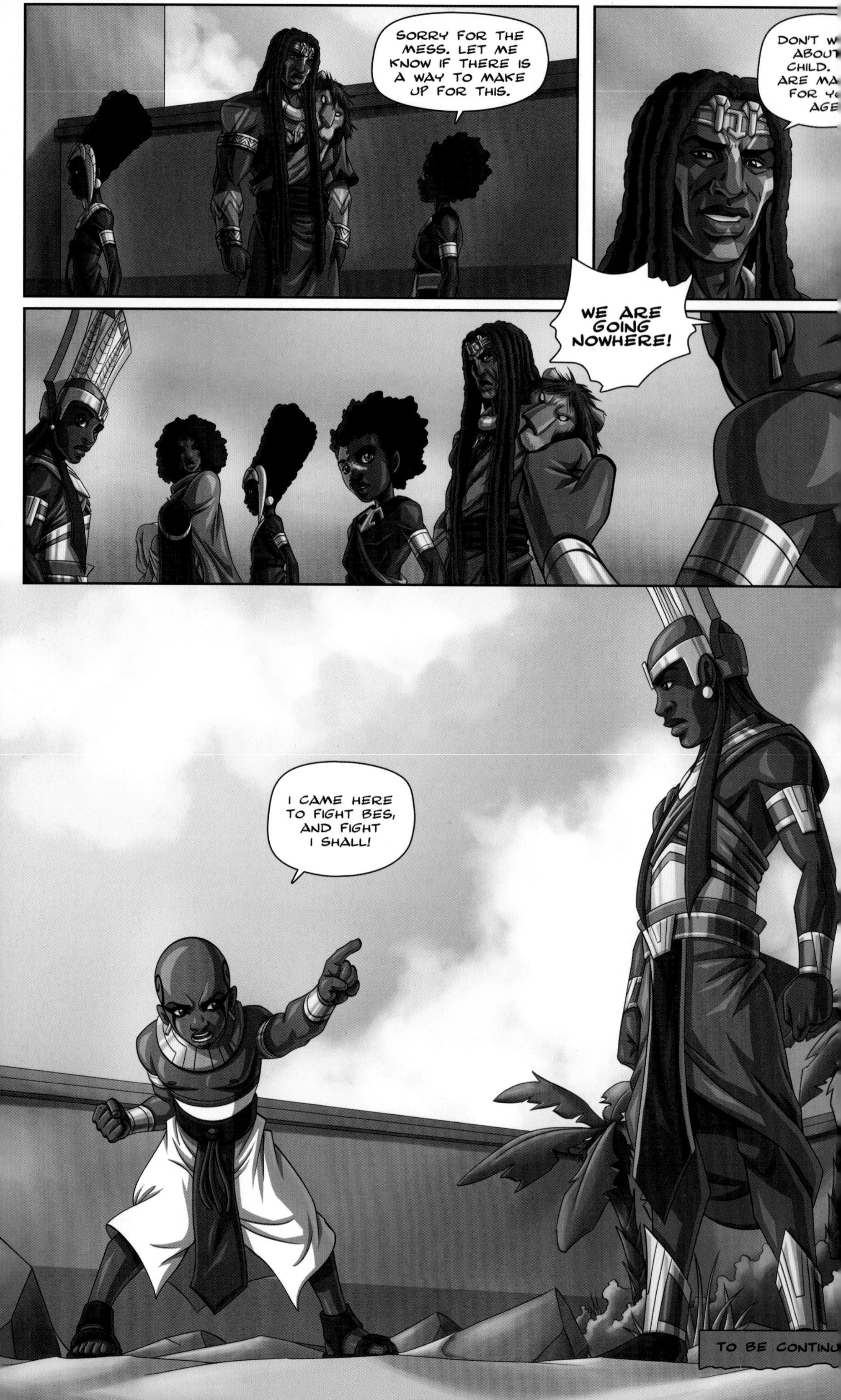
SORRY FOR THE MESS. LET ME KNOW IF THERE IS A WAY TO MAKE UP FOR THIS.
DON'T W ABOUT CHILD. ARE MA FOR Y AGE
WE ARE GOING NOWHERE!
I CAME HERE TO FIGHT BES, AND FIGHT I SHALL!
TO BE CONTINU

he City of Kerma

rma was the capital city of
e Kushite civilization in the
rd millennia BCE. It dominated
e region's gold trade and the
thways down the Nile. This
evated the Kushite culture to a
mpetitive level with their north-
n brothers in Kemet. The cul-
re of the Kushites was not
ich different from Kemet but
ey started using written hiero-
phs much later in their king-
m, making early recounts of
eir achievements and culture
to their neighbors in Kush.

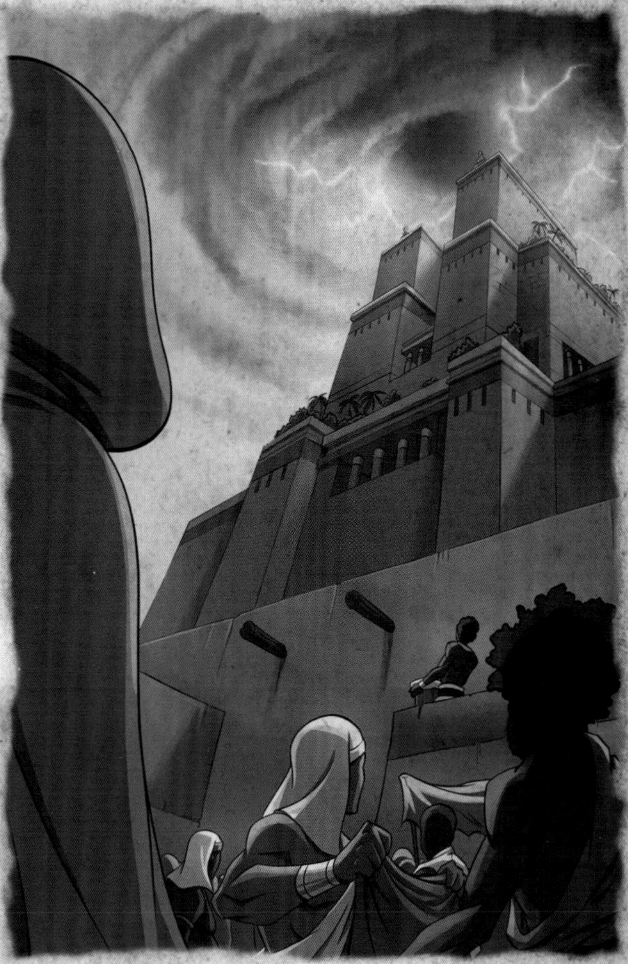

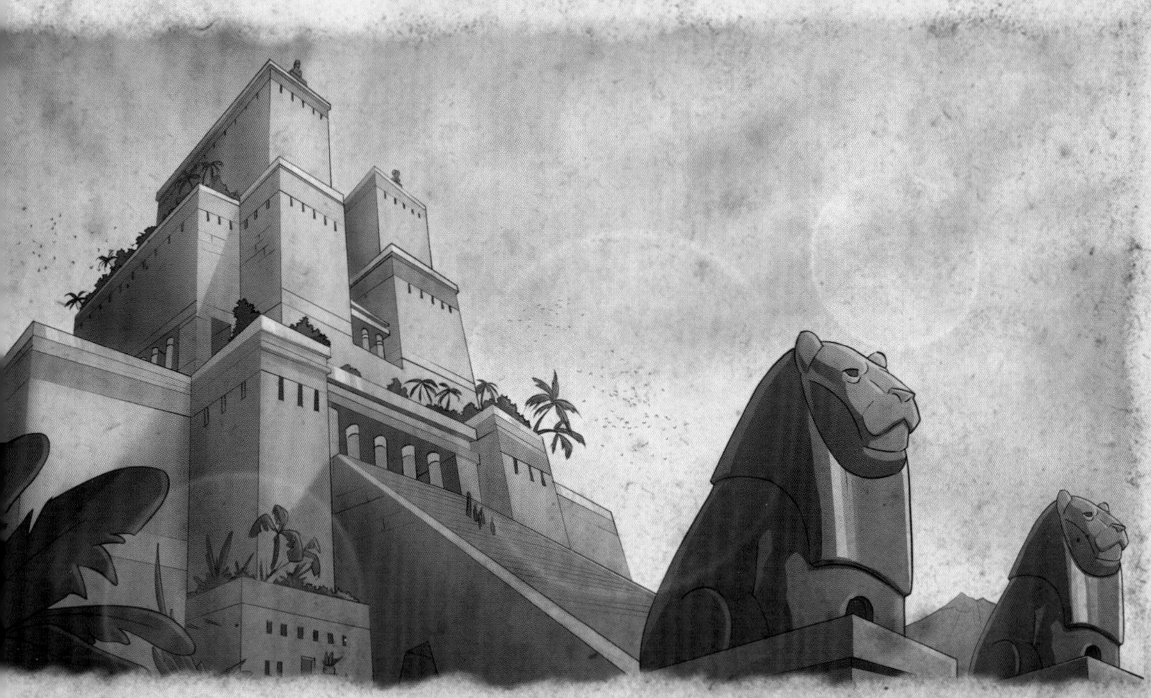

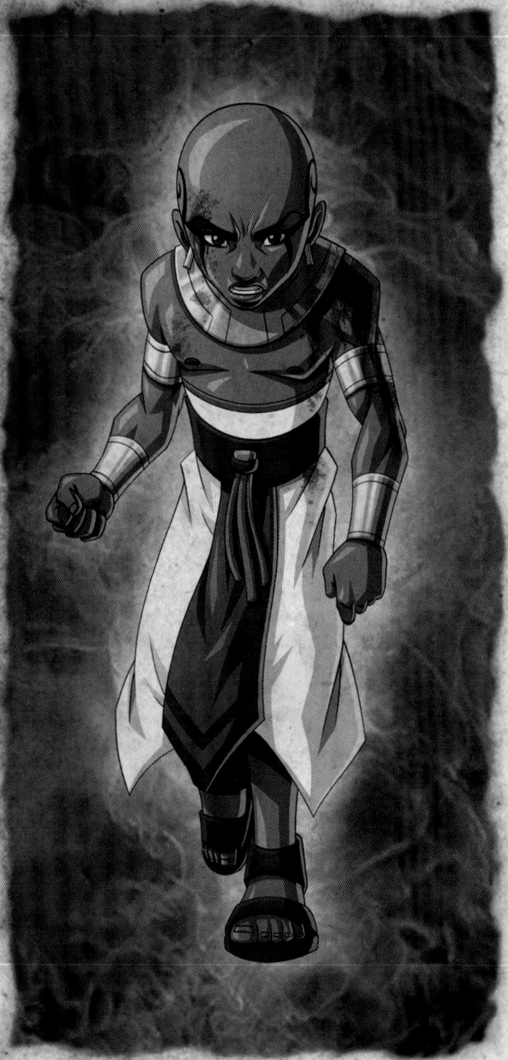

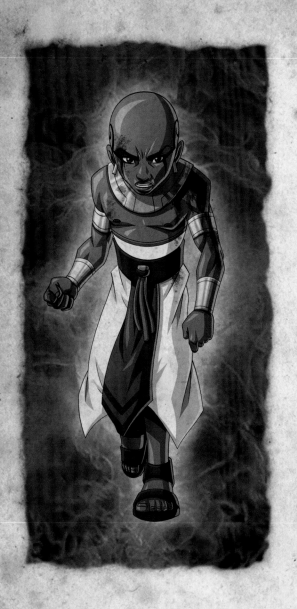

Ausar, The Bringer of Orde

In Kemetic mythology, Ausar is saic to be the Pharaoh who brought Kemet civilization. Before his reign, the people of Kemet were unruly a had savage customs. He forged the empire, with the aid of Tehuti, into thriving civilization and reigned for many years in piece before traged struck.

This is why in Black Sands, he is a prince with an insane amount of re sponsibility on his shoulders and ar undomitable will. What will become the boy who wishes to become kin

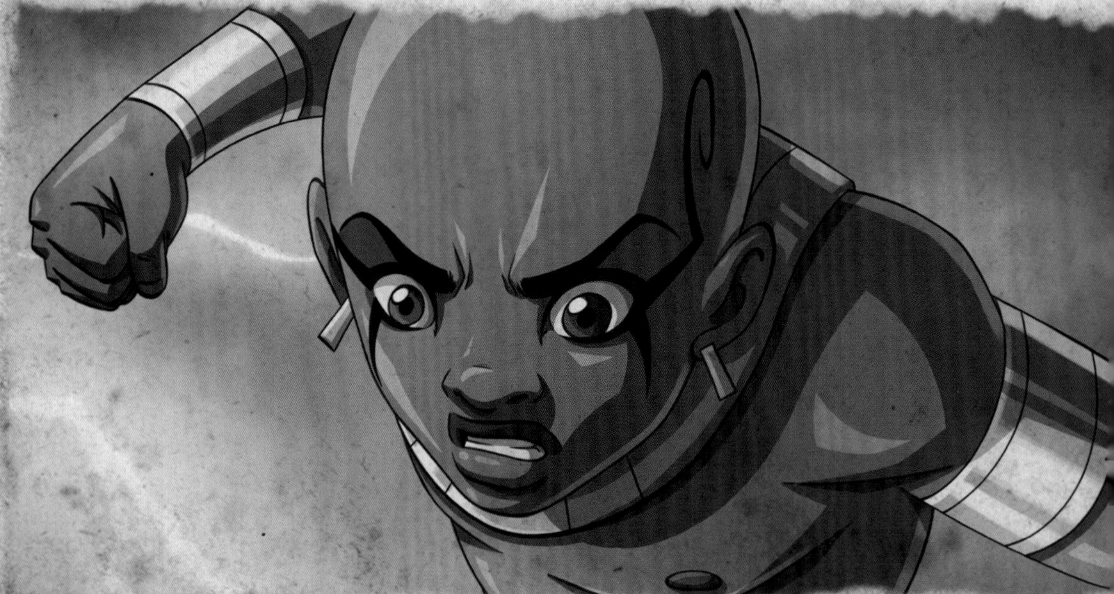

The Queens of the North and the South

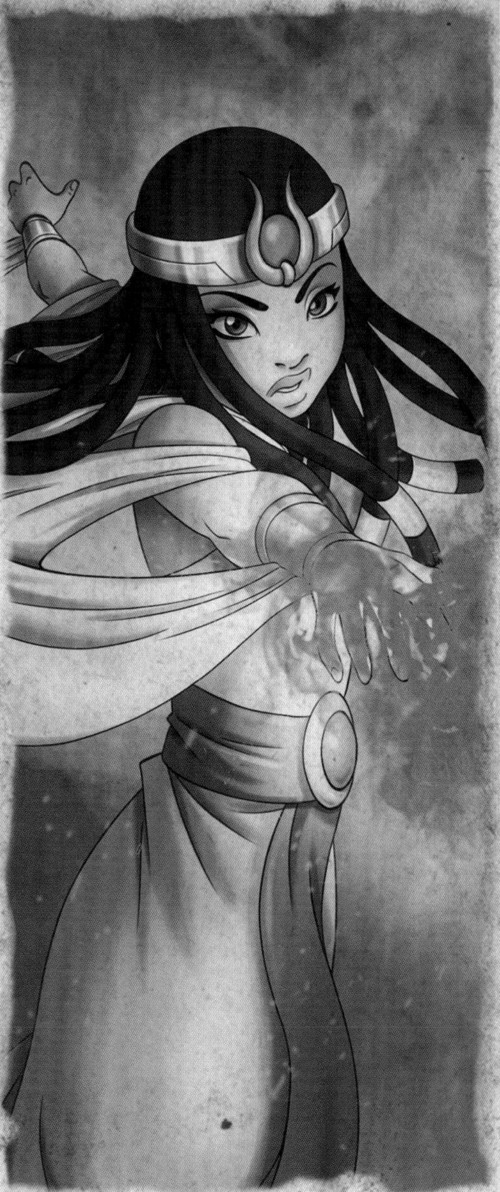

n mythology, Auset and Amesemi are both queens of their own kingdoms. Some say that Amesemi is the equivalent of Auset to the Kushites. They both play a critical role in the protection and guidance of their male counterparts and wield wild magic that has no comparison to other gods.

n Black Sands, Amesemi is the current Queen while Auset is still a child. Amesemi sees potential in the young woman but also feels her child-like attitude is dangerous, especially given the power she wields.

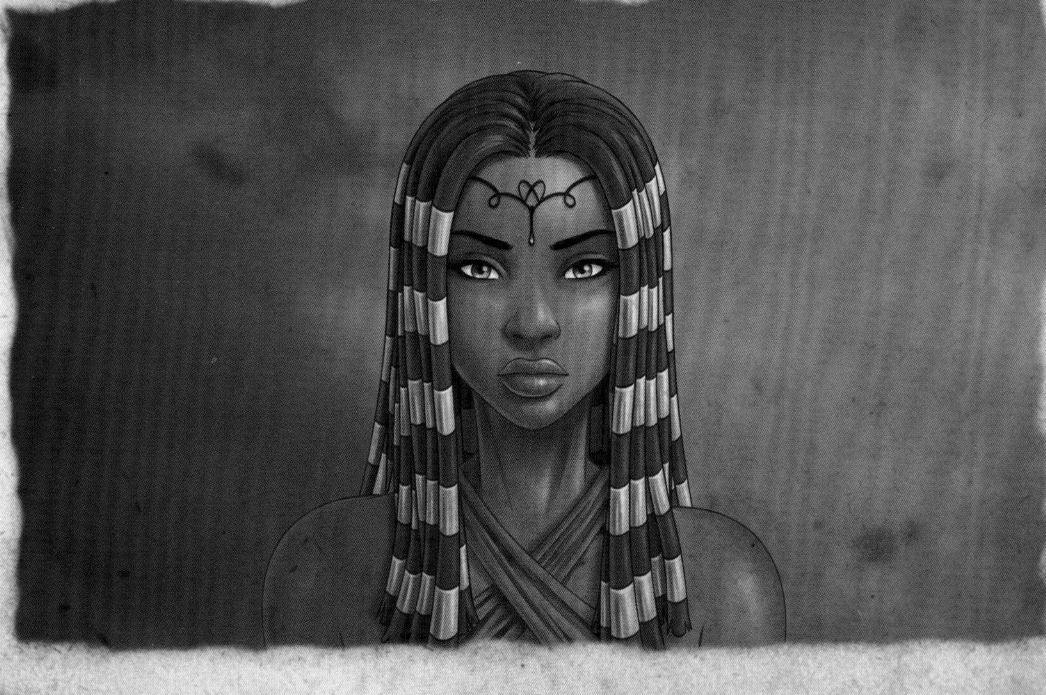

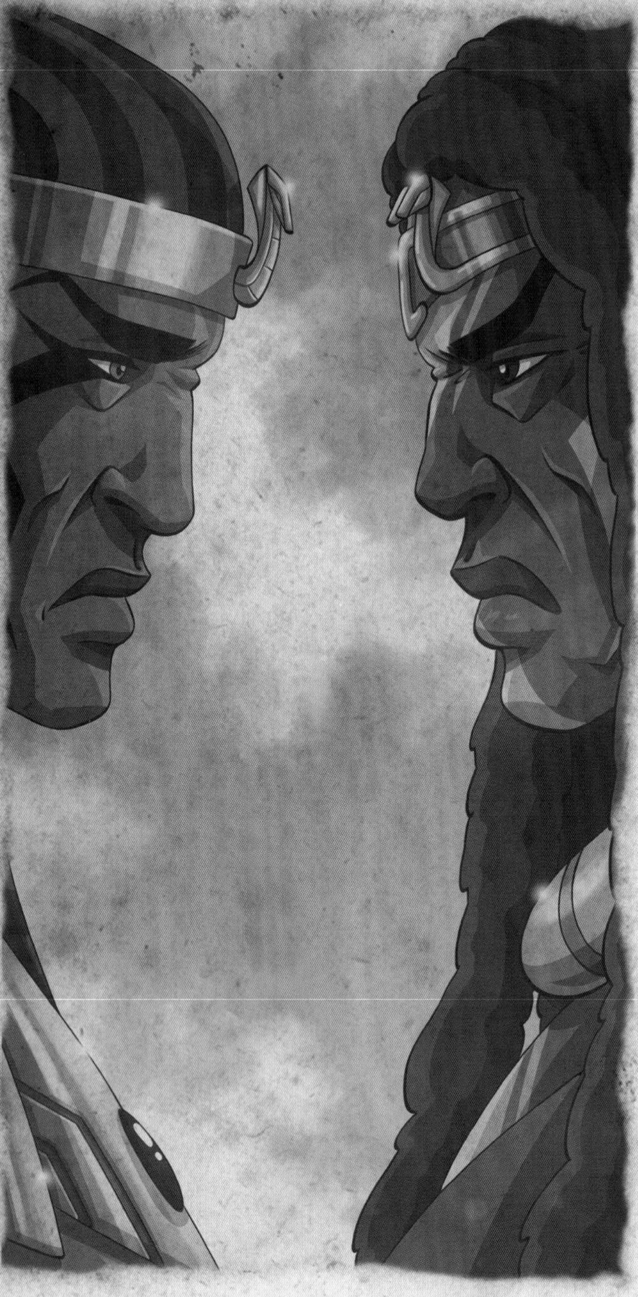

Diplomacy between Kingdoms

In history, Kush and Kemet have had a confusing relationship. At times they are known for long periods of peace,and at other times they are destroying each other. This complicated relationship has been going on for thousands of years throughout their history. In Black Sands, we made the conflict more understandable by having the leaders, Rah and Apedemak, be brothers who fiercely hated one another. What could be more complicated than that?

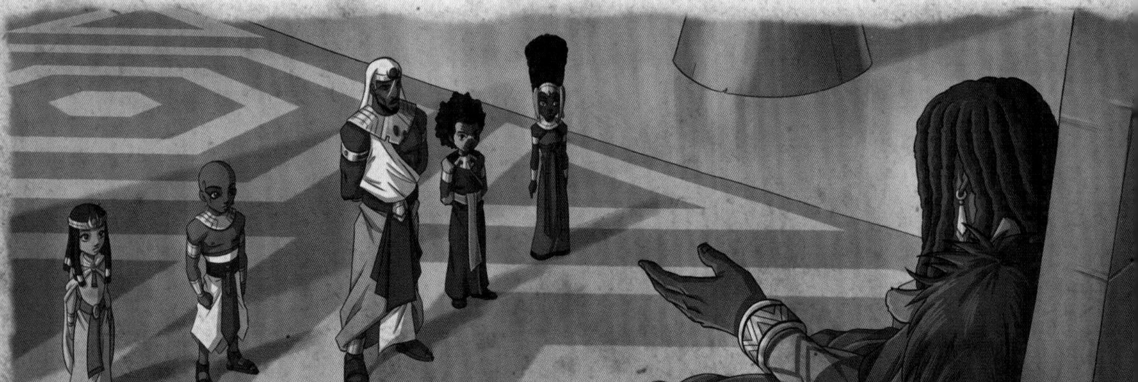

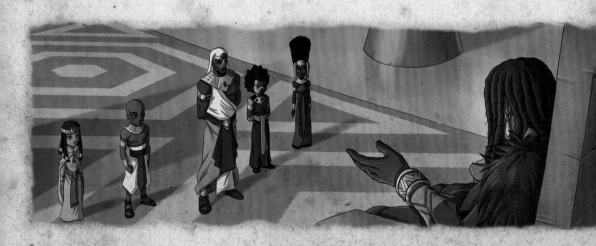

pedemak,
e Protector
Kush

mythology, Apedemak
symbolized by a lion
tecting the throne. Many
ictions also showed him
a lion-headed man. His
n attributes were that of
rotector and a wartime
y, destroying the ene-
s of Kush. It is also
wn that his exploits were
orded by Kemetic scribes,
king him an unusual case
Kush as a god that was
atly respected by his
als.

s is why in Black Sands he is the first true Pharaoh of Kush and is known
oughout both Kemet and Kush for his exploits. His fame has reached the very
ps of Memphis,and that bothers Rah, his brother, considerably.

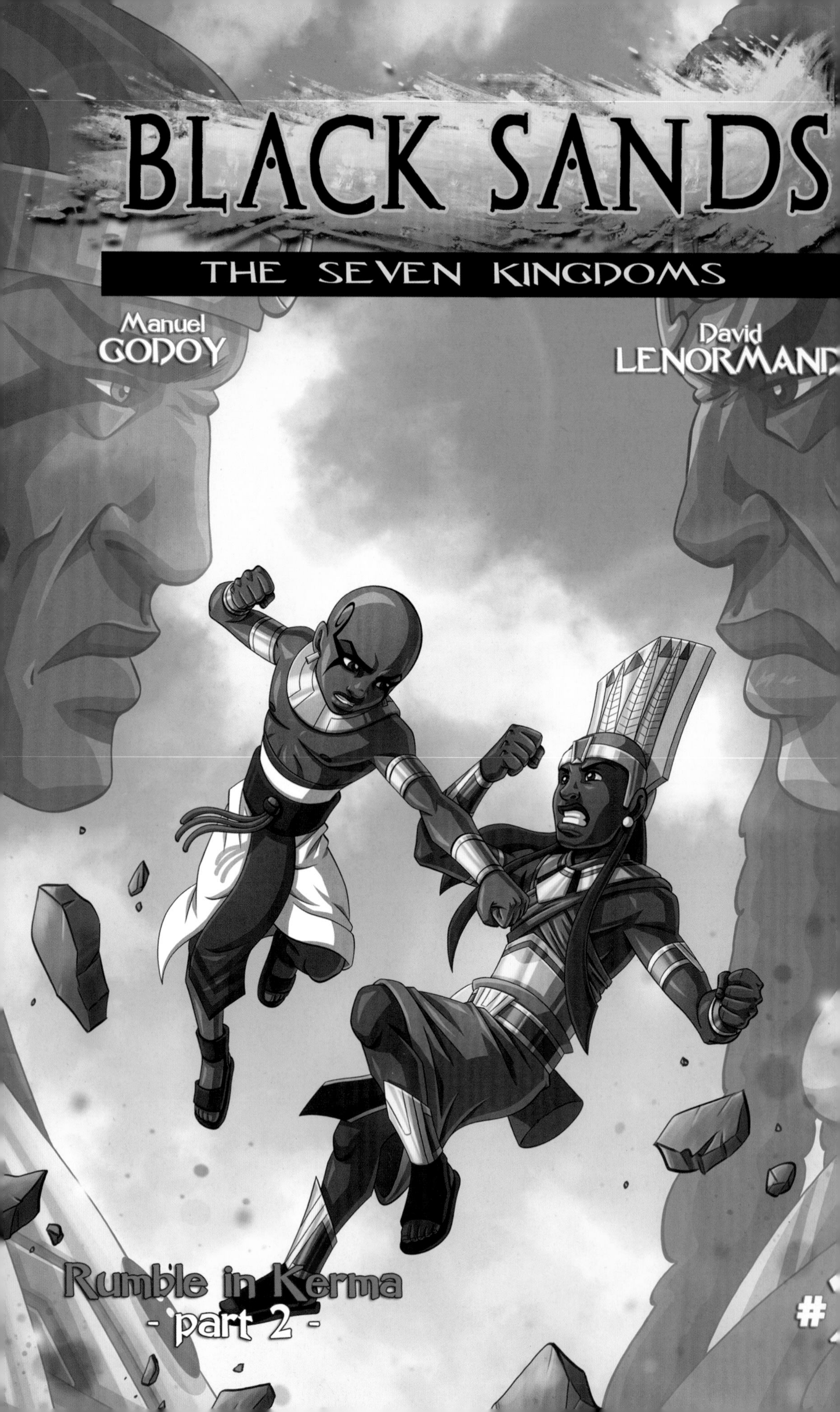
BLACK SANDS
THE SEVEN KINGDOMS
Manuel GODOY
David LENORMAND
Rumble in Kerma
- part 2 -
#

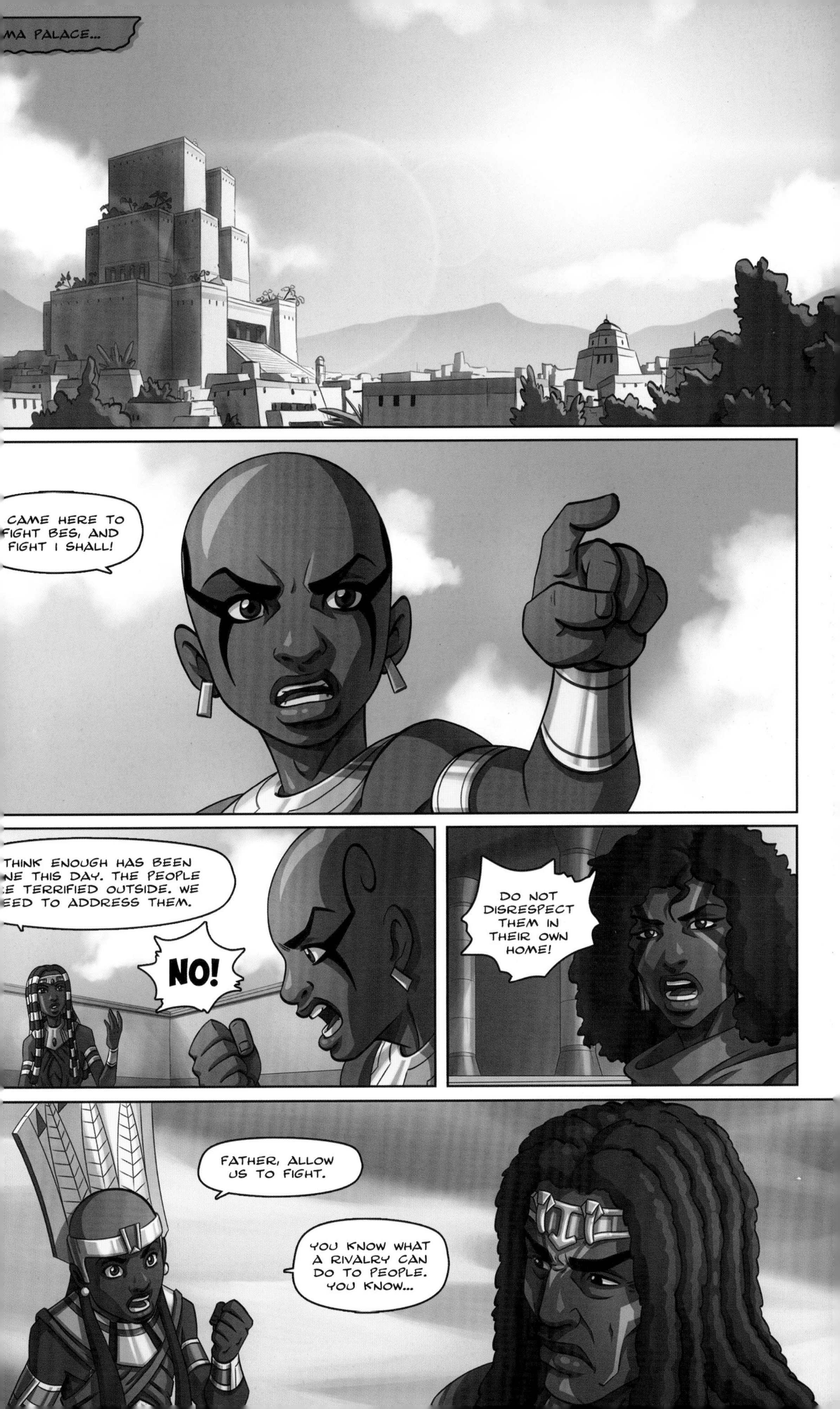
MA PALACE...
CAME HERE TO FIGHT BES, AND FIGHT I SHALL!
THINK ENOUGH HAS BEEN NE THIS DAY. THE PEOPLE E TERRIFIED OUTSIDE. WE EED TO ADDRESS THEM.
NO!
DO NOT DISRESPECT THEM IN THEIR OWN HOME!
FATHER, ALLOW US TO FIGHT.
YOU KNOW WHAT A RIVALRY CAN DO TO PEOPLE. YOU KNOW...

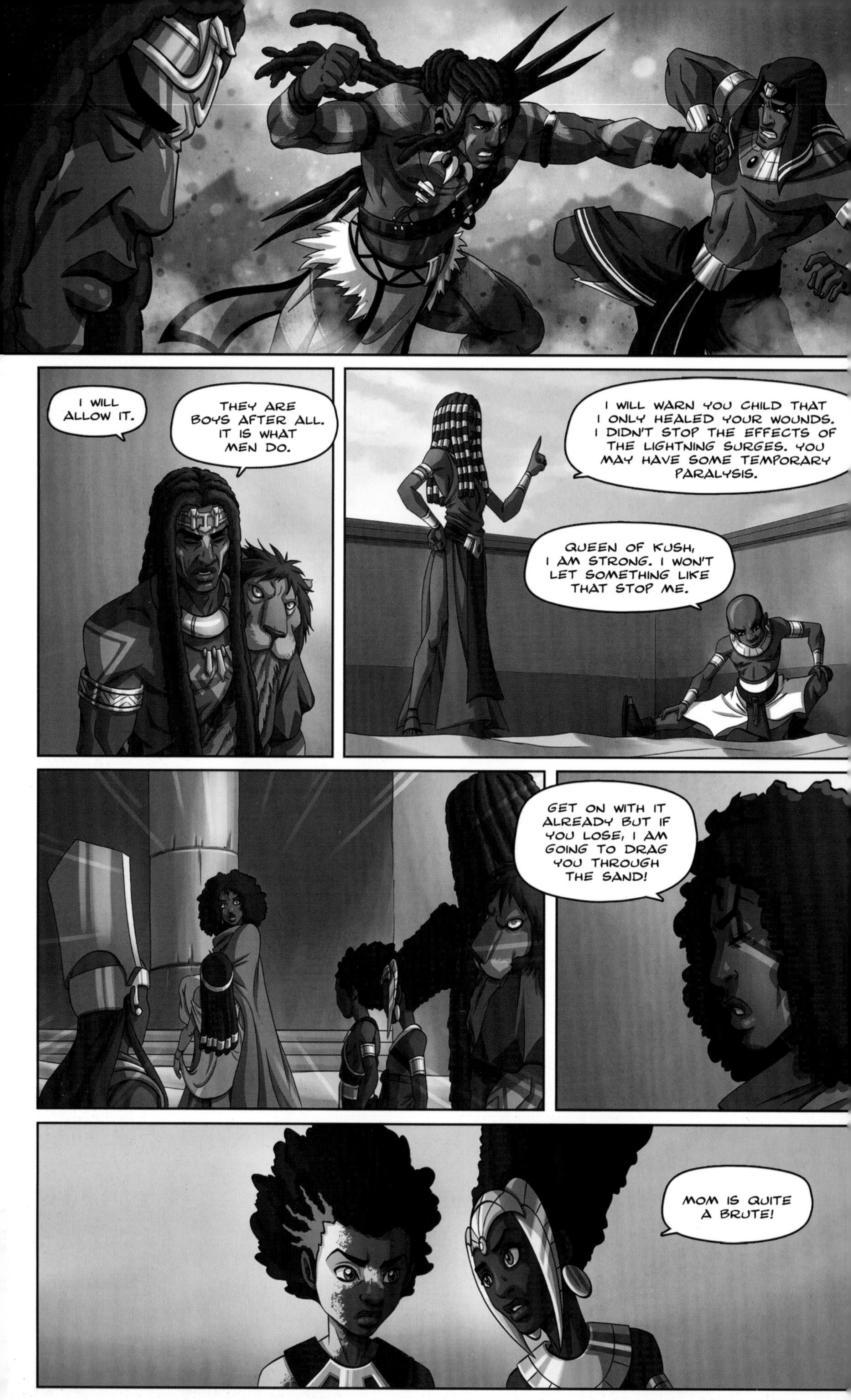
I WILL ALLOW IT.
THEY ARE BOYS AFTER ALL. IT IS WHAT MEN DO.
I WILL WARN YOU CHILD THAT I ONLY HEALED YOUR WOUNDS. I DIDN'T STOP THE EFFECTS OF THE LIGHTNING SURGES. YOU MAY HAVE SOME TEMPORARY PARALYSIS.
QUEEN OF KUSH, I AM STRONG. I WON'T LET SOMETHING LIKE THAT STOP ME.
GET ON WITH IT ALREADY BUT IF YOU LOSE, I AM GOING TO DRAG YOU THROUGH THE SAND!
MOM IS QUITE A BRUTE!

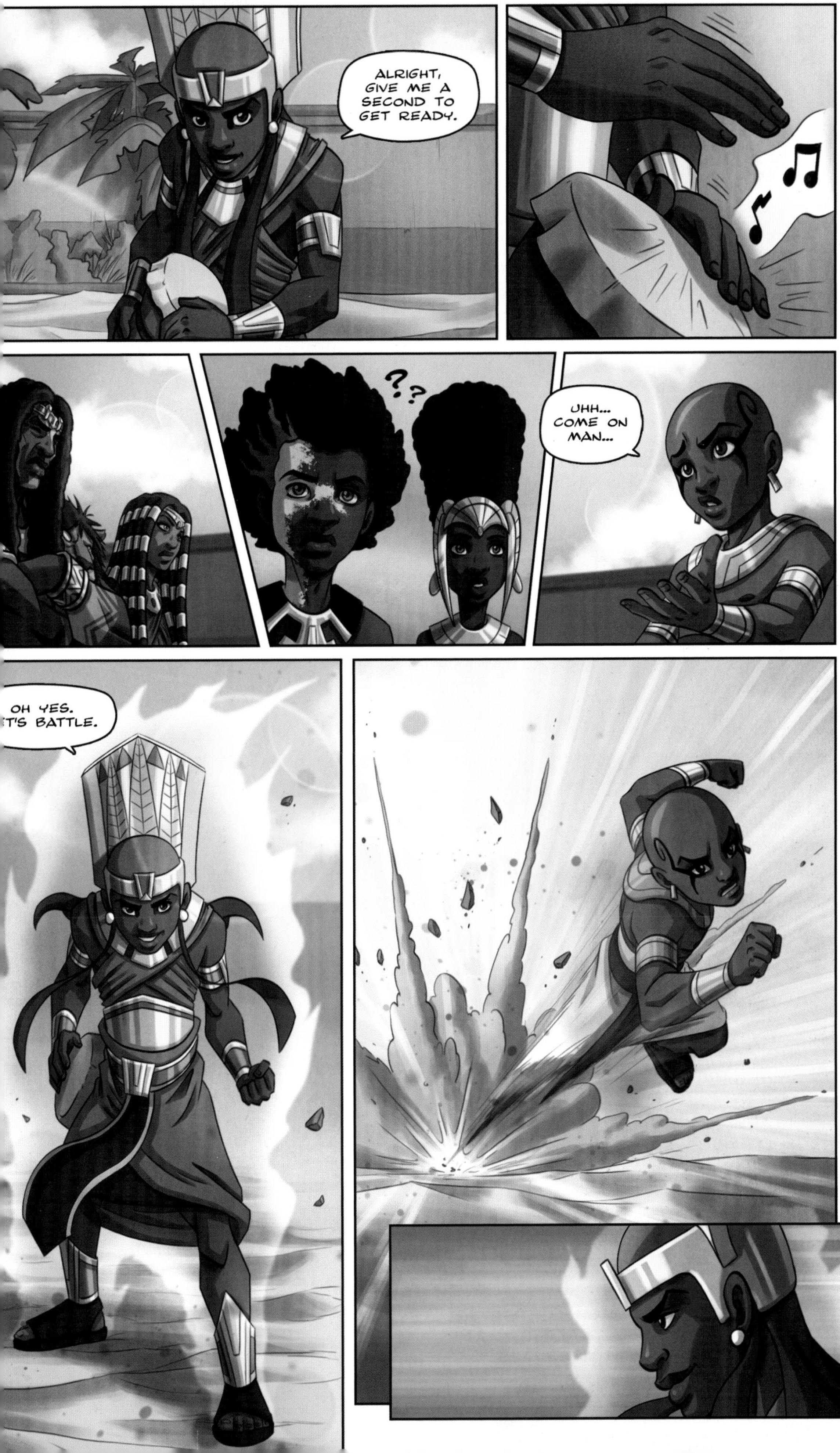
ALRIGHT, GIVE ME A SECOND TO GET READY.
??
UHH... COME ON MAN...
OH YES. T'S BATTLE.

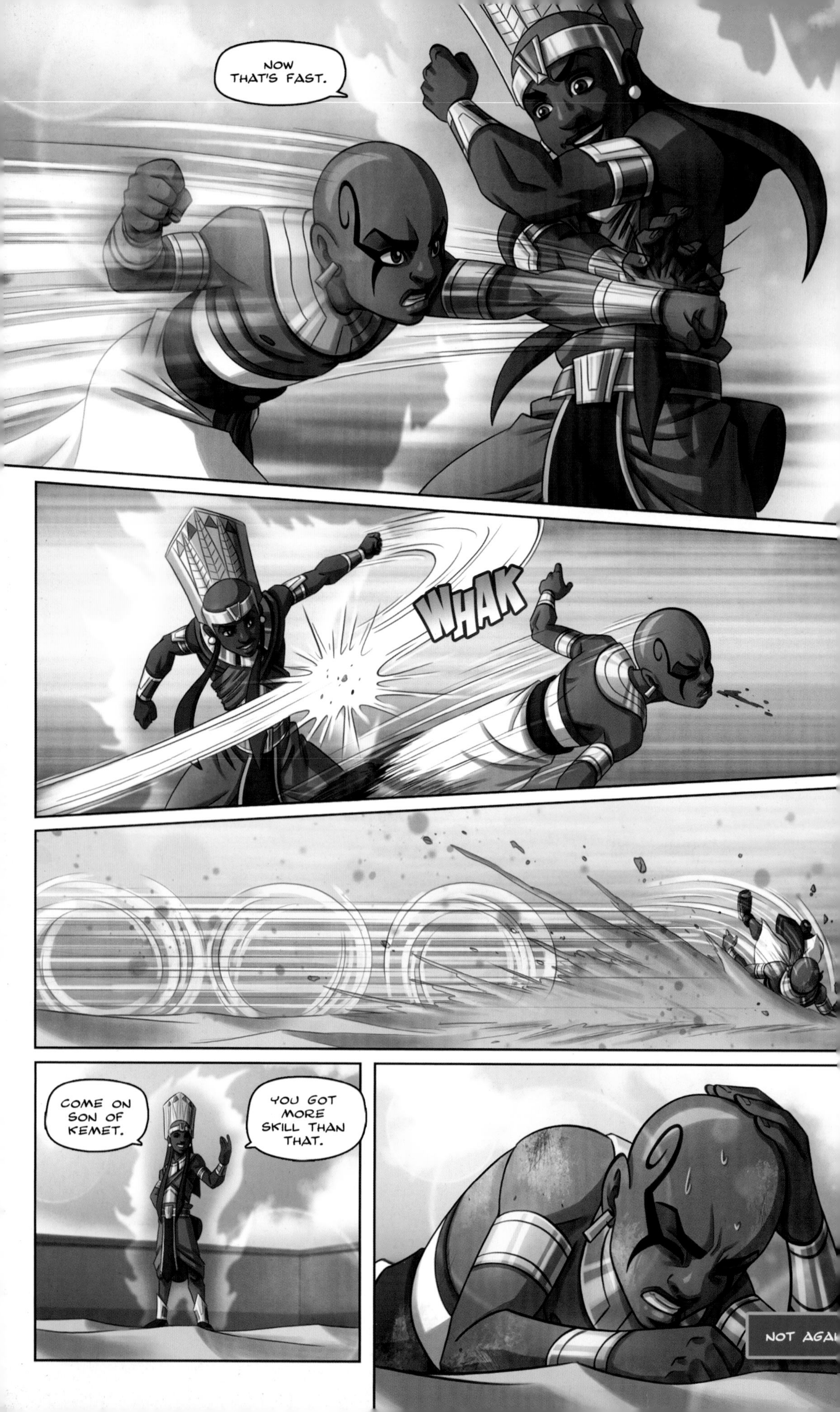
NOW THAT'S FAST.
WHAK
COME ON SON OF KEMET.
YOU GOT MORE SKILL THAN THAT.
NOT AGA

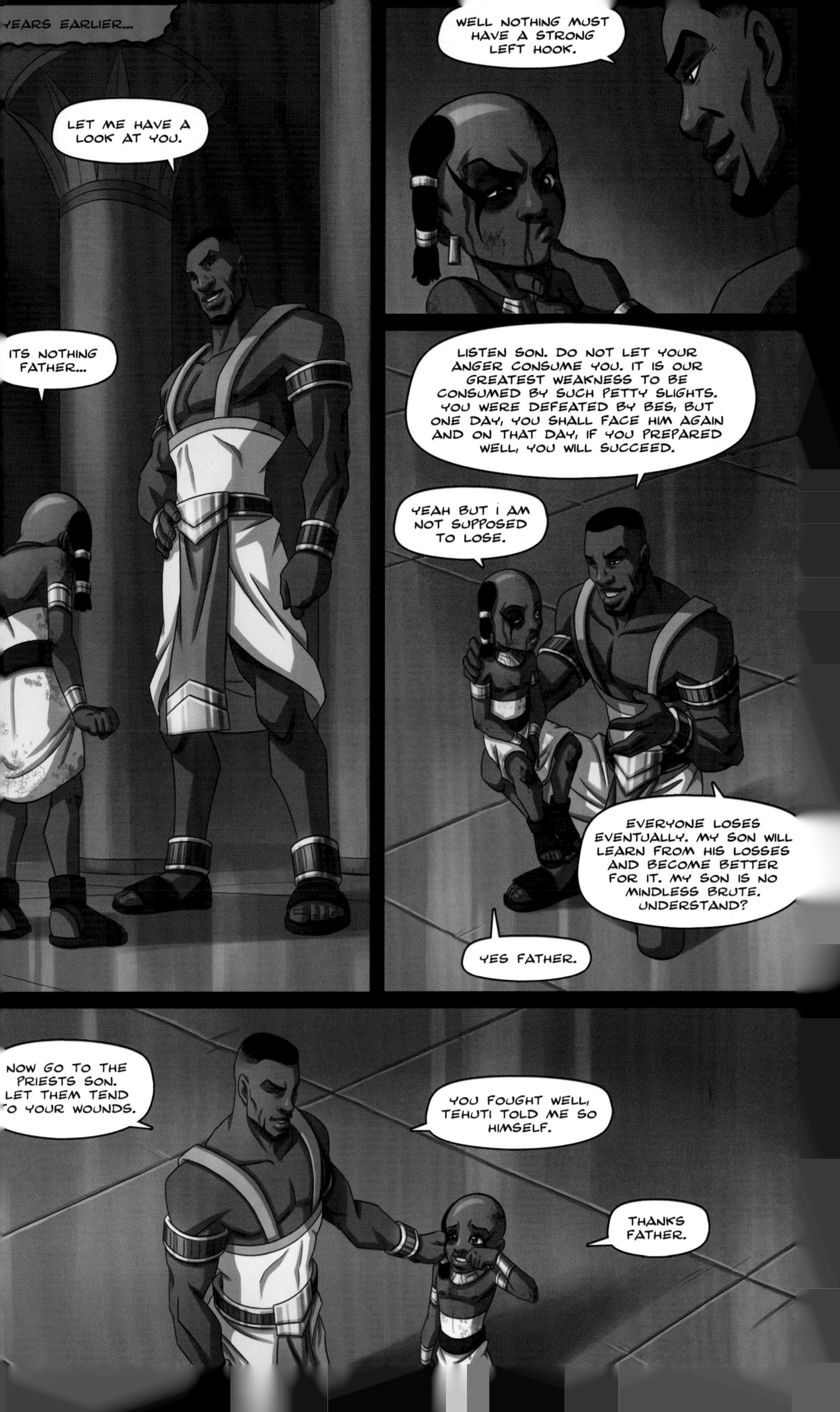
YEARS EARLIER...
LET ME HAVE A LOOK AT YOU.
ITS NOTHING FATHER...
WELL NOTHING MUST HAVE A STRONG LEFT HOOK.
LISTEN SON. DO NOT LET YOUR ANGER CONSUME YOU. IT IS OUR GREATEST WEAKNESS TO BE CONSUMED BY SUCH PETTY SLIGHTS. YOU WERE DEFEATED BY BES, BUT ONE DAY, YOU SHALL FACE HIM AGAIN AND ON THAT DAY, IF YOU PREPARED WELL, YOU WILL SUCCEED.
YEAH BUT I AM NOT SUPPOSED TO LOSE.
EVERYONE LOSES EVENTUALLY. MY SON WILL LEARN FROM HIS LOSSES AND BECOME BETTER FOR IT. MY SON IS NO MINDLESS BRUTE. UNDERSTAND?
YES FATHER.
NOW GO TO THE PRIESTS SON. LET THEM TEND TO YOUR WOUNDS.
YOU FOUGHT WELL, TEHUTI TOLD ME SO HIMSELF.
THANKS FATHER.

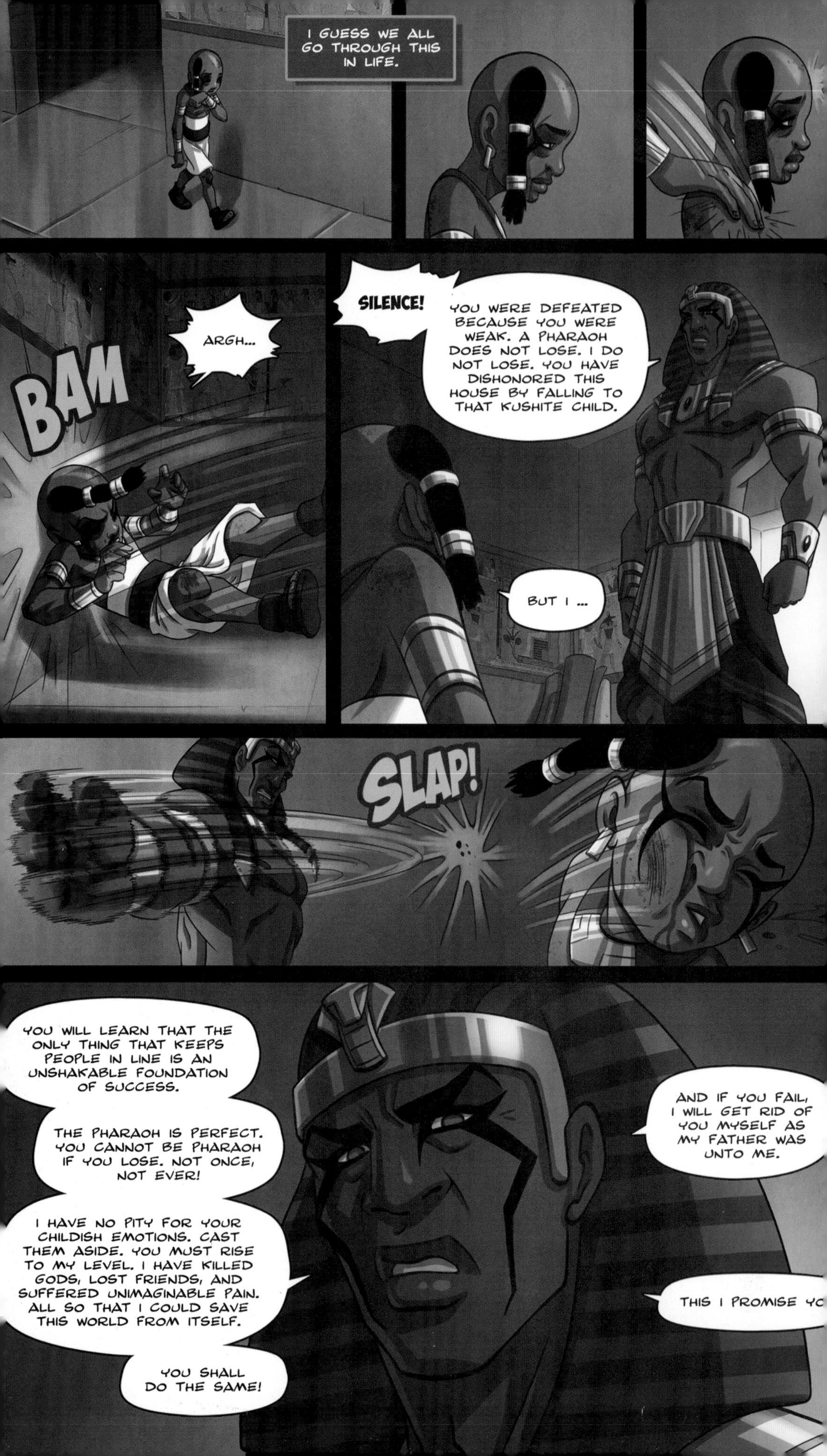
I GUESS WE ALL GO THROUGH THIS IN LIFE.
BAM
ARGH...
SILENCE!
YOU WERE DEFEATED BECAUSE YOU WERE WEAK. A PHARAOH DOES NOT LOSE. I DO NOT LOSE. YOU HAVE DISHONORED THIS HOUSE BY FALLING TO THAT KUSHITE CHILD.
BUT I ...
SLAP!
YOU WILL LEARN THAT THE ONLY THING THAT KEEPS PEOPLE IN LINE IS AN UNSHAKABLE FOUNDATION OF SUCCESS.
THE PHARAOH IS PERFECT. YOU CANNOT BE PHARAOH IF YOU LOSE. NOT ONCE, NOT EVER!
I HAVE NO PITY FOR YOUR CHILDISH EMOTIONS. CAST THEM ASIDE. YOU MUST RISE TO MY LEVEL. I HAVE KILLED GODS, LOST FRIENDS, AND SUFFERED UNIMAGINABLE PAIN. ALL SO THAT I COULD SAVE THIS WORLD FROM ITSELF.
YOU SHALL DO THE SAME!
AND IF YOU FAIL, I WILL GET RID OF YOU MYSELF AS MY FATHER WAS UNTO ME.
THIS I PROMISE YO

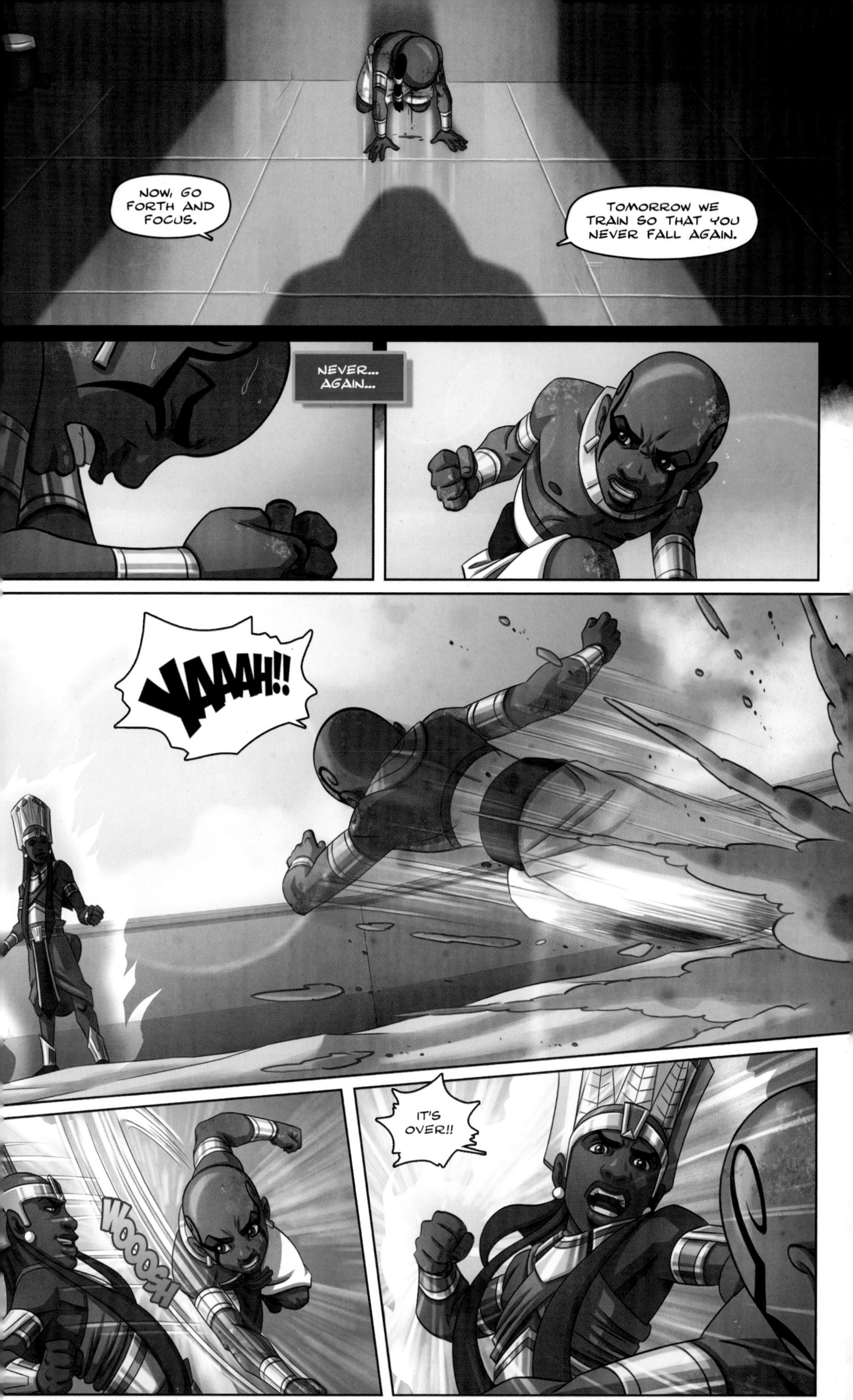
NOW, GO FORTH AND FOCUS.
TOMORROW WE TRAIN SO THAT YOU NEVER FALL AGAIN.
NEVER... AGAIN...
YAAAH!!
WOOOSH
IT'S OVER!!

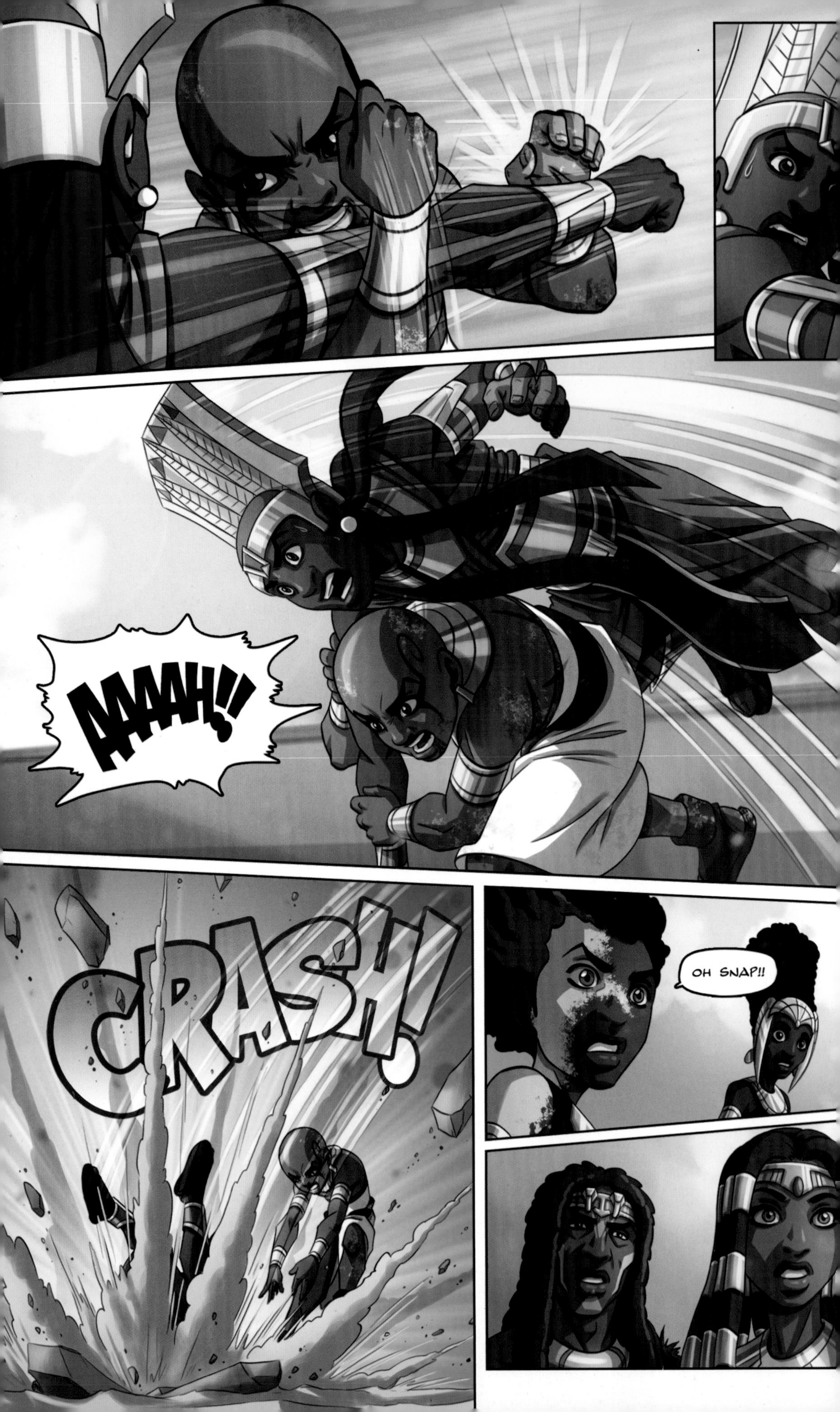
AAAAH!!
CRASH!
OH SNAP!!

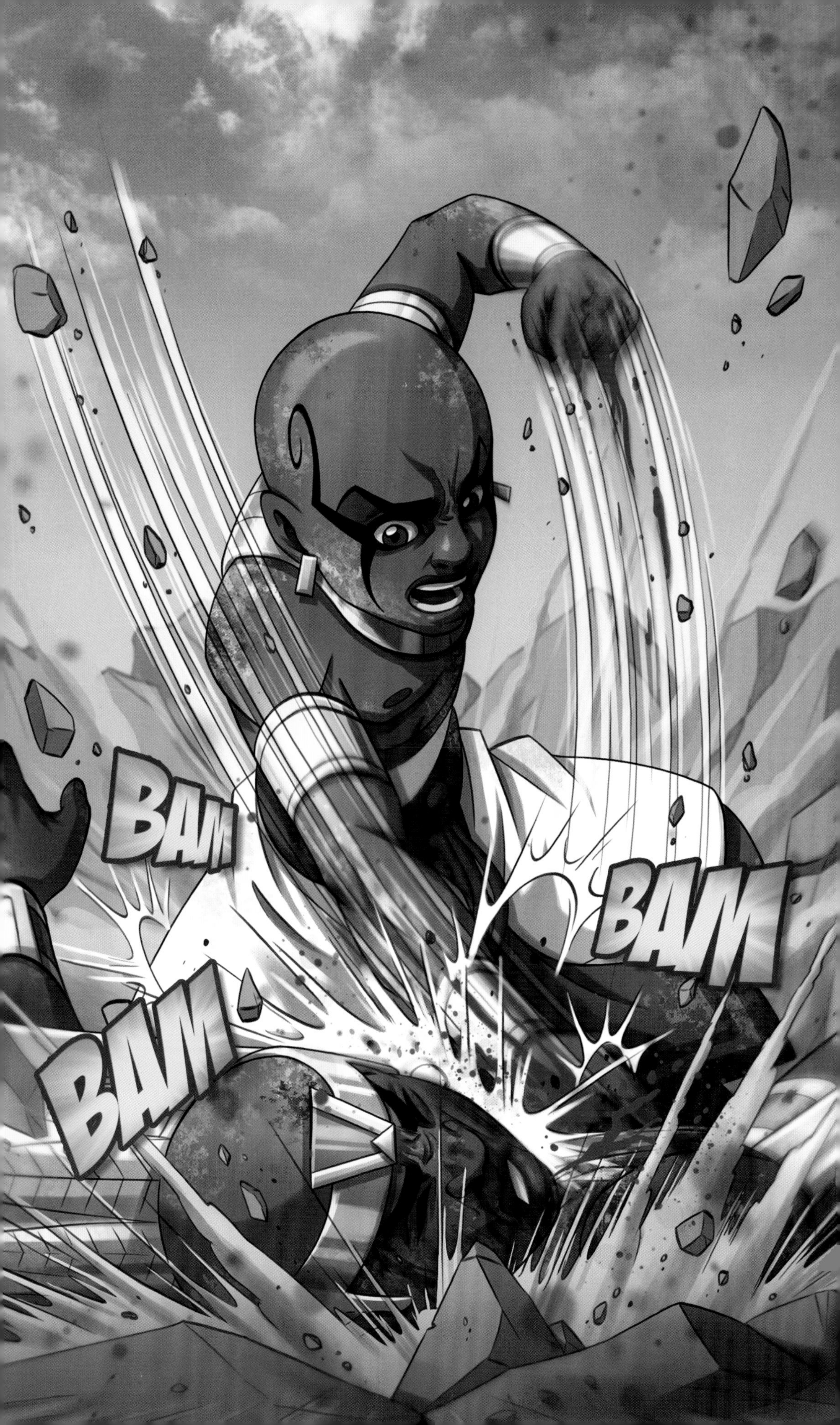
BAM
BAM
BAM

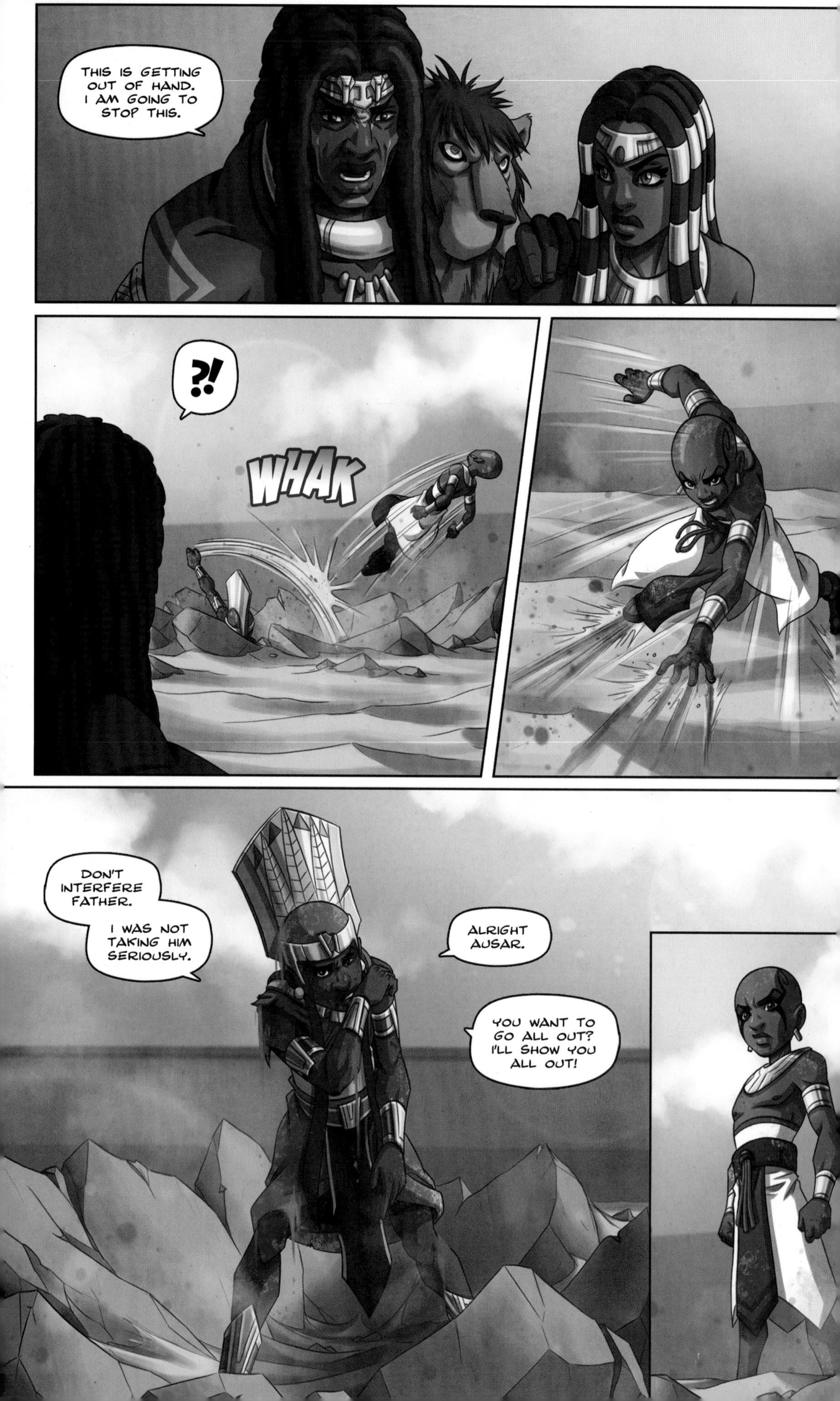
THIS IS GETTING OUT OF HAND. I AM GOING TO STOP THIS.
?!
WHAK
DON'T INTERFERE FATHER.
I WAS NOT TAKING HIM SERIOUSLY.
ALRIGHT AUSAR.
YOU WANT TO GO ALL OUT? I'LL SHOW YOU ALL OUT!

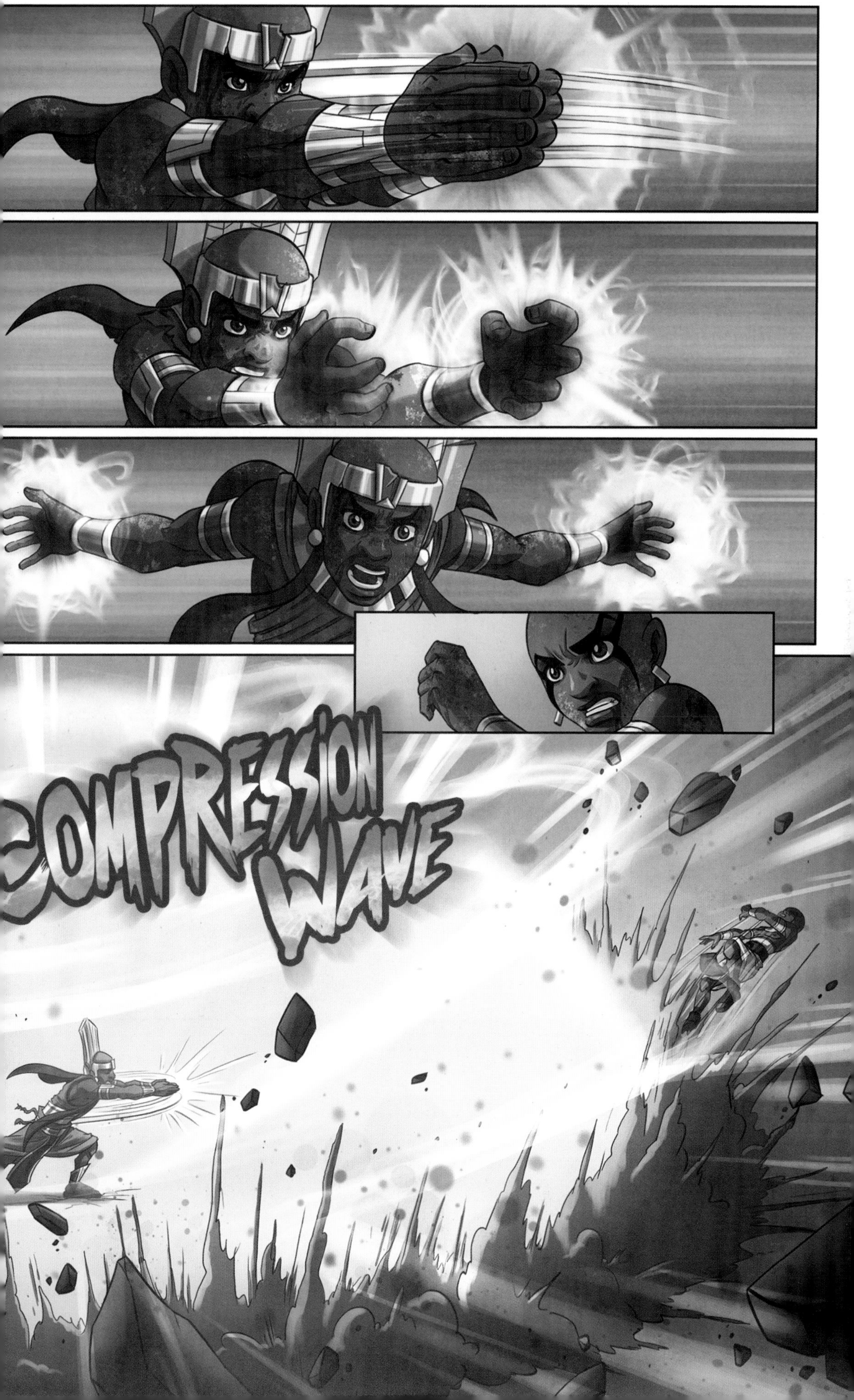
COMPRESSION WAVE

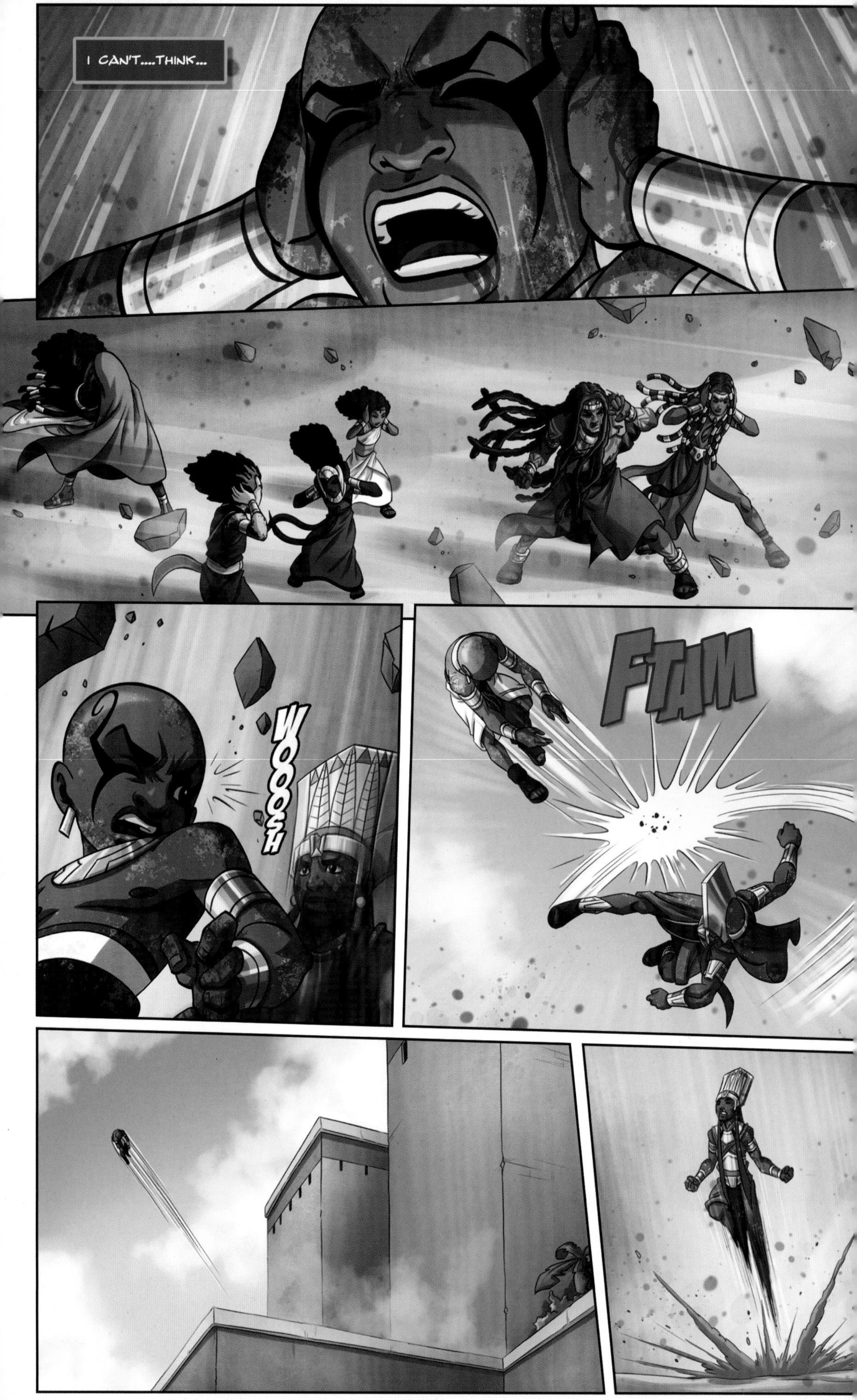
I CAN'T....THINK...
WOOOOSH
FTAM

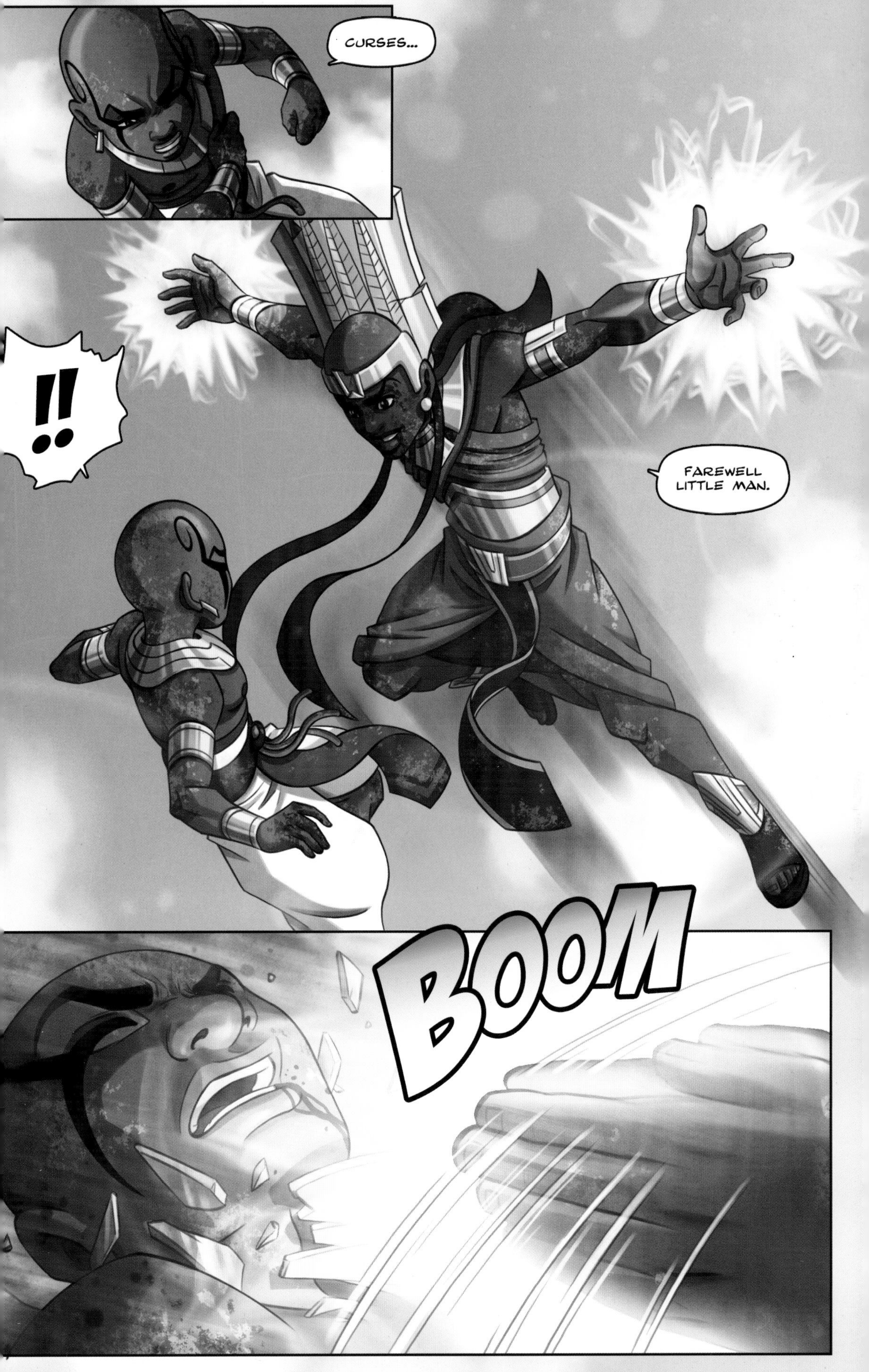
CURSES...
!!
FAREWELL LITTLE MAN.
BOOM

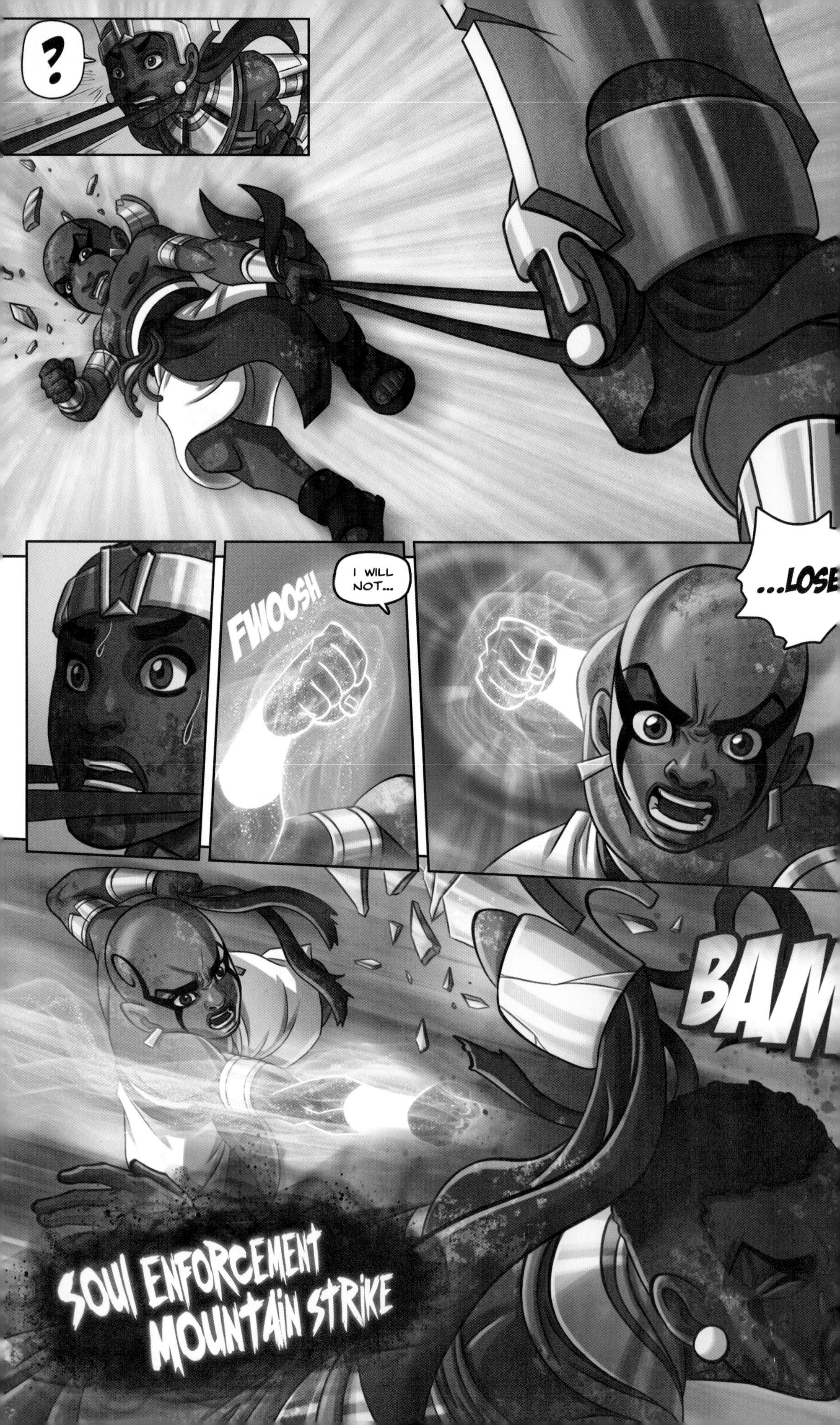
?
FWOOSH
I WILL NOT...
...LOSE
BAM
SOUL ENFORCEMENT MOUNTAIN STRIKE

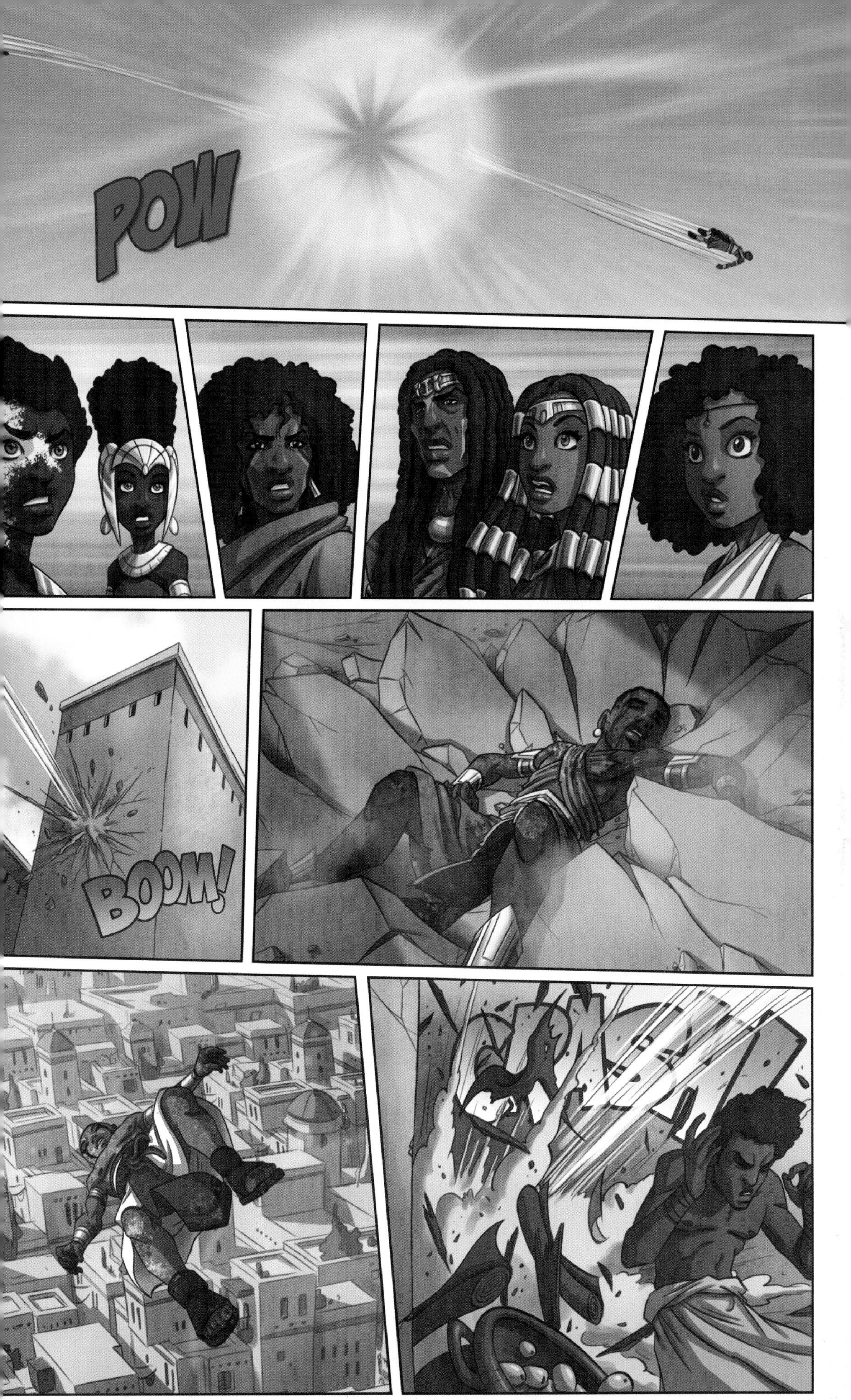
POW
BOOM!

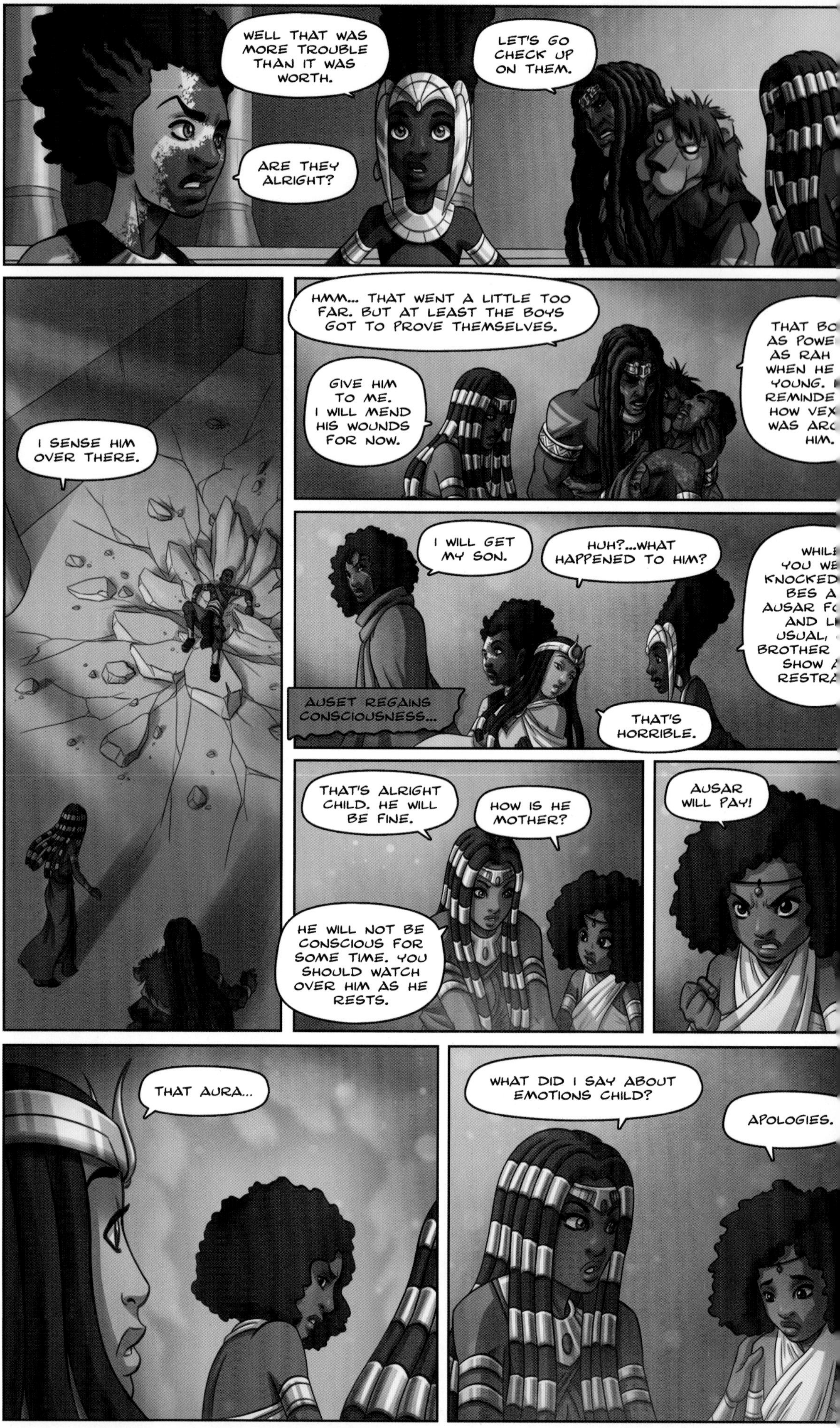

WELL THAT WAS MORE TROUBLE THAN IT WAS WORTH.
LET'S GO CHECK UP ON THEM.
ARE THEY ALRIGHT?
I SENSE HIM OVER THERE.
HMM... THAT WENT A LITTLE TOO FAR. BUT AT LEAST THE BOYS GOT TO PROVE THEMSELVES.
GIVE HIM TO ME. I WILL MEND HIS WOUNDS FOR NOW.
THAT BO AS POWE AS RAH WHEN HE YOUNG. REMINDE HOW VEX WAS ARC HIM.
I WILL GET MY SON.
HUH?...WHAT HAPPENED TO HIM?
WHIL YOU WE KNOCKED BES A AUSAR F AND L USUAL, BROTHER SHOW RESTRA
AUSET REGAINS CONSCIOUSNESS...
THAT'S HORRIBLE.
THAT'S ALRIGHT CHILD. HE WILL BE FINE.
HOW IS HE MOTHER?
HE WILL NOT BE CONSCIOUS FOR SOME TIME. YOU SHOULD WATCH OVER HIM AS HE RESTS.
AUSAR WILL PAY!
THAT AURA...
WHAT DID I SAY ABOUT EMOTIONS CHILD?
APOLOGIES.

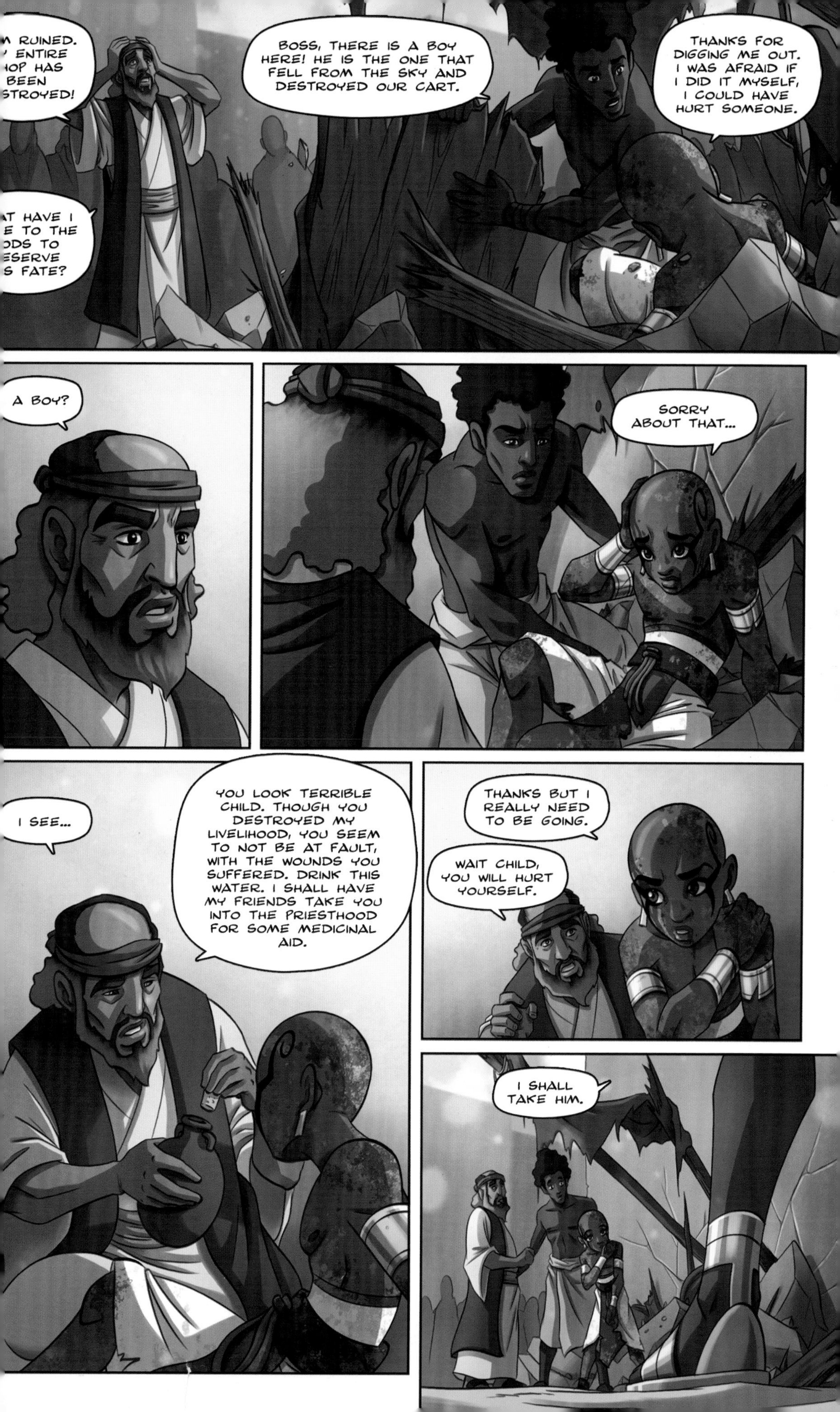
M RUINED. ENTIRE HOP HAS BEEN STROYED!
BOSS, THERE IS A BOY HERE! HE IS THE ONE THAT FELL FROM THE SKY AND DESTROYED OUR CART.
THANKS FOR DIGGING ME OUT. I WAS AFRAID IF I DID IT MYSELF, I COULD HAVE HURT SOMEONE.
AT HAVE I E TO THE ODS TO ESERVE S FATE?
A BOY?
SORRY ABOUT THAT...
I SEE...
YOU LOOK TERRIBLE CHILD. THOUGH YOU DESTROYED MY LIVELIHOOD, YOU SEEM TO NOT BE AT FAULT, WITH THE WOUNDS YOU SUFFERED. DRINK THIS WATER. I SHALL HAVE MY FRIENDS TAKE YOU INTO THE PRIESTHOOD FOR SOME MEDICINAL AID.
THANKS BUT I REALLY NEED TO BE GOING.
WAIT CHILD, YOU WILL HURT YOURSELF.
I SHALL TAKE HIM.

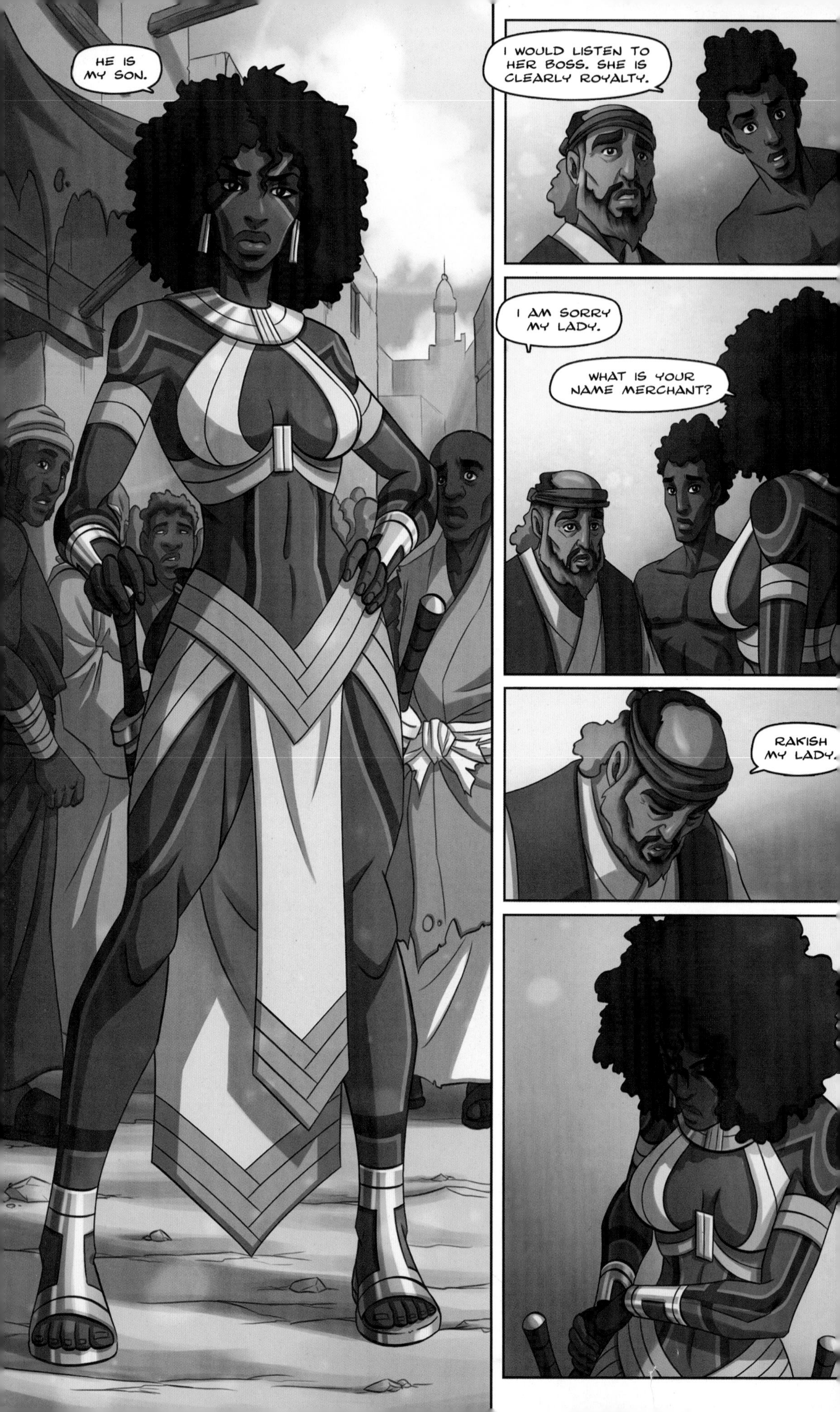
HE IS MY SON.
I WOULD LISTEN TO HER BOSS. SHE IS CLEARLY ROYALTY.
I AM SORRY MY LADY.
WHAT IS YOUR NAME MERCHANT?
RAKISH MY LADY.

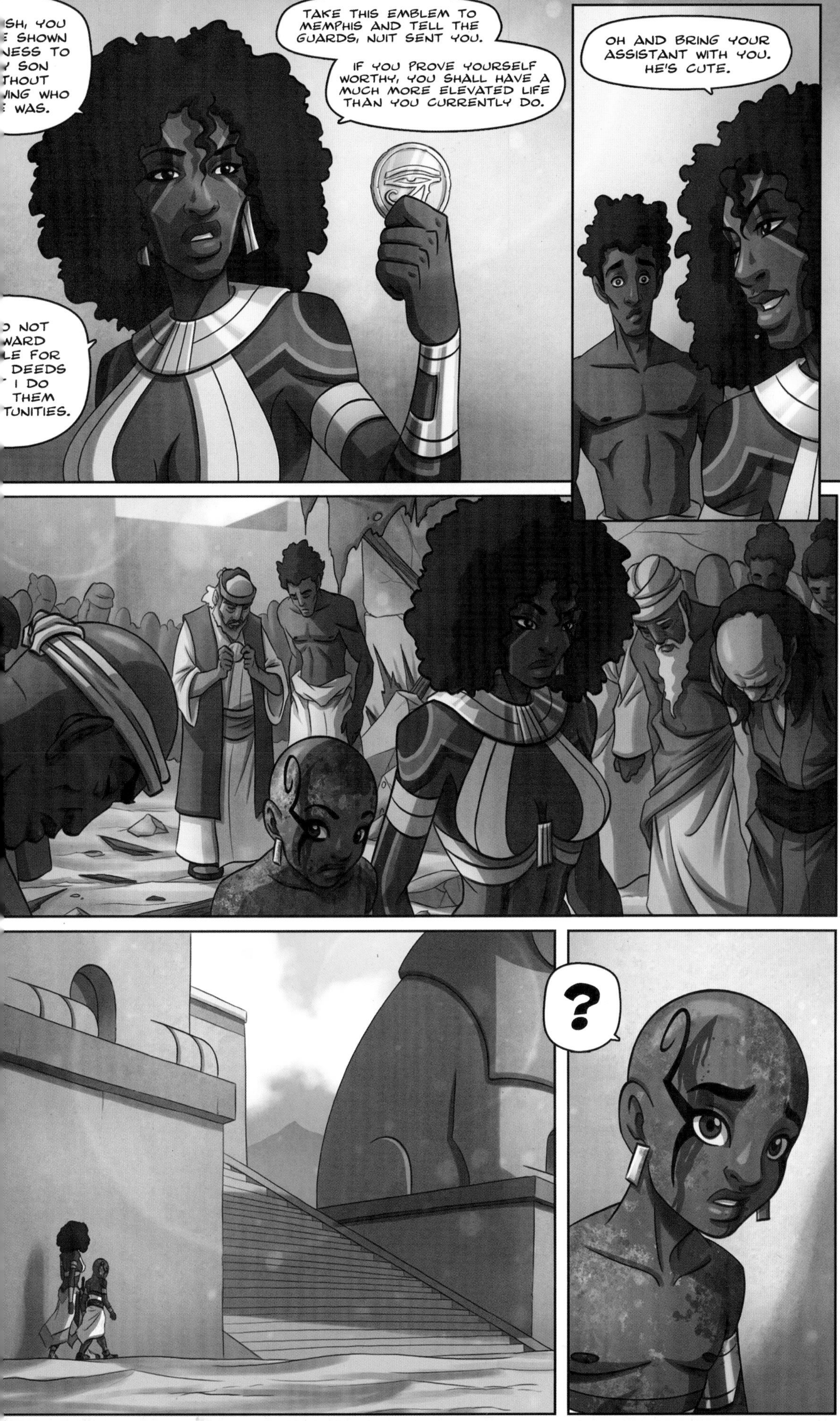

SH, YOU E SHOWN NESS TO Y SON THOUT WING WHO E WAS.
O NOT WARD LE FOR DEEDS I DO THEM TUNITIES.
TAKE THIS EMBLEM TO MEMPHIS AND TELL THE GUARDS, NUIT SENT YOU.
IF YOU PROVE YOURSELF WORTHY, YOU SHALL HAVE A MUCH MORE ELEVATED LIFE THAN YOU CURRENTLY DO.
OH AND BRING YOUR ASSISTANT WITH YOU. HE'S CUTE.
?

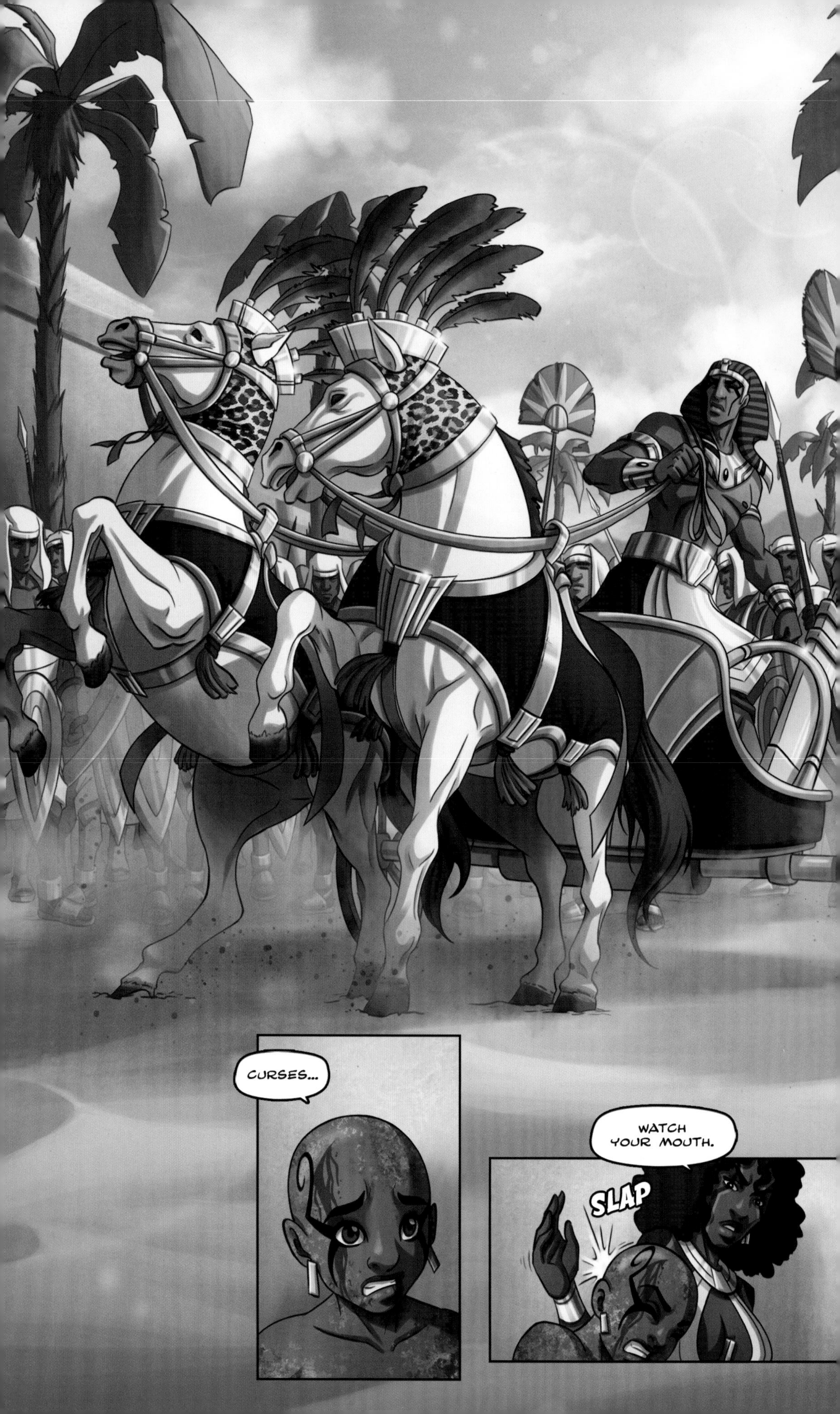
CURSES...
WATCH YOUR MOUTH.
SLAP

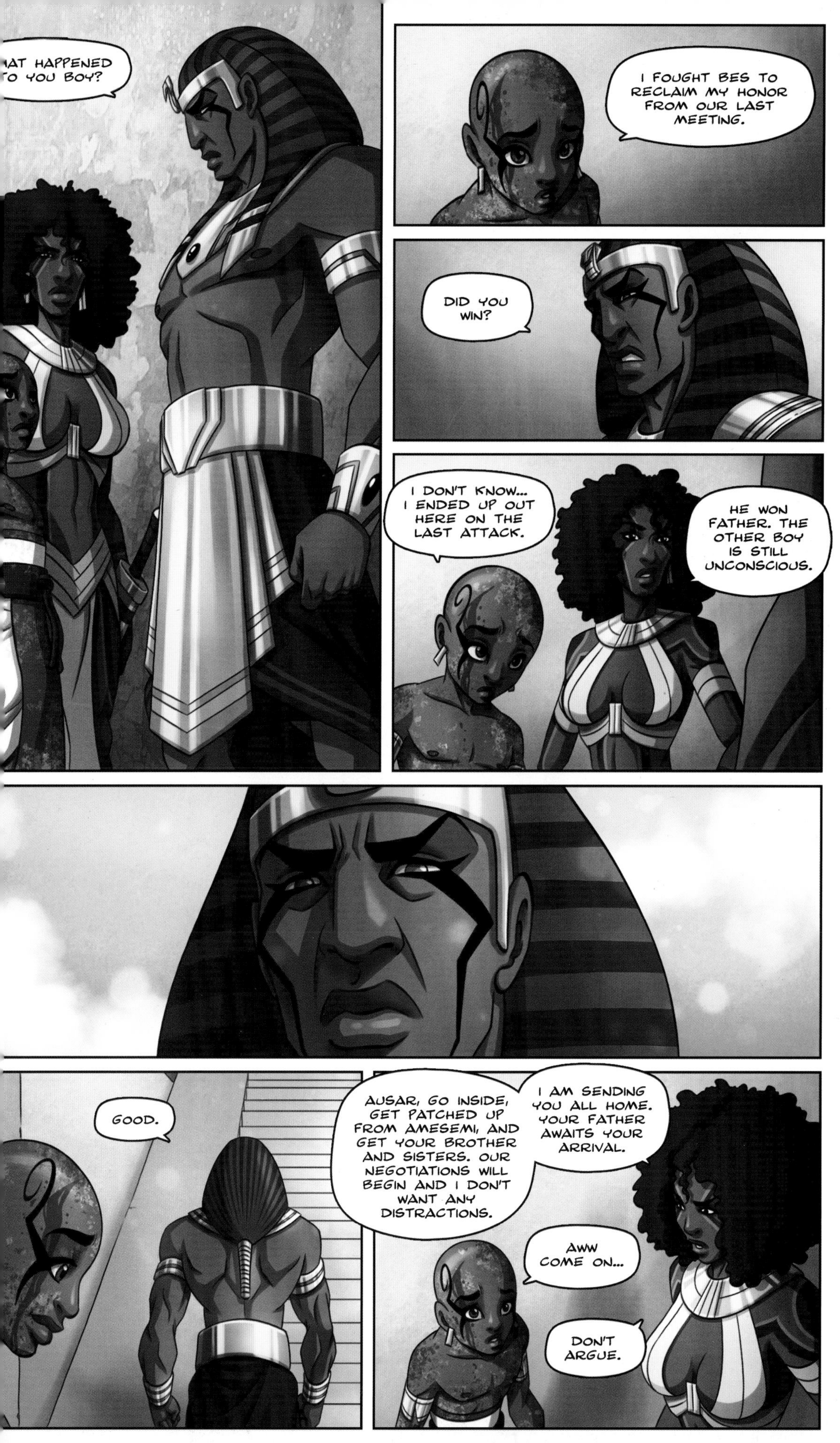
HAT HAPPENED TO YOU BOY?
I FOUGHT BES TO RECLAIM MY HONOR FROM OUR LAST MEETING.
DID YOU WIN?
I DON'T KNOW... I ENDED UP OUT HERE ON THE LAST ATTACK.
HE WON FATHER. THE OTHER BOY IS STILL UNCONSCIOUS.
GOOD.
AUSAR, GO INSIDE, GET PATCHED UP FROM AMESEMI, AND GET YOUR BROTHER AND SISTERS. OUR NEGOTIATIONS WILL BEGIN AND I DON'T WANT ANY DISTRACTIONS.
I AM SENDING YOU ALL HOME. YOUR FATHER AWAITS YOUR ARRIVAL.
AWW COME ON...
DON'T ARGUE.

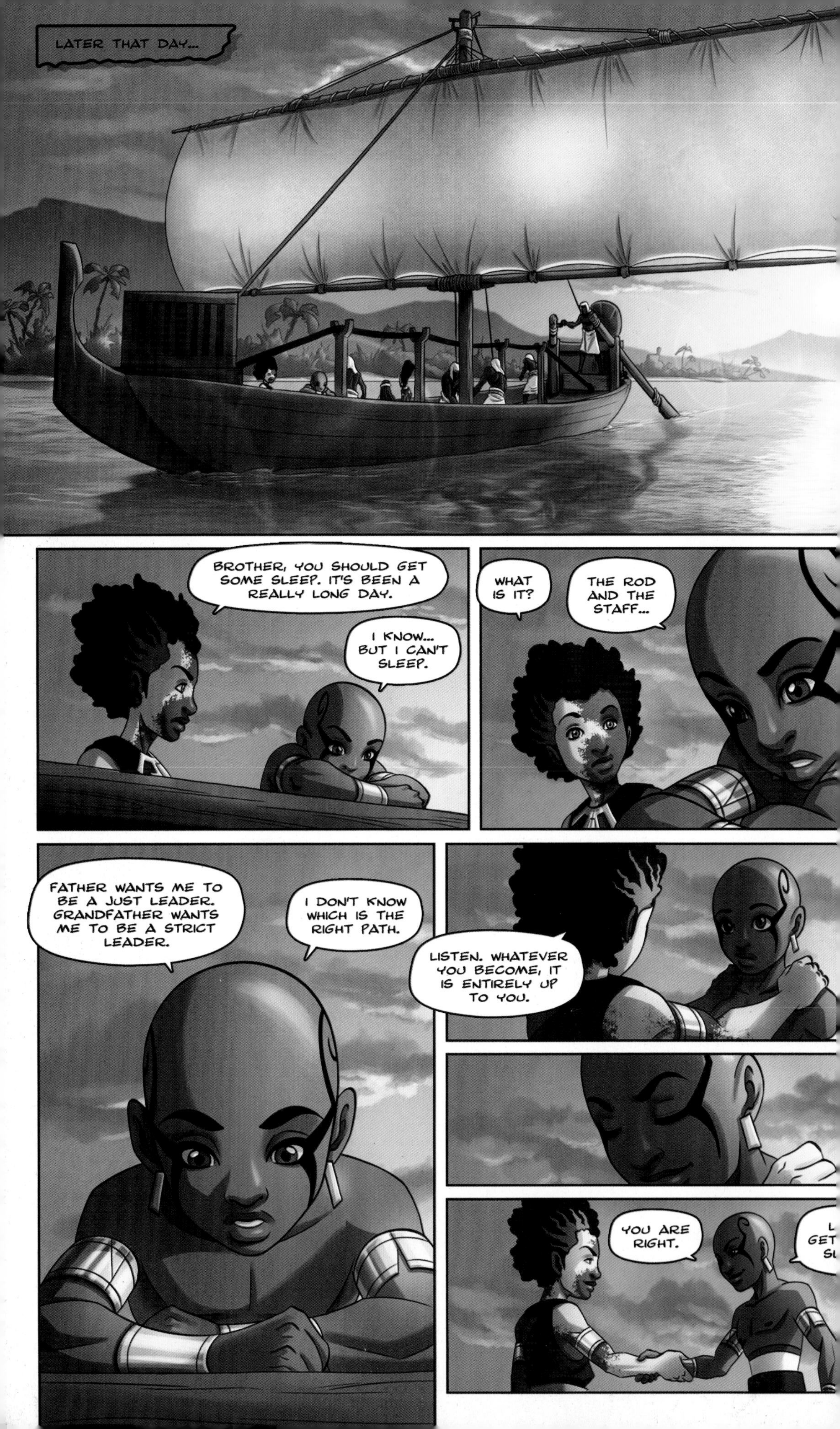
LATER THAT DAY...
BROTHER, YOU SHOULD GET SOME SLEEP. IT'S BEEN A REALLY LONG DAY.
I KNOW... BUT I CAN'T SLEEP.
WHAT IS IT?
THE ROD AND THE STAFF...
FATHER WANTS ME TO BE A JUST LEADER. GRANDFATHER WANTS ME TO BE A STRICT LEADER.
I DON'T KNOW WHICH IS THE RIGHT PATH.
LISTEN. WHATEVER YOU BECOME, IT IS ENTIRELY UP TO YOU.
YOU ARE RIGHT.

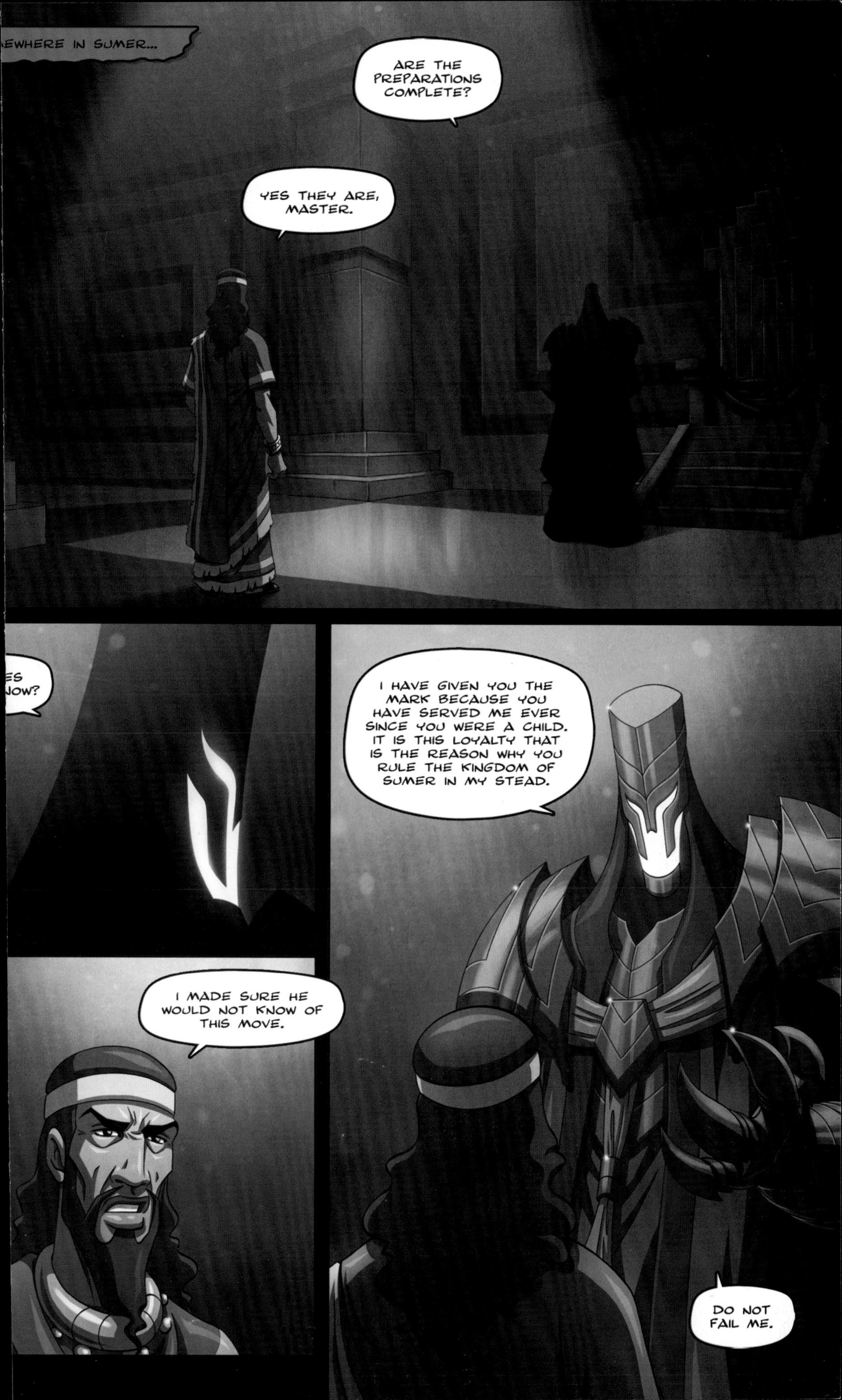
EWHERE IN SUMER...
ARE THE PREPARATIONS COMPLETE?
YES THEY ARE, MASTER.
I HAVE GIVEN YOU THE MARK BECAUSE YOU HAVE SERVED ME EVER SINCE YOU WERE A CHILD. IT IS THIS LOYALTY THAT IS THE REASON WHY YOU RULE THE KINGDOM OF SUMER IN MY STEAD.
I MADE SURE HE WOULD NOT KNOW OF THIS MOVE.
DO NOT FAIL ME.

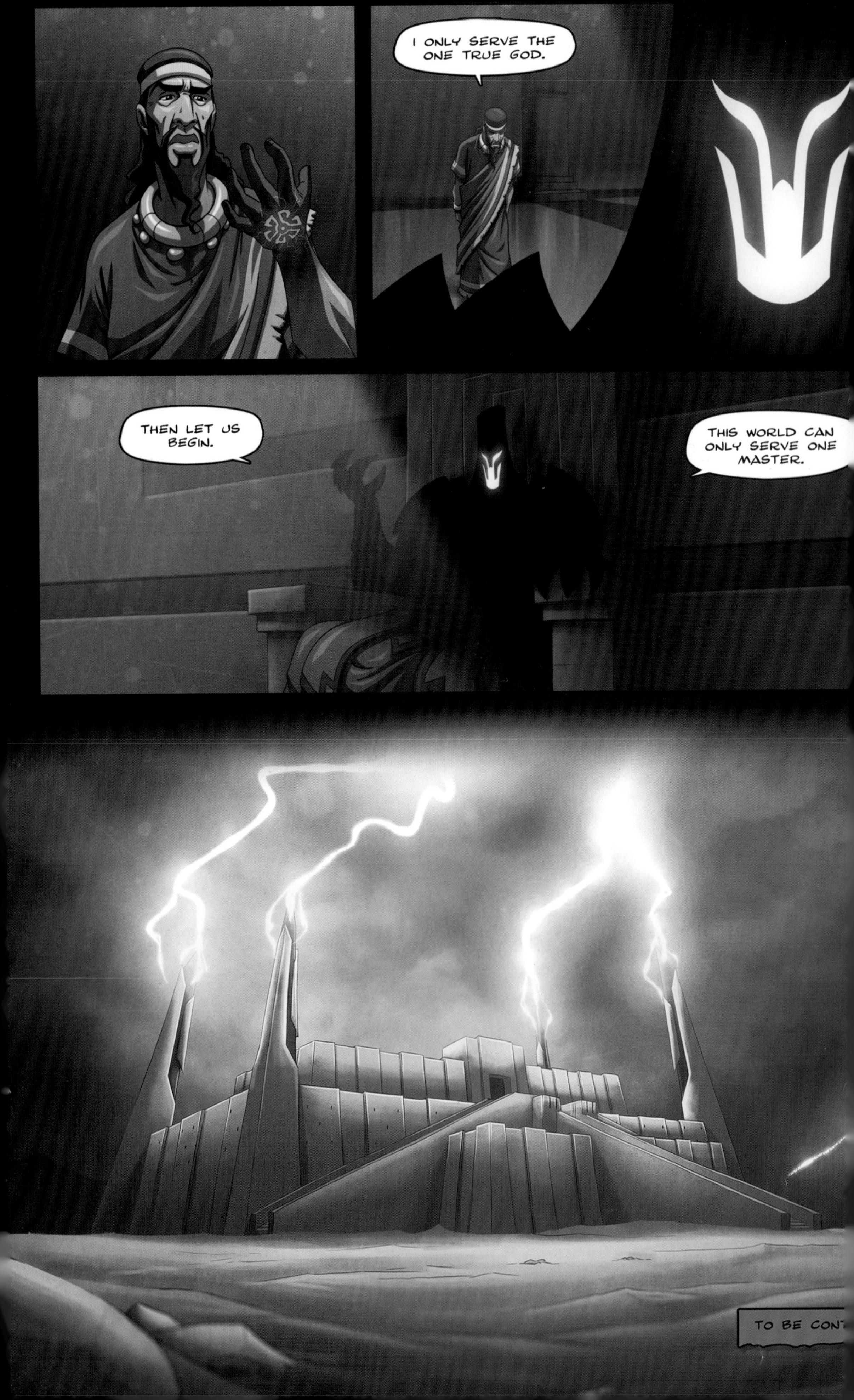
I ONLY SERVE THE ONE TRUE GOD.
THEN LET US BEGIN.
THIS WORLD CAN ONLY SERVE ONE MASTER.
TO BE CONT

he War Between
lods and Men

Black Sands,
ancient gods of
piru are alien
aders, but in
tory, they were
culously
werful gods of
  kingdoms.

e Titans, Deva, and Anunnaki wielded terrible powers that could wipe out
tire civilizations,and their personal actions caused many calamities in the
rld. It is for this reason that we separated those old gods from the demi-gods
Kemet and Sumer. In Akkadian and Kemetic texts, the gods ruled as men and
people. They died very normal deaths and lived on in spirit to guide humanity
t no longer took an active role, unlike the gods of old.

The Kushite Empire

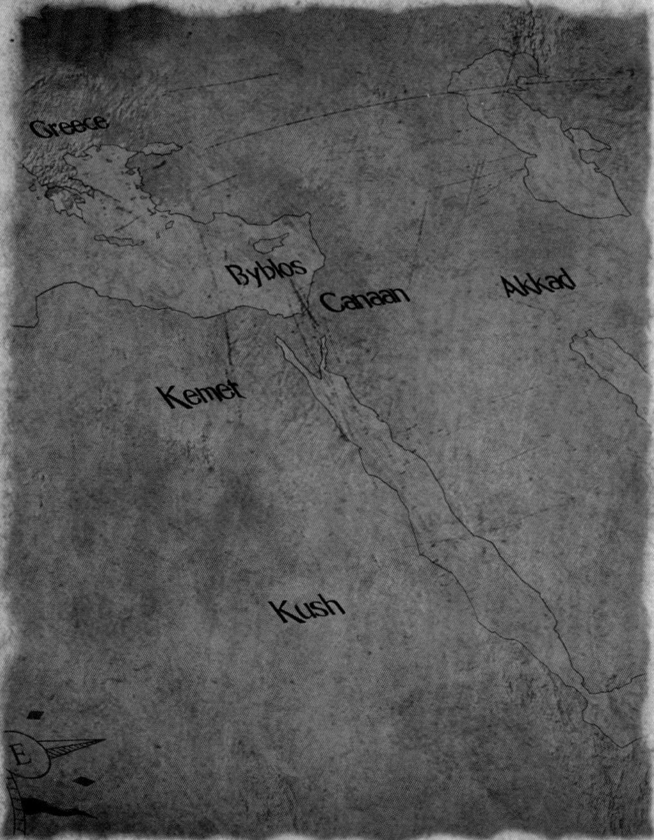
Greece
Byblos
Canaan
Akkad
Kemet
Kush

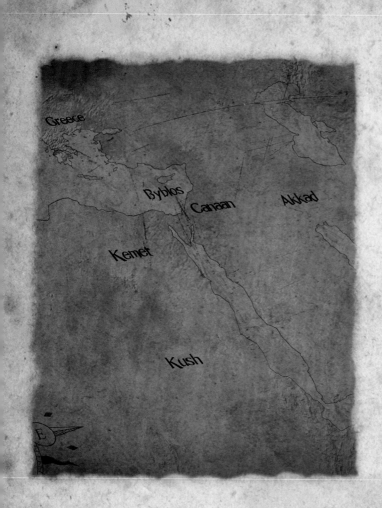

Established around 2500 BC the Kushite Empire started i the region around the city o Kerma. Known for their incredible archers and domin in the gold trade, Kush was strong rival to Kemet and st on par with their neighbors f thousands of years. With th exception of burial practices the Kushites tended to shar cultural norms with their Ke neighbors due to their comm origins. The Kushites buried their royalty with commoners mass graves as a symbol of unity for the people.

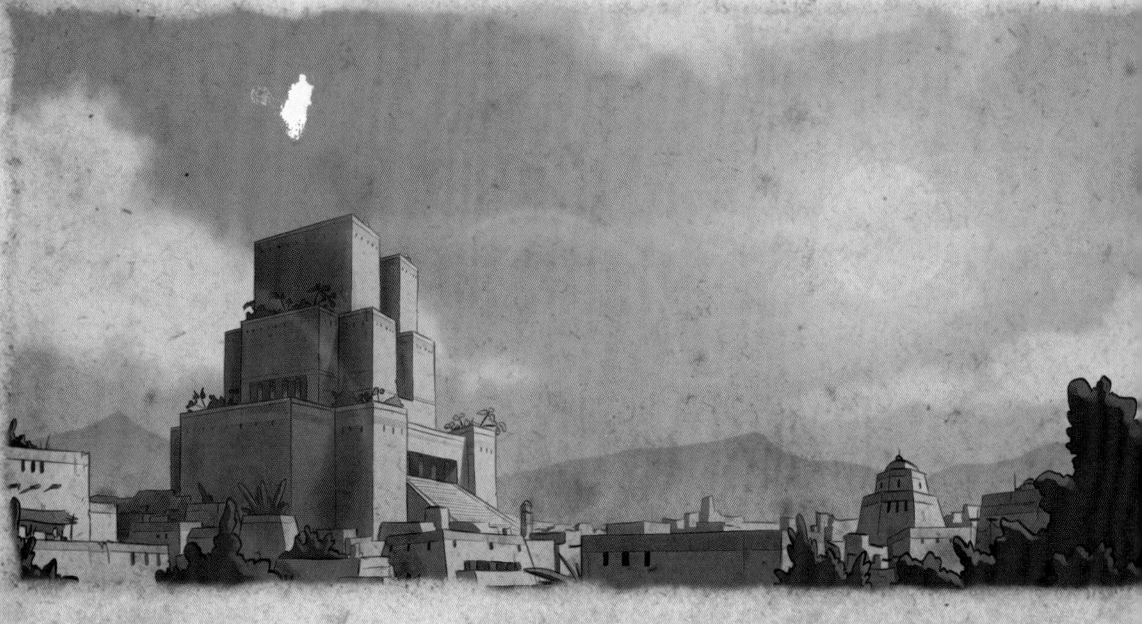

'he Kingdom of umer

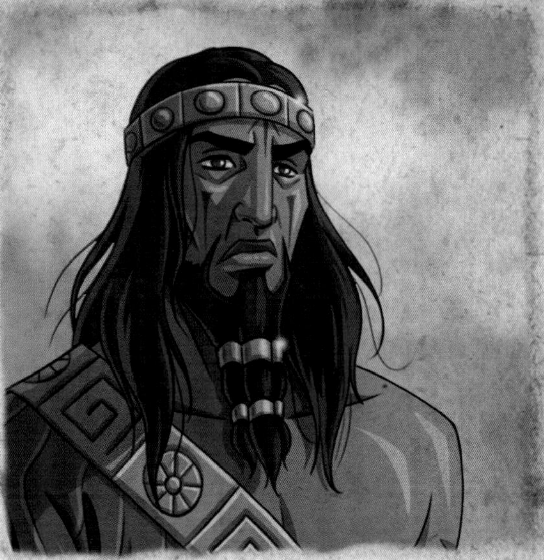

ıe successors of the Akkadian vilization, Sumer was a highly ligious society. The Kings were so considered the high priest and d a sacred pact to keep order and ability for the gods. Many cities ose from this civilization and It Is ıown to be first Empire in the orld.

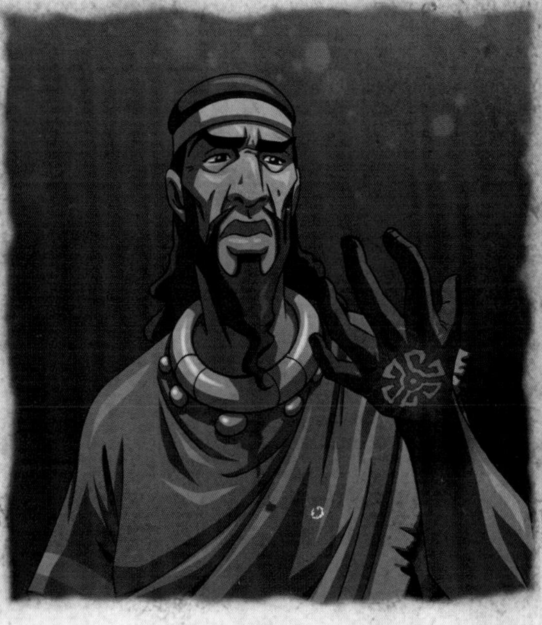

Black Sands, we incorporate their ligious beliefs of the Gods bringing der to a very real state. Their ds, the Anunnaki, are the true lers of Sumer but they allow the gh priest to rule in their stead to ot panic the people. As such, the ingdom runs highly efficiently but so has a deep mysterious aura ound everyday life.

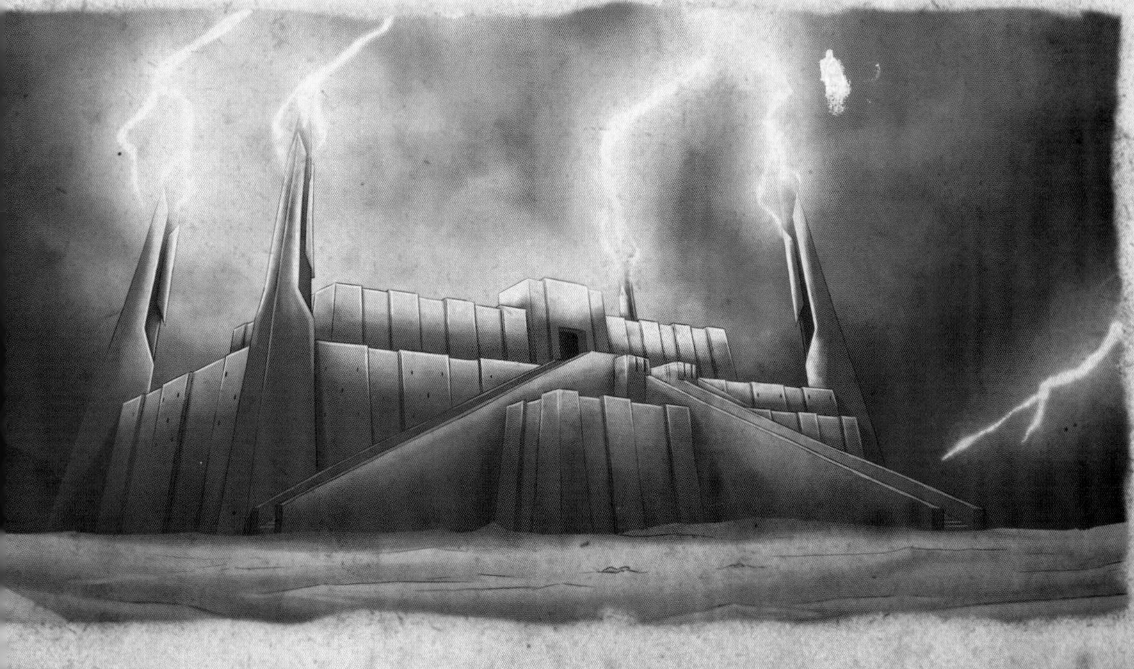

The Dark Pharaoh

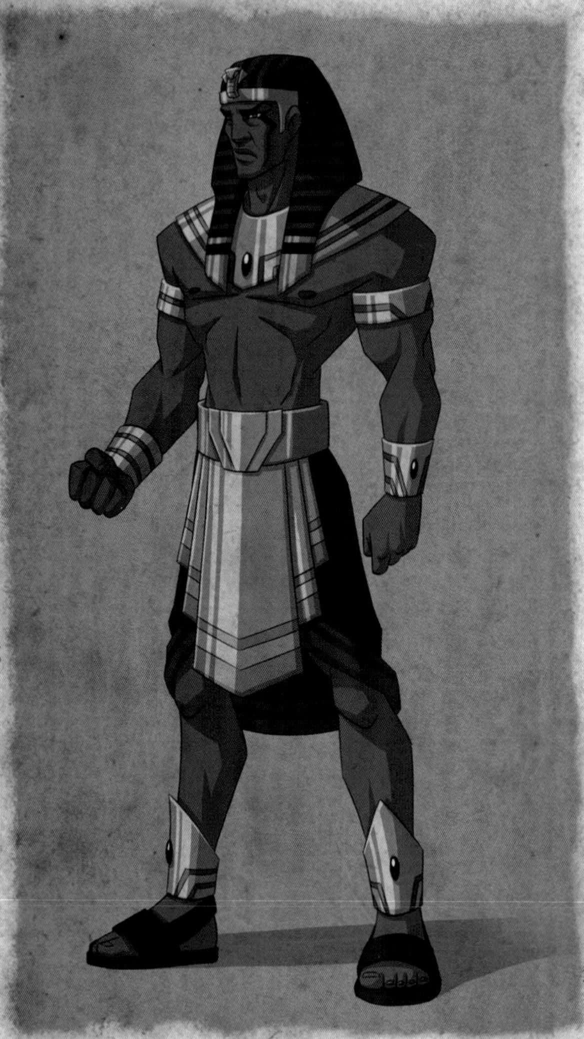

Known as the first mortal Pharaoh Kemet, Rah is said to have aided in creation in the world before taking mortal form and ruling for a thousa years. His influence over the Keme system of justice has left a mark o their society for thousands of year with many living their entire lives in status of they were given at birth. Unlike In most caste societies, the lower class were treated with resp due to the
teachings of the first Pharaoh. He serves the kingdom and performs exactly as expected is worthy of eternal life. This is why many hold as the true first Pharaoh and not ju some mythological character.

It is of note, that many Kings that followed thousands of years later h myths written of them similar to Ra even though we know they existed without question.

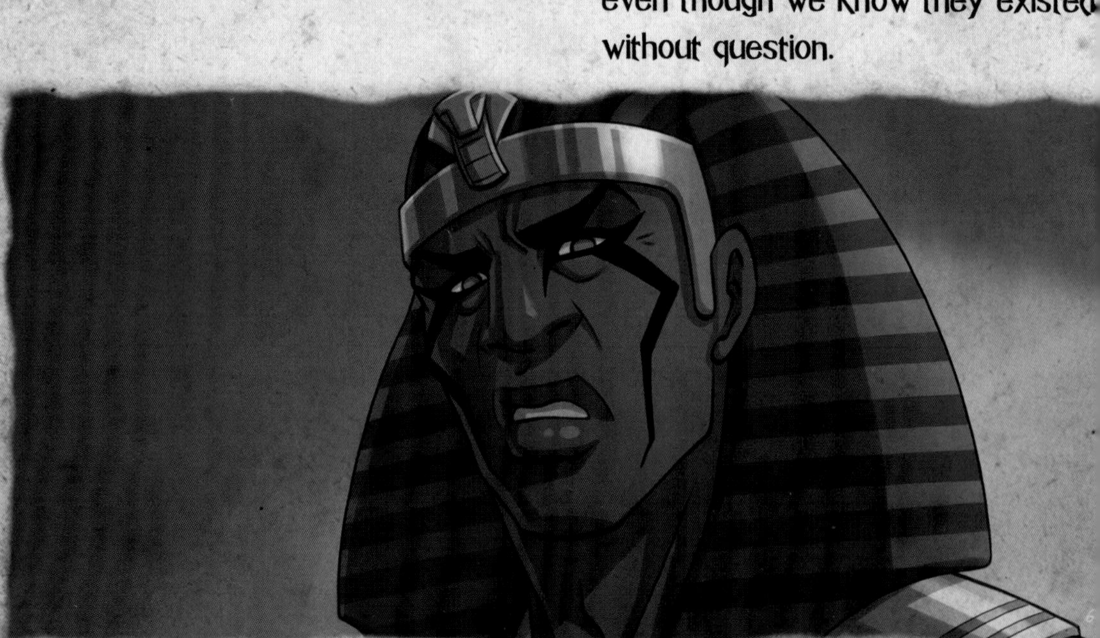

e Anunnaki

e said to rule Sumer and world, the Anunnaki are the ike deities of ancient er. Their leader was named 'duk and he had immense er over the elements, com- ly being referred to as the ger of storms. Legends say Anunaki created humanity o menial tasks they did not to do. Some say it was to precious metals. Whatever reason, they clearly wanted anity to serve them.

lack Sands, the Anunnaki ancient gods from the et Nibiru. The creation changes a bit, but the re- of the kingdom's rule re- s the same. The people ve the gods unquestionably.

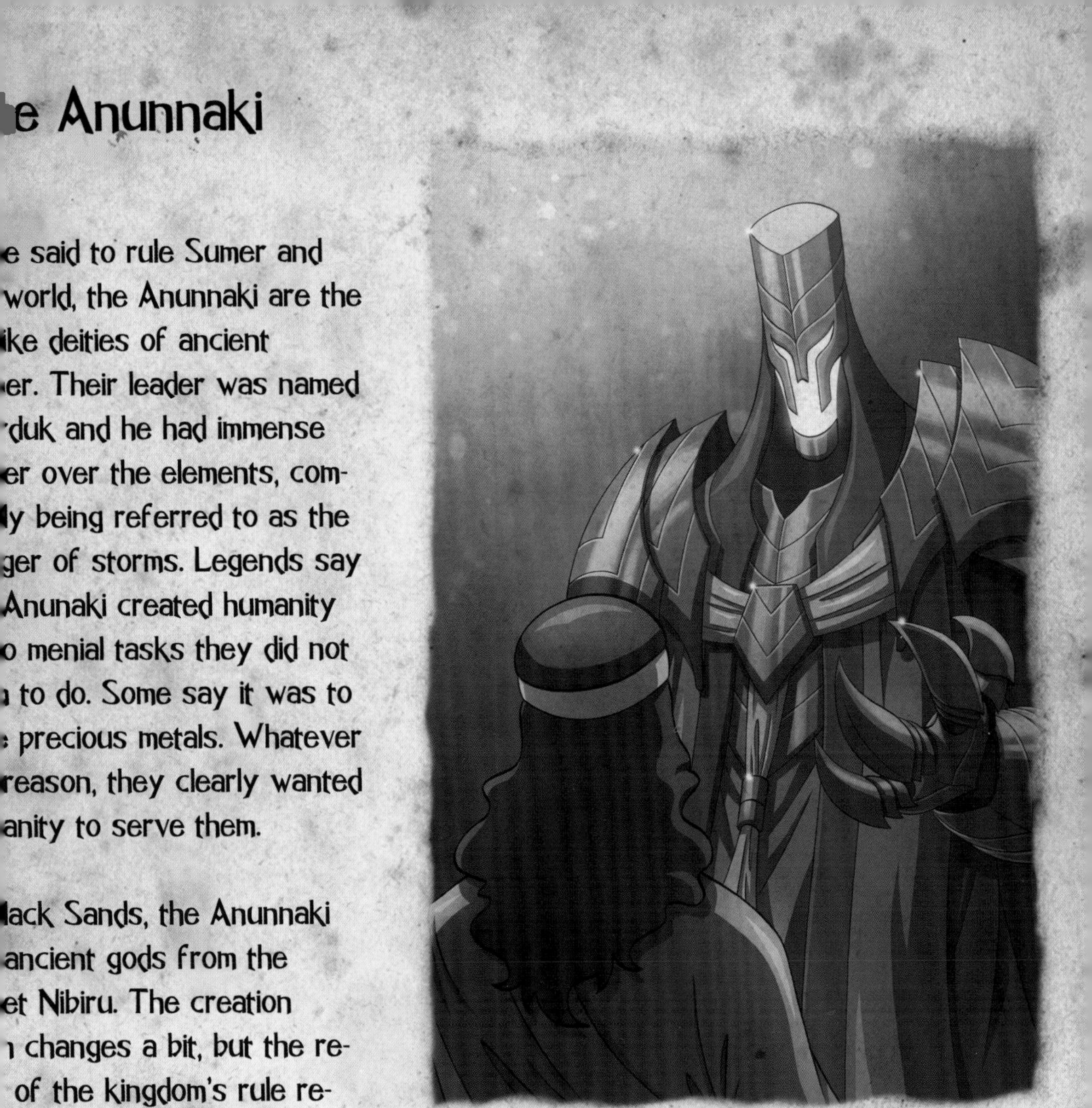

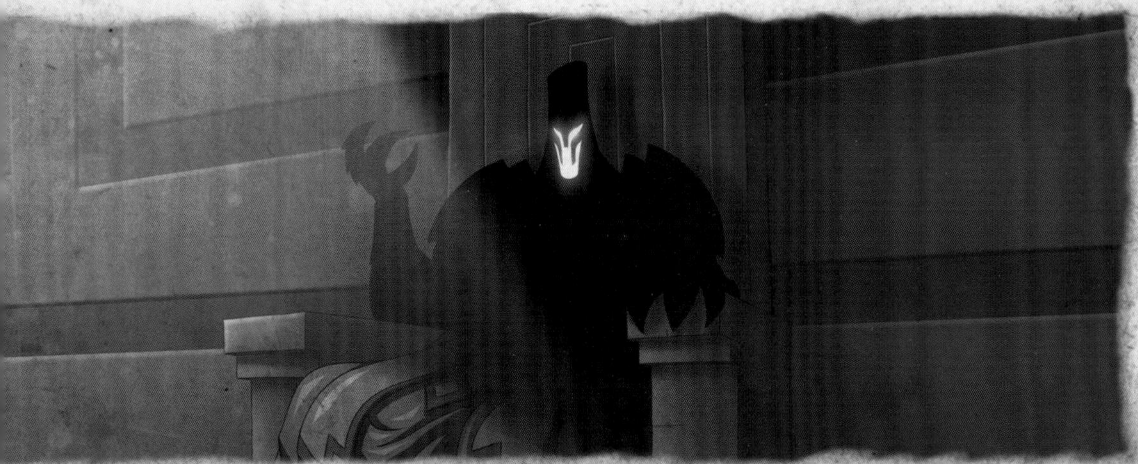

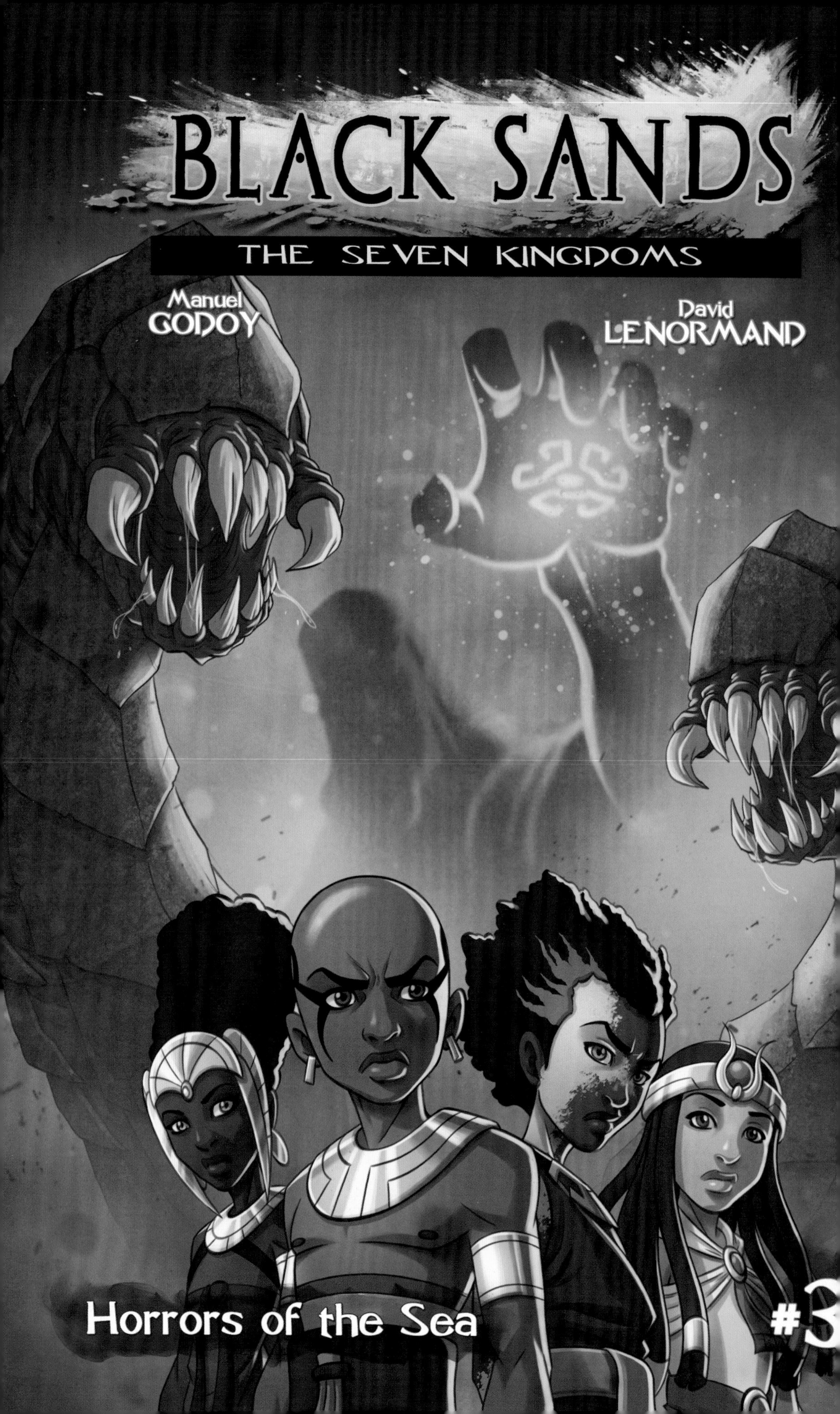
BLACK SANDS
THE SEVEN KINGDOMS
Manuel GODOY
David LENORMAND
Horrors of the Sea
#3

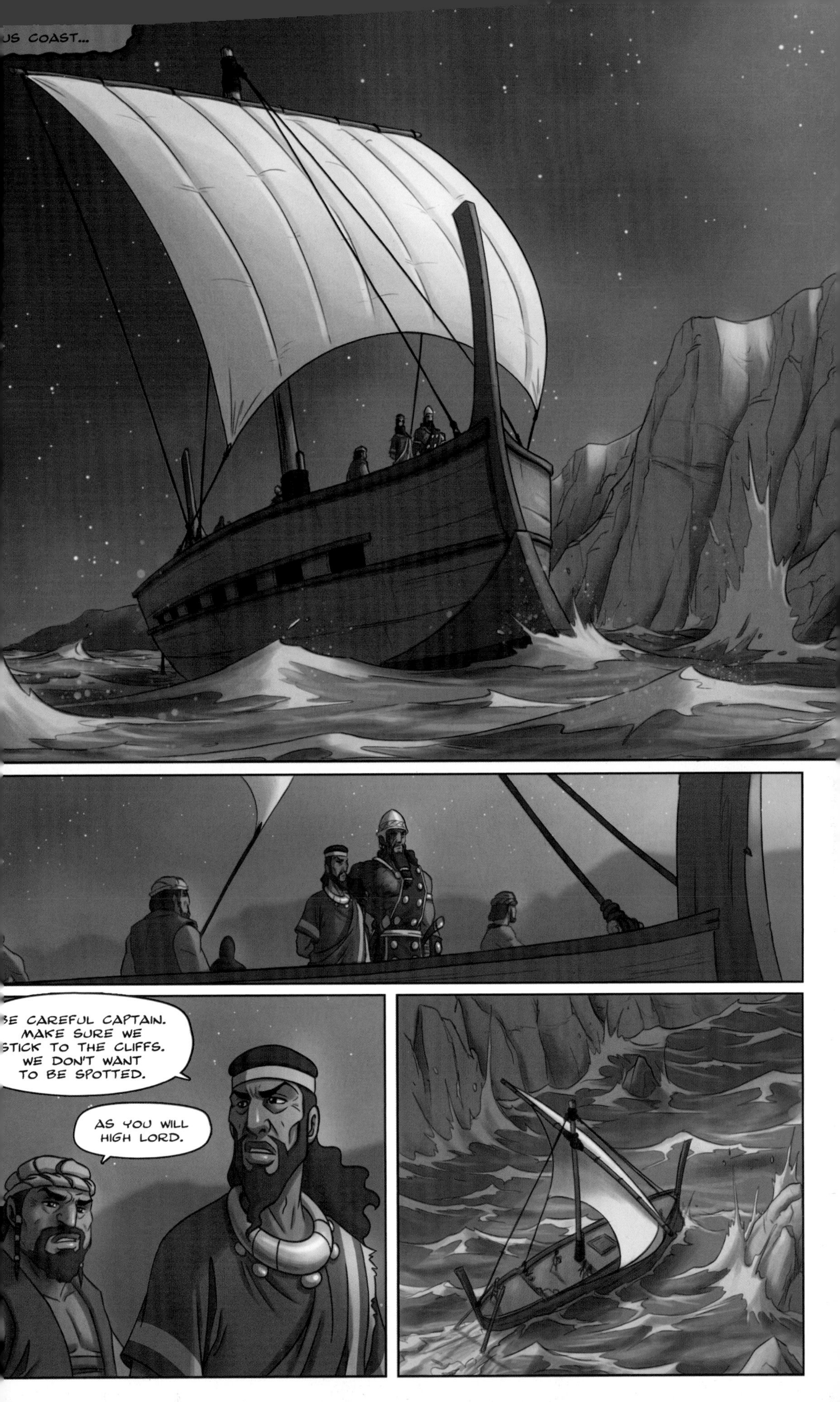
US COAST...
BE CAREFUL CAPTAIN. MAKE SURE WE STICK TO THE CLIFFS. WE DON'T WANT TO BE SPOTTED.
AS YOU WILL HIGH LORD.

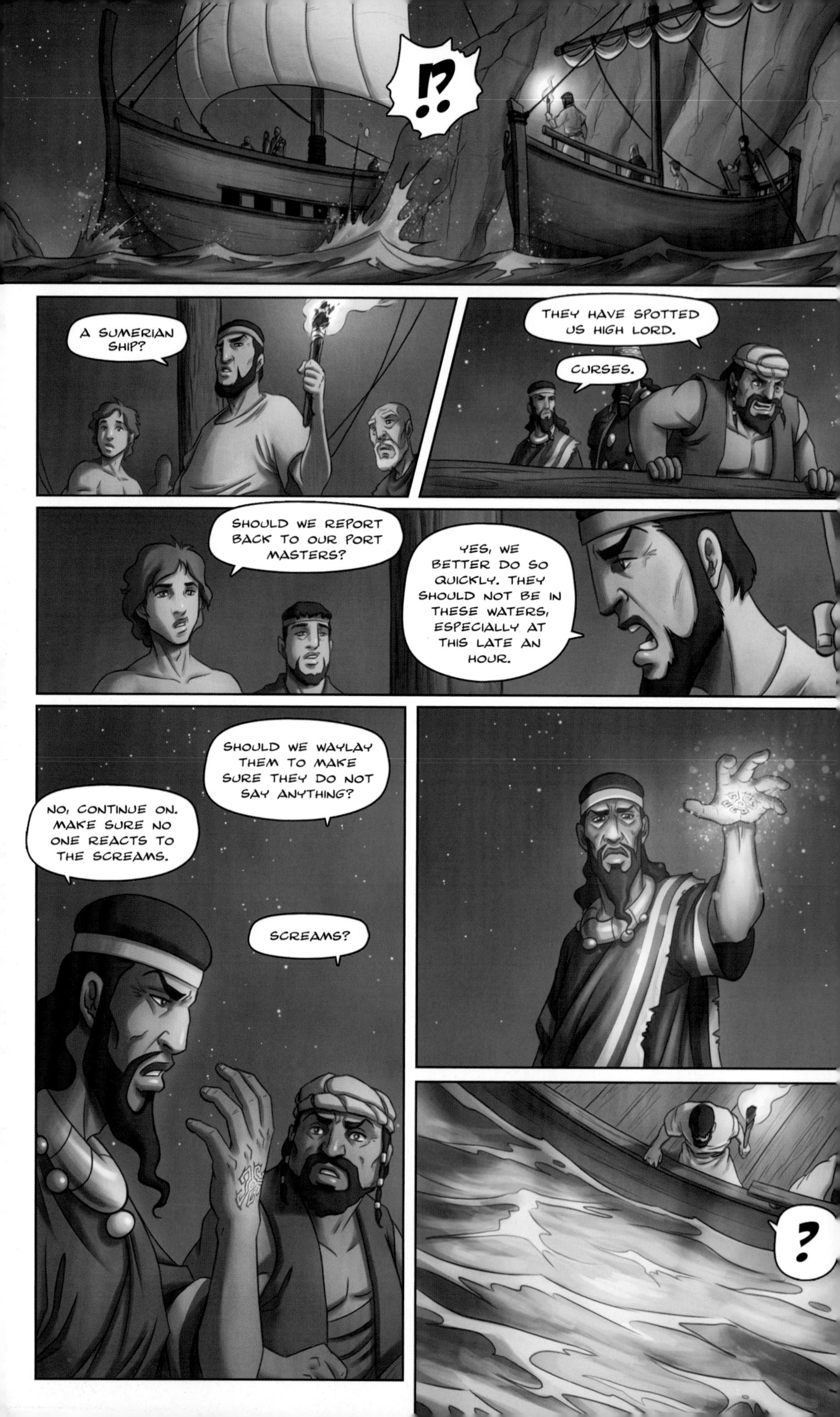
!?
A SUMERIAN SHIP?
THEY HAVE SPOTTED US HIGH LORD.
CURSES.
SHOULD WE REPORT BACK TO OUR PORT MASTERS?
YES, WE BETTER DO SO QUICKLY. THEY SHOULD NOT BE IN THESE WATERS, ESPECIALLY AT THIS LATE AN HOUR.
SHOULD WE WAYLAY THEM TO MAKE SURE THEY DO NOT SAY ANYTHING?
NO, CONTINUE ON. MAKE SURE NO ONE REACTS TO THE SCREAMS.
SCREAMS?
?

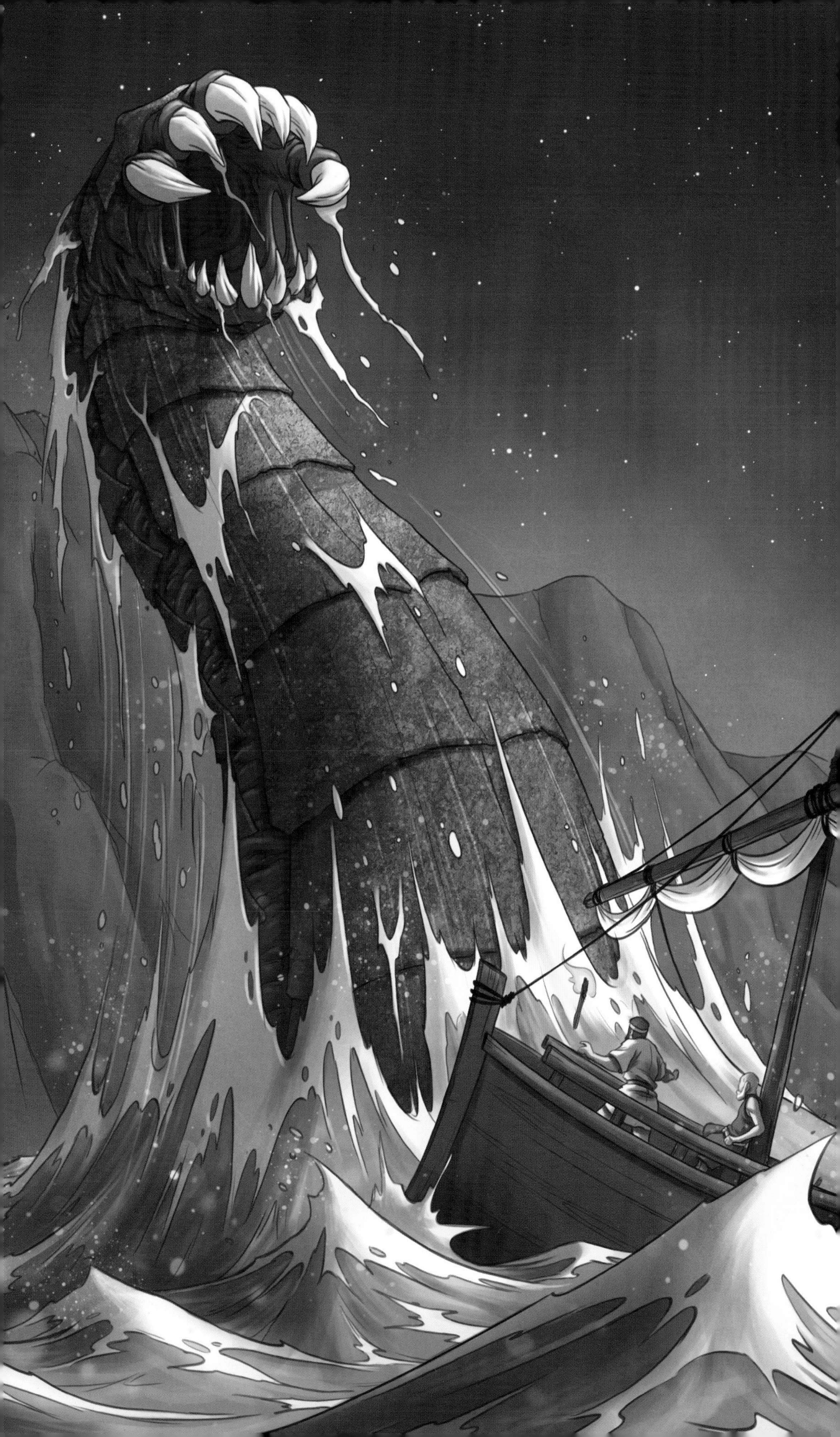

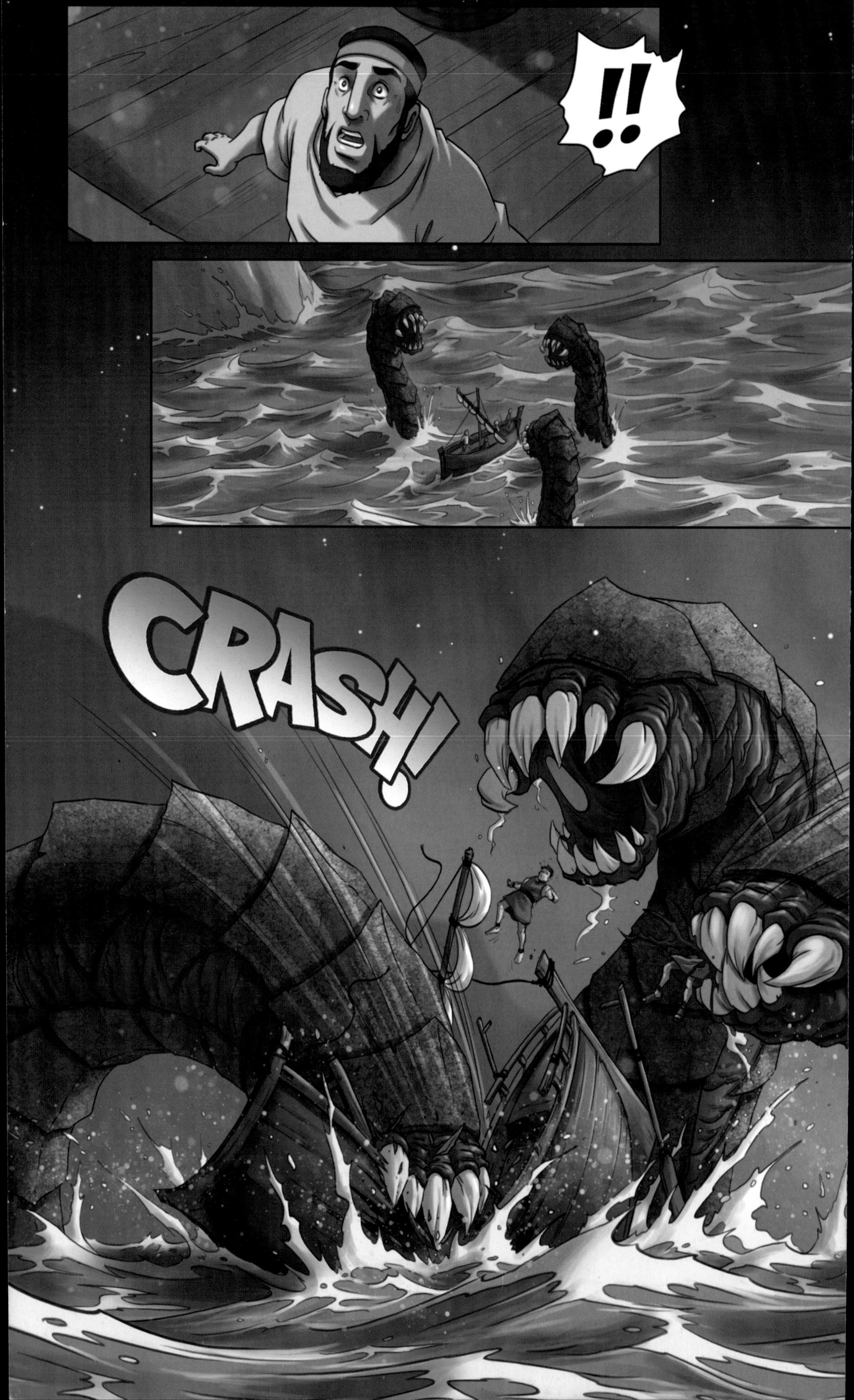
!!
CRASH!

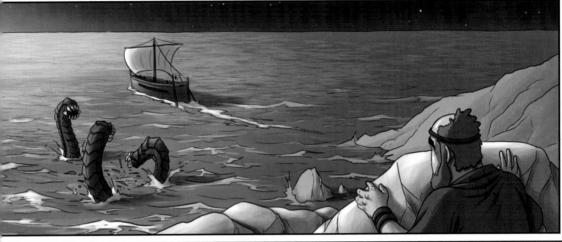

ROTIRI...

THE NEXT MORNING...

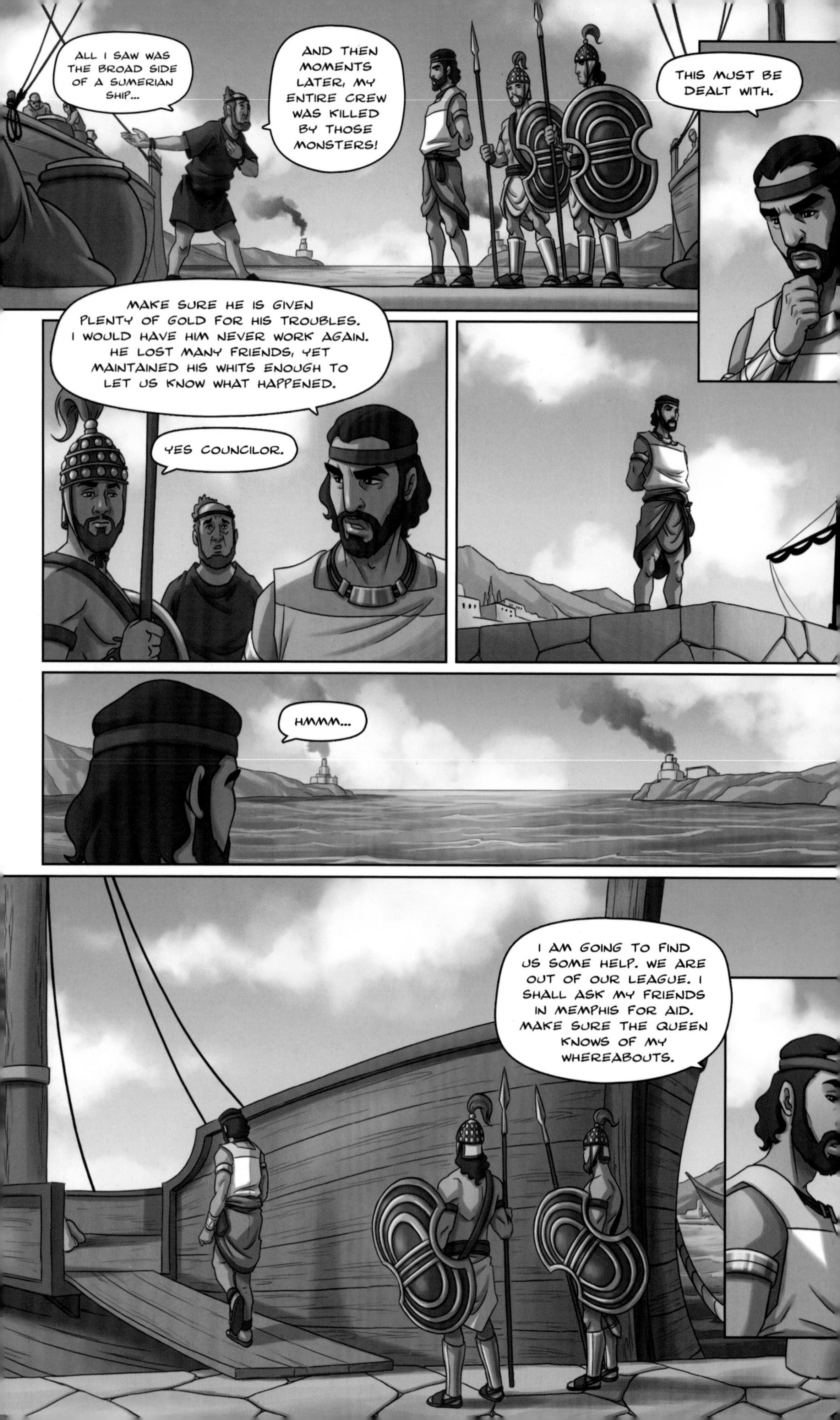
ALL I SAW WAS THE BROAD SIDE OF A SUMERIAN SHIP...
AND THEN MOMENTS LATER, MY ENTIRE CREW WAS KILLED BY THOSE MONSTERS!
THIS MUST BE DEALT WITH.
MAKE SURE HE IS GIVEN PLENTY OF GOLD FOR HIS TROUBLES. I WOULD HAVE HIM NEVER WORK AGAIN. HE LOST MANY FRIENDS, YET MAINTAINED HIS WHITS ENOUGH TO LET US KNOW WHAT HAPPENED.
YES COUNCILOR.
HMMM...
I AM GOING TO FIND US SOME HELP. WE ARE OUT OF OUR LEAGUE. I SHALL ASK MY FRIENDS IN MEMPHIS FOR AID. MAKE SURE THE QUEEN KNOWS OF MY WHEREABOUTS.

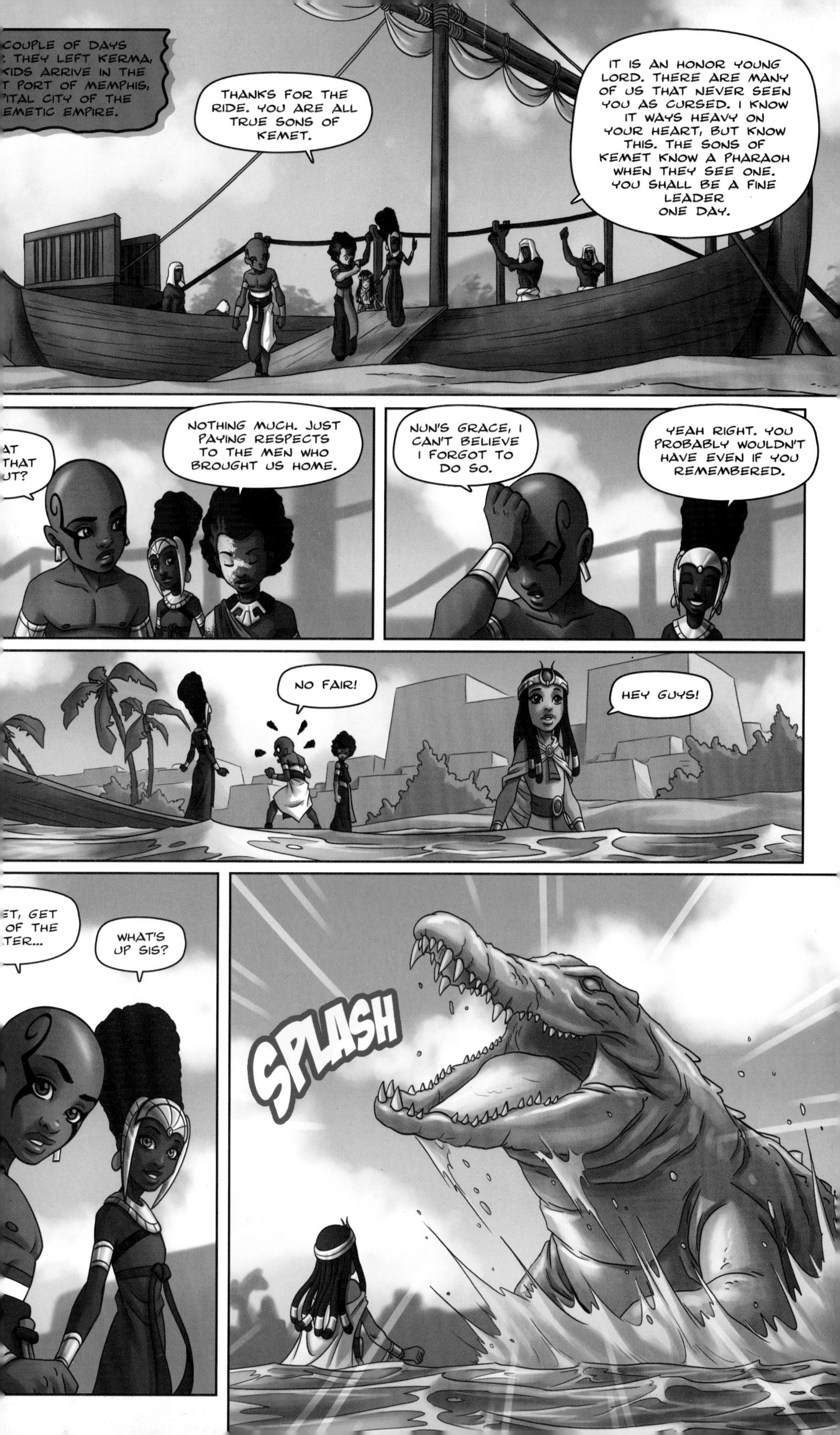

COUPLE OF DAYS : THEY LEFT KERMA, KIDS ARRIVE IN THE T PORT OF MEMPHIS, PITAL CITY OF THE EMETIC EMPIRE.
THANKS FOR THE RIDE. YOU ARE ALL TRUE SONS OF KEMET.
IT IS AN HONOR YOUNG LORD. THERE ARE MANY OF US THAT NEVER SEEN YOU AS CURSED. I KNOW IT WAYS HEAVY ON YOUR HEART, BUT KNOW THIS. THE SONS OF KEMET KNOW A PHARAOH WHEN THEY SEE ONE. YOU SHALL BE A FINE LEADER ONE DAY.
AT THAT UT?
NOTHING MUCH. JUST PAYING RESPECTS TO THE MEN WHO BROUGHT US HOME.
NUN'S GRACE, I CAN'T BELIEVE I FORGOT TO DO SO.
YEAH RIGHT. YOU PROBABLY WOULDN'T HAVE EVEN IF YOU REMEMBERED.
NO FAIR!
HEY GUYS!
ET, GET OF THE TER...
WHAT'S UP SIS?
SPLASH

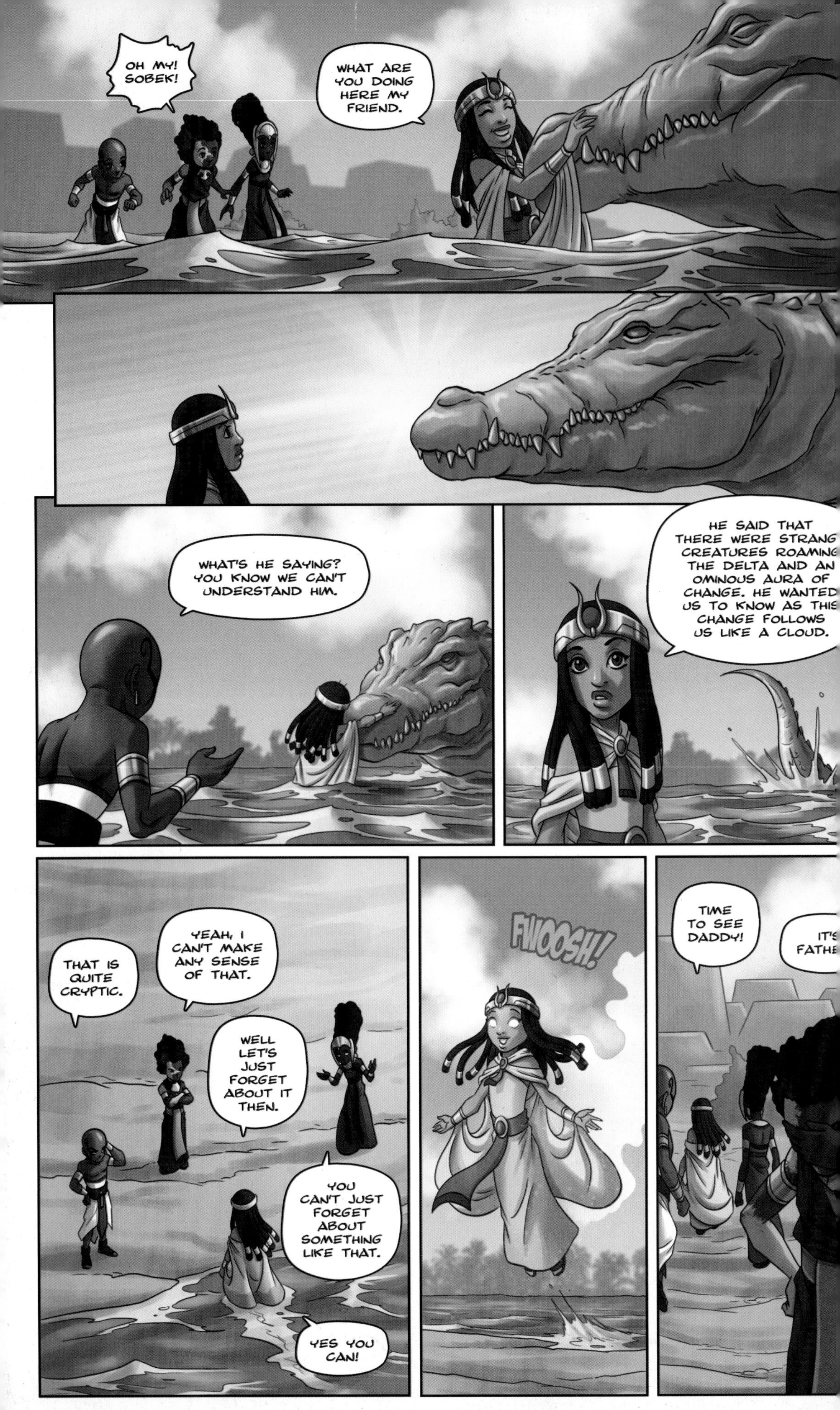
OH MY! SOBEK!
WHAT ARE YOU DOING HERE MY FRIEND.
WHAT'S HE SAYING? YOU KNOW WE CAN'T UNDERSTAND HIM.
HE SAID THAT THERE WERE STRANG CREATURES ROAMING THE DELTA AND AN OMINOUS AURA OF CHANGE. HE WANTED US TO KNOW AS THIS CHANGE FOLLOWS US LIKE A CLOUD.
THAT IS QUITE CRYPTIC.
YEAH, I CAN'T MAKE ANY SENSE OF THAT.
WELL LET'S JUST FORGET ABOUT IT THEN.
YOU CAN'T JUST FORGET ABOUT SOMETHING LIKE THAT.
YES YOU CAN!
FWOOSH!
TIME TO SEE DADDY!
IT'S FATHE

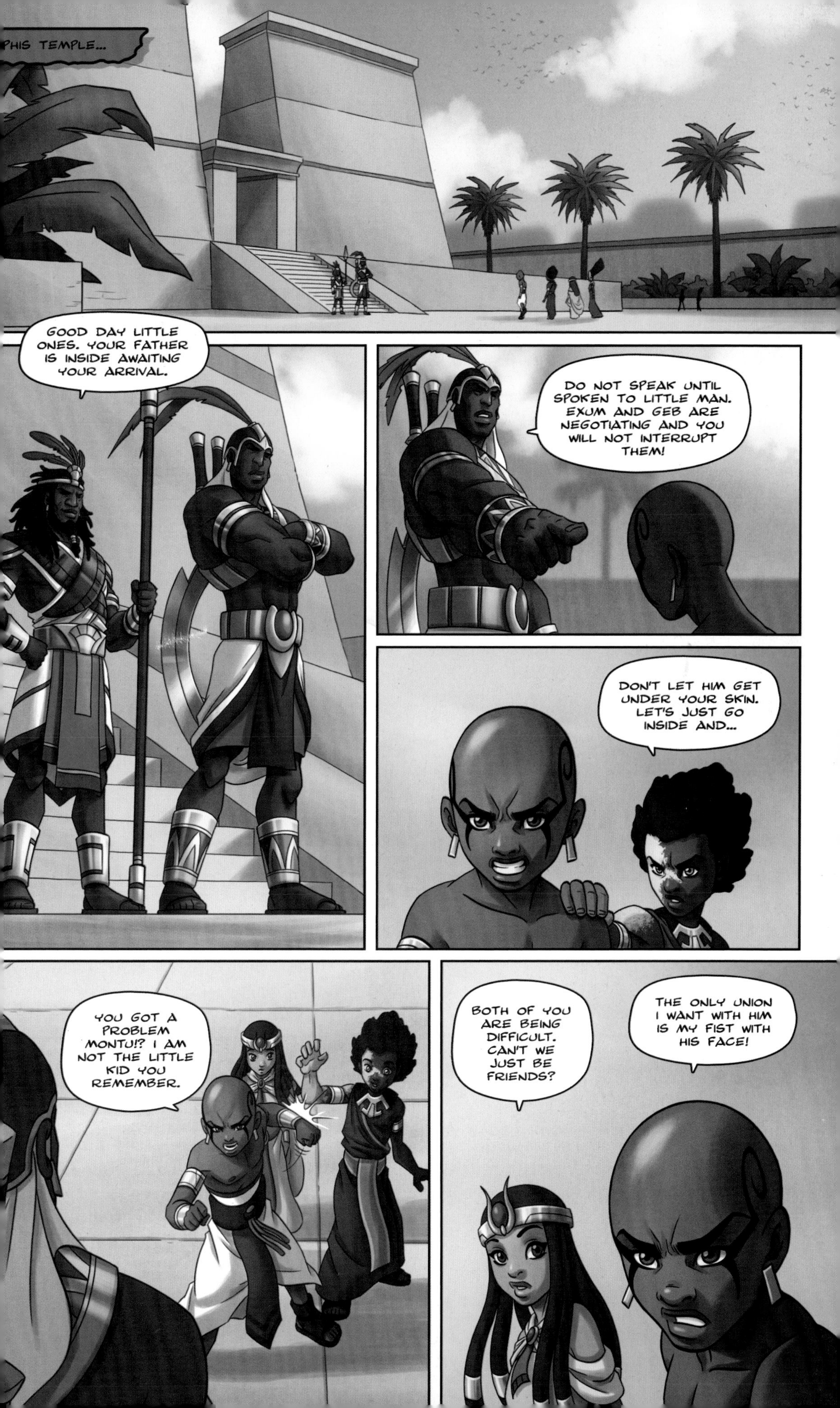

PHIS TEMPLE...
GOOD DAY LITTLE ONES. YOUR FATHER IS INSIDE AWAITING YOUR ARRIVAL.
DO NOT SPEAK UNTIL SPOKEN TO LITTLE MAN. EXUM AND GEB ARE NEGOTIATING AND YOU WILL NOT INTERRUPT THEM!
DON'T LET HIM GET UNDER YOUR SKIN. LET'S JUST GO INSIDE AND...
YOU GOT A PROBLEM MONTU!? I AM NOT THE LITTLE KID YOU REMEMBER.
BOTH OF YOU ARE BEING DIFFICULT. CAN'T WE JUST BE FRIENDS?
THE ONLY UNION I WANT WITH HIM IS MY FIST WITH HIS FACE!

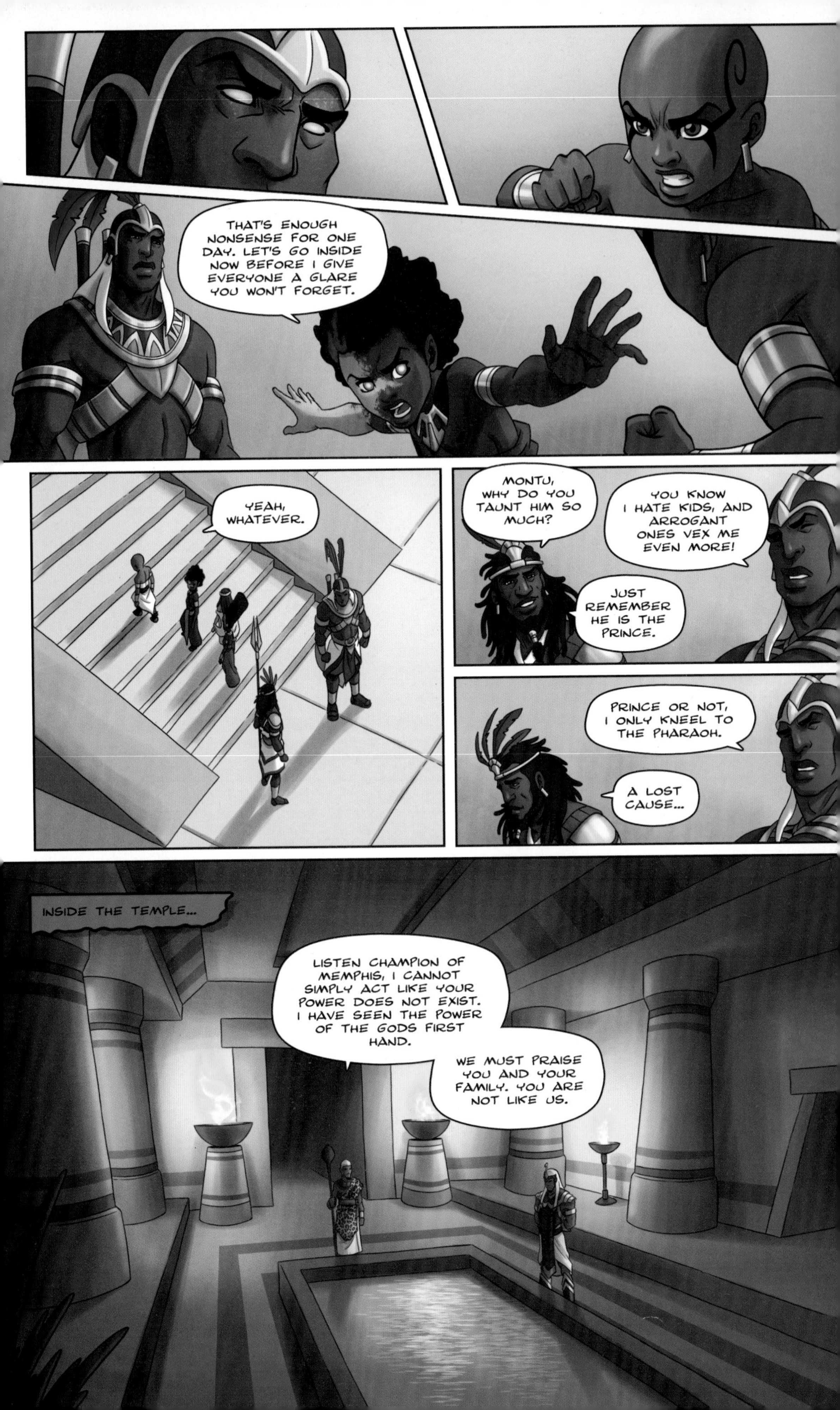
THAT'S ENOUGH NONSENSE FOR ONE DAY. LET'S GO INSIDE NOW BEFORE I GIVE EVERYONE A GLARE YOU WON'T FORGET.
YEAH, WHATEVER.
MONTU, WHY DO YOU TAUNT HIM SO MUCH?
YOU KNOW I HATE KIDS, AND ARROGANT ONES VEX ME EVEN MORE!
JUST REMEMBER HE IS THE PRINCE.
PRINCE OR NOT, I ONLY KNEEL TO THE PHARAOH.
A LOST CAUSE...
INSIDE THE TEMPLE...
LISTEN CHAMPION OF MEMPHIS, I CANNOT SIMPLY ACT LIKE YOUR POWER DOES NOT EXIST. I HAVE SEEN THE POWER OF THE GODS FIRST HAND.
WE MUST PRAISE YOU AND YOUR FAMILY. YOU ARE NOT LIKE US.

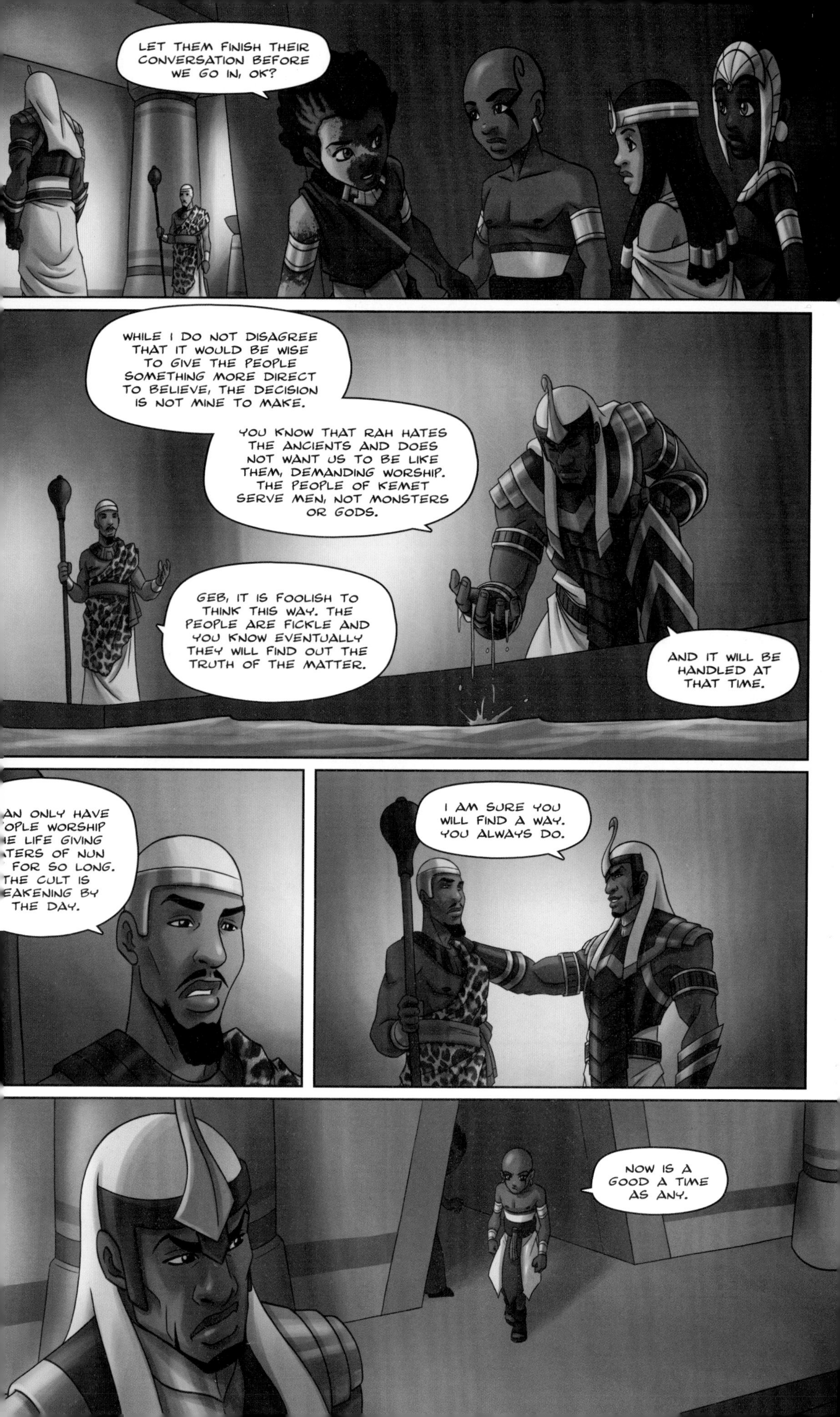
LET THEM FINISH THEIR CONVERSATION BEFORE WE GO IN, OK?
WHILE I DO NOT DISAGREE THAT IT WOULD BE WISE TO GIVE THE PEOPLE SOMETHING MORE DIRECT TO BELIEVE, THE DECISION IS NOT MINE TO MAKE.
YOU KNOW THAT RAH HATES THE ANCIENTS AND DOES NOT WANT US TO BE LIKE THEM, DEMANDING WORSHIP. THE PEOPLE OF KEMET SERVE MEN, NOT MONSTERS OR GODS.
GEB, IT IS FOOLISH TO THINK THIS WAY. THE PEOPLE ARE FICKLE AND YOU KNOW EVENTUALLY THEY WILL FIND OUT THE TRUTH OF THE MATTER.
AND IT WILL BE HANDLED AT THAT TIME.
AN ONLY HAVE OPLE WORSHIP IE LIFE GIVING ATERS OF NUN FOR SO LONG. THE CULT IS EAKENING BY THE DAY.
I AM SURE YOU WILL FIND A WAY. YOU ALWAYS DO.
NOW IS A GOOD A TIME AS ANY.

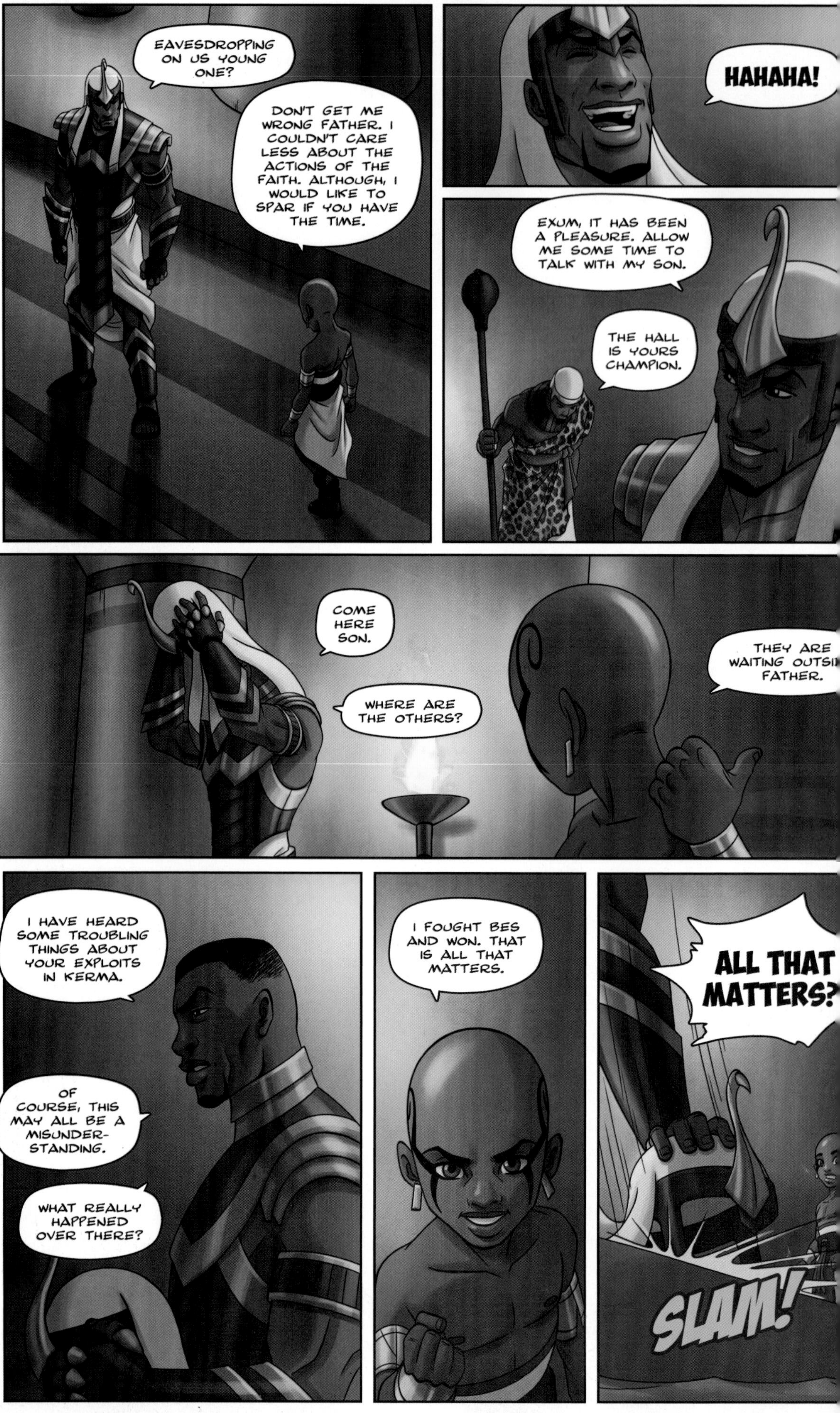

EAVESDROPPING ON US YOUNG ONE?
DON'T GET ME WRONG FATHER. I COULDN'T CARE LESS ABOUT THE ACTIONS OF THE FAITH. ALTHOUGH, I WOULD LIKE TO SPAR IF YOU HAVE THE TIME.
HAHAHA!
EXUM, IT HAS BEEN A PLEASURE. ALLOW ME SOME TIME TO TALK WITH MY SON.
THE HALL IS YOURS CHAMPION.
COME HERE SON.
WHERE ARE THE OTHERS?
THEY ARE WAITING OUTSI
FATHER.
I HAVE HEARD SOME TROUBLING THINGS ABOUT YOUR EXPLOITS IN KERMA.
OF COURSE, THIS MAY ALL BE A MISUNDER-STANDING.
WHAT REALLY HAPPENED OVER THERE?
I FOUGHT BES AND WON. THAT IS ALL THAT MATTERS.
ALL THAT MATTERS?
SLAM!

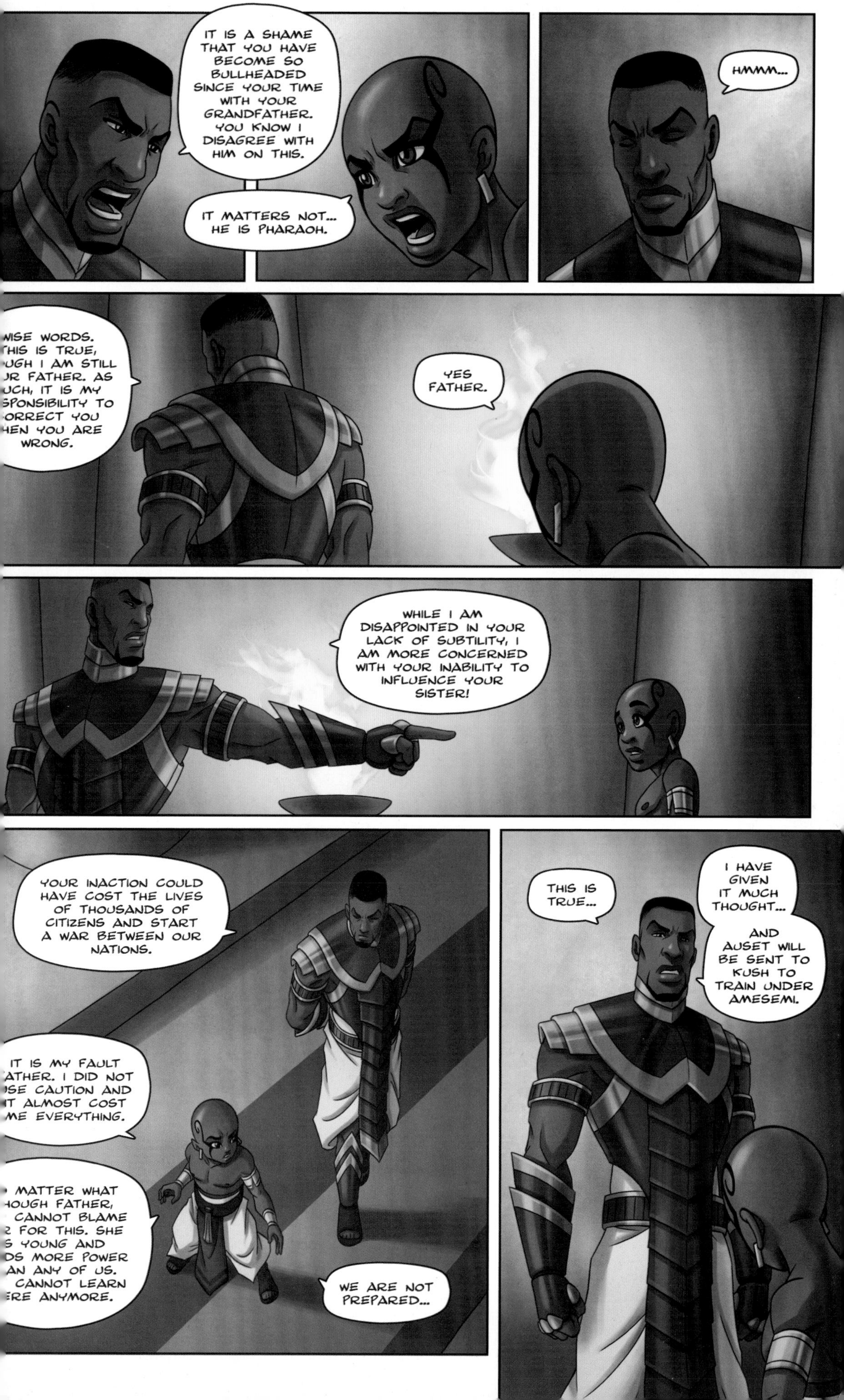

IT IS A SHAME THAT YOU HAVE BECOME SO BULLHEADED SINCE YOUR TIME WITH YOUR GRANDFATHER. YOU KNOW I DISAGREE WITH HIM ON THIS.
IT MATTERS NOT... HE IS PHARAOH.
HMMM...
WISE WORDS. THIS IS TRUE, UGH I AM STILL UR FATHER. AS UCH, IT IS MY SPONSIBILITY TO ORRECT YOU HEN YOU ARE WRONG.
YES FATHER.
WHILE I AM DISAPPOINTED IN YOUR LACK OF SUBTILITY, I AM MORE CONCERNED WITH YOUR INABILITY TO INFLUENCE YOUR SISTER!
YOUR INACTION COULD HAVE COST THE LIVES OF THOUSANDS OF CITIZENS AND START A WAR BETWEEN OUR NATIONS.
IT IS MY FAULT FATHER. I DID NOT USE CAUTION AND IT ALMOST COST ME EVERYTHING.
MATTER WHAT HOUGH FATHER, CANNOT BLAME FOR THIS. SHE S YOUNG AND DS MORE POWER AN ANY OF US. CANNOT LEARN ERE ANYMORE.
WE ARE NOT PREPARED...
THIS IS TRUE...
I HAVE GIVEN IT MUCH THOUGHT...
AND AUSET WILL BE SENT TO KUSH TO TRAIN UNDER AMESEMI.

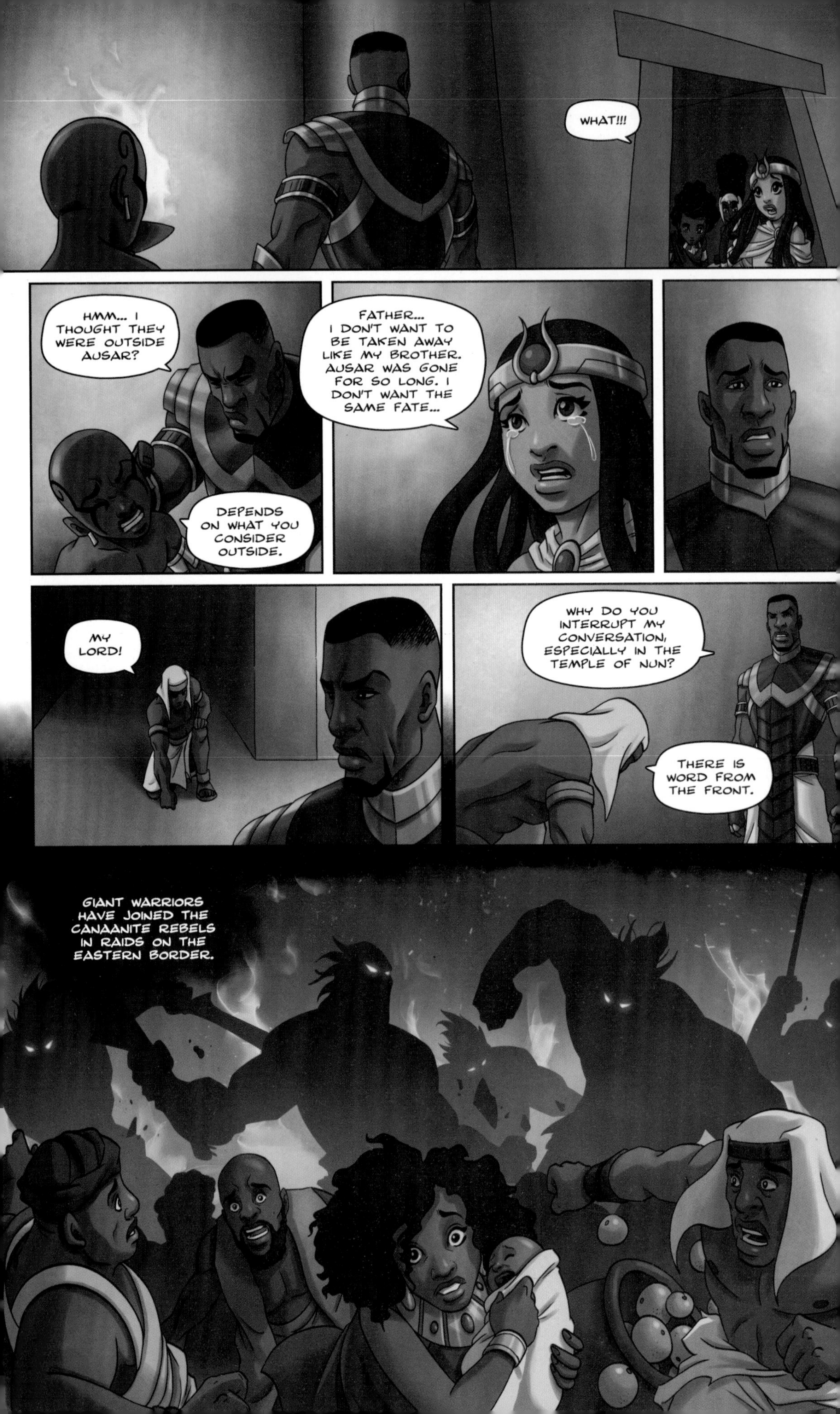
WHAT!!!
HMM... I THOUGHT THEY WERE OUTSIDE AUSAR?
DEPENDS ON WHAT YOU CONSIDER OUTSIDE.
FATHER... I DON'T WANT TO BE TAKEN AWAY LIKE MY BROTHER. AUSAR WAS GONE FOR SO LONG. I DON'T WANT THE SAME FATE...
MY LORD!
WHY DO YOU INTERRUPT MY CONVERSATION, ESPECIALLY IN THE TEMPLE OF NUN?
THERE IS WORD FROM THE FRONT.
GIANT WARRIORS HAVE JOINED THE CANAANITE REBELS IN RAIDS ON THE EASTERN BORDER.

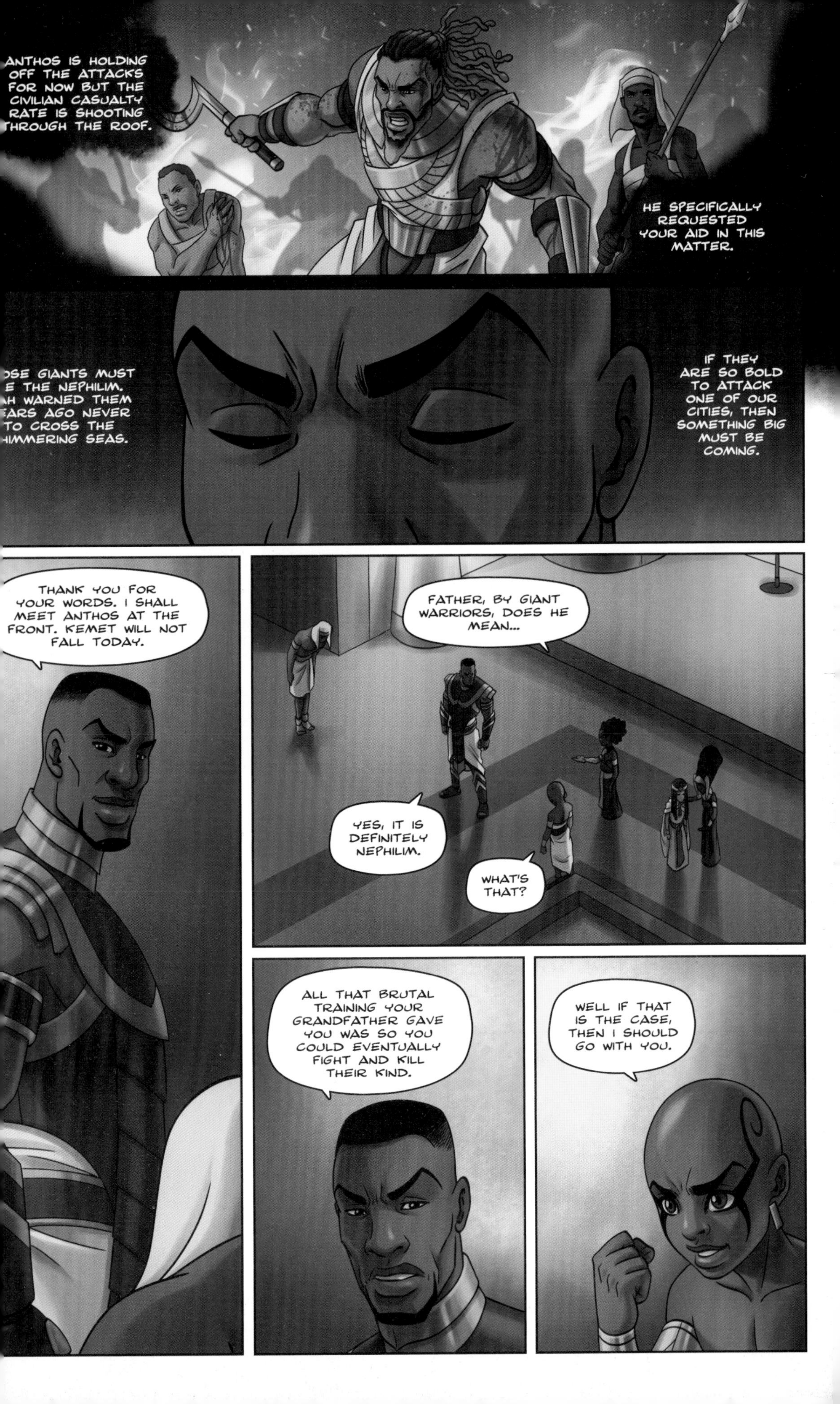

ANTHOS IS HOLDING OFF THE ATTACKS FOR NOW BUT THE CIVILIAN CASUALTY RATE IS SHOOTING THROUGH THE ROOF.
HE SPECIFICALLY REQUESTED YOUR AID IN THIS MATTER.
OSE GIANTS MUST E THE NEPHILIM. AH WARNED THEM EARS AGO NEVER TO CROSS THE HIMMERING SEAS.
IF THEY ARE SO BOLD TO ATTACK ONE OF OUR CITIES, THEN SOMETHING BIG MUST BE COMING.
THANK YOU FOR YOUR WORDS. I SHALL MEET ANTHOS AT THE FRONT. KEMET WILL NOT FALL TODAY.
FATHER, BY GIANT WARRIORS, DOES HE MEAN...
YES, IT IS DEFINITELY NEPHILIM.
WHAT'S THAT?
ALL THAT BRUTAL TRAINING YOUR GRANDFATHER GAVE YOU WAS SO YOU COULD EVENTUALLY FIGHT AND KILL THEIR KIND.
WELL IF THAT IS THE CASE, THEN I SHOULD GO WITH YOU.

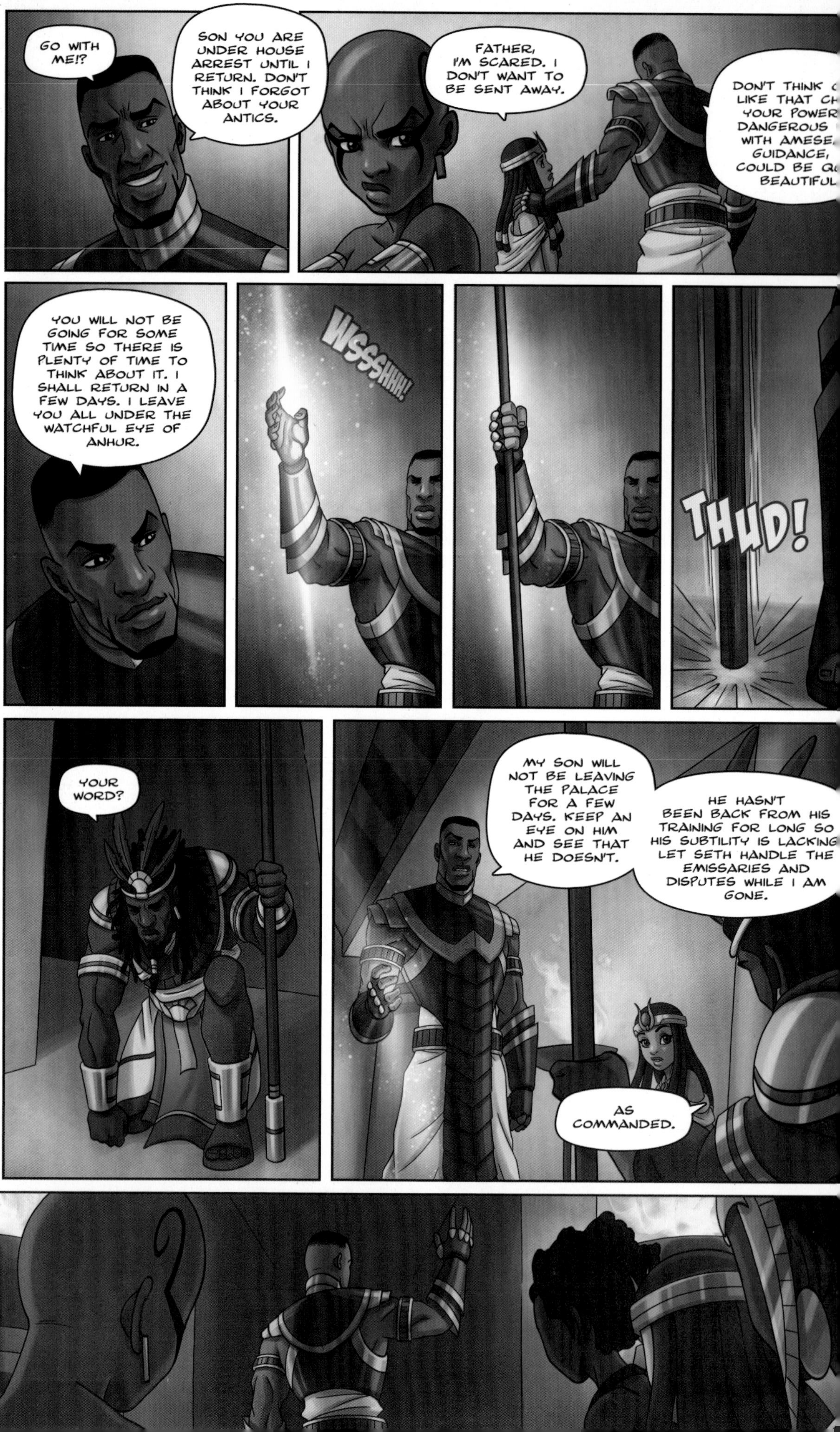
GO WITH ME!?
SON YOU ARE UNDER HOUSE ARREST UNTIL I RETURN. DON'T THINK I FORGOT ABOUT YOUR ANTICS.
FATHER, I'M SCARED. I DON'T WANT TO BE SENT AWAY.
DON'T THINK LIKE THAT YOUR POWER DANGEROUS WITH AMESE GUIDANCE, COULD BE BEAUTIFUL
YOU WILL NOT BE GOING FOR SOME TIME SO THERE IS PLENTY OF TIME TO THINK ABOUT IT. I SHALL RETURN IN A FEW DAYS. I LEAVE YOU ALL UNDER THE WATCHFUL EYE OF ANHUR.
WSSSHHH!
THUD!
YOUR WORD?
MY SON WILL NOT BE LEAVING THE PALACE FOR A FEW DAYS. KEEP AN EYE ON HIM AND SEE THAT HE DOESN'T.
HE HASN'T BEEN BACK FROM HIS TRAINING FOR LONG SO HIS SUBTILITY IS LACKING LET SETH HANDLE THE EMISSARIES AND DISPUTES WHILE I AM GONE.
AS COMMANDED.

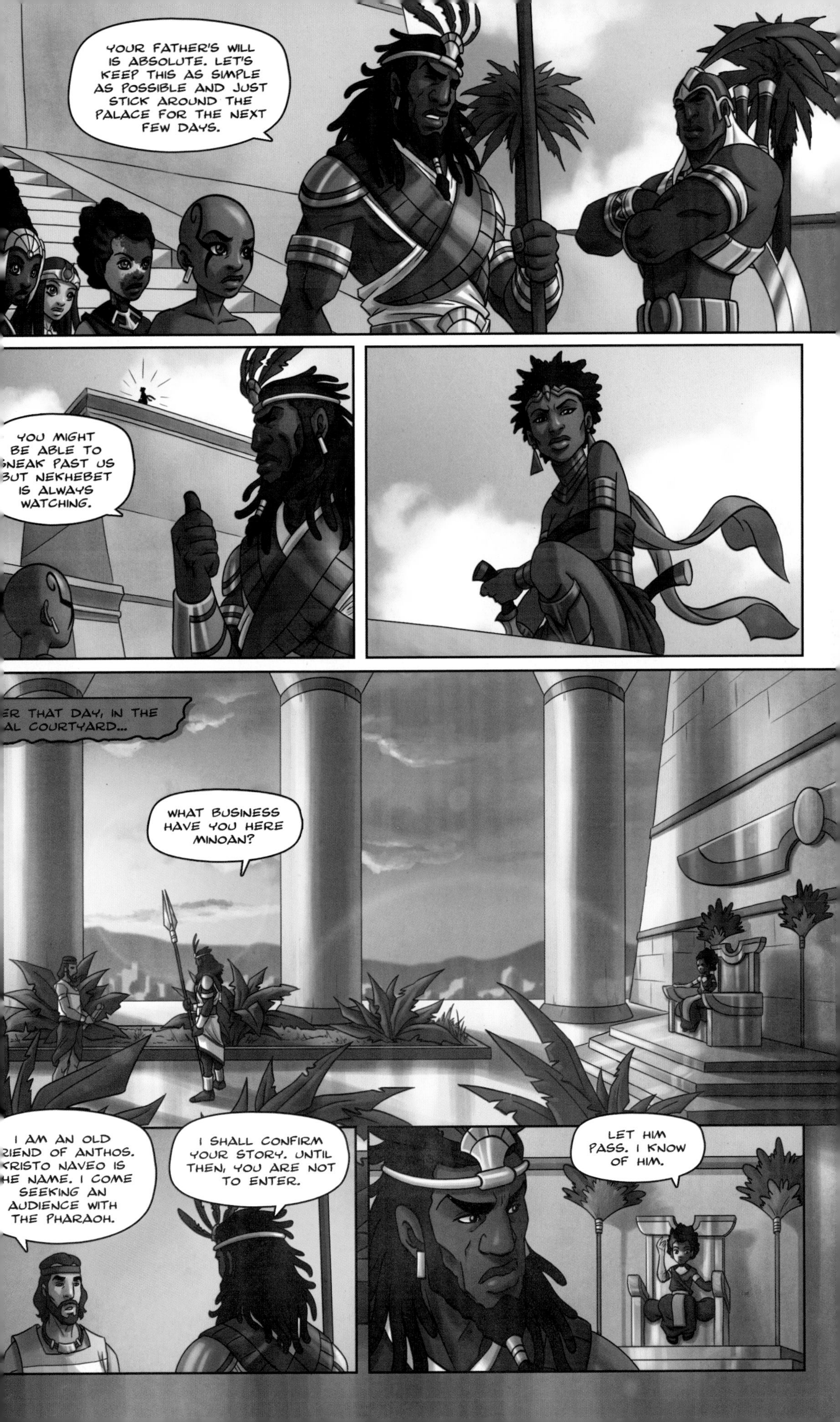

YOUR FATHER'S WILL IS ABSOLUTE. LET'S KEEP THIS AS SIMPLE AS POSSIBLE AND JUST STICK AROUND THE PALACE FOR THE NEXT FEW DAYS.
YOU MIGHT BE ABLE TO SNEAK PAST US BUT NEKHEBET IS ALWAYS WATCHING.
ER THAT DAY, IN THE AL COURTYARD...
WHAT BUSINESS HAVE YOU HERE MINOAN?
I AM AN OLD RIEND OF ANTHOS. KRISTO NAVEO IS HE NAME. I COME SEEKING AN AUDIENCE WITH THE PHARAOH.
I SHALL CONFIRM YOUR STORY. UNTIL THEN, YOU ARE NOT TO ENTER.
LET HIM PASS. I KNOW OF HIM.

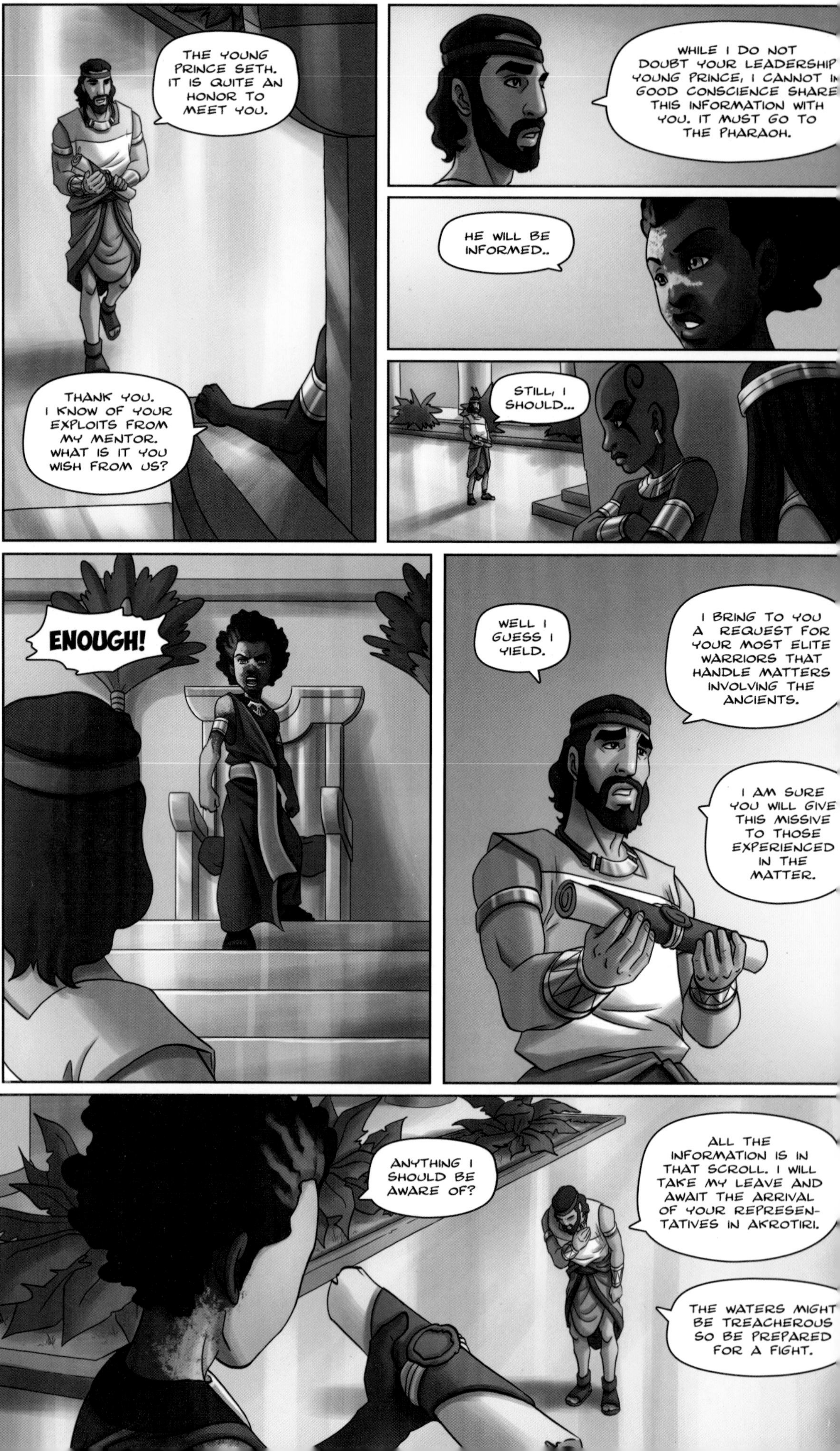
THE YOUNG PRINCE SETH. IT IS QUITE AN HONOR TO MEET YOU.
THANK YOU. I KNOW OF YOUR EXPLOITS FROM MY MENTOR. WHAT IS IT YOU WISH FROM US?
WHILE I DO NOT DOUBT YOUR LEADERSHIP YOUNG PRINCE, I CANNOT IN GOOD CONSCIENCE SHARE THIS INFORMATION WITH YOU. IT MUST GO TO THE PHARAOH.
HE WILL BE INFORMED..
STILL, I SHOULD...
ENOUGH!
WELL I GUESS I YIELD.
I BRING TO YOU A REQUEST FOR YOUR MOST ELITE WARRIORS THAT HANDLE MATTERS INVOLVING THE ANCIENTS.
I AM SURE YOU WILL GIVE THIS MISSIVE TO THOSE EXPERIENCED IN THE MATTER.
ANYTHING I SHOULD BE AWARE OF?
ALL THE INFORMATION IS IN THAT SCROLL. I WILL TAKE MY LEAVE AND AWAIT THE ARRIVAL OF YOUR REPRESEN-TATIVES IN AKROTIRI.
THE WATERS MIGHT BE TREACHEROUS SO BE PREPARED FOR A FIGHT.

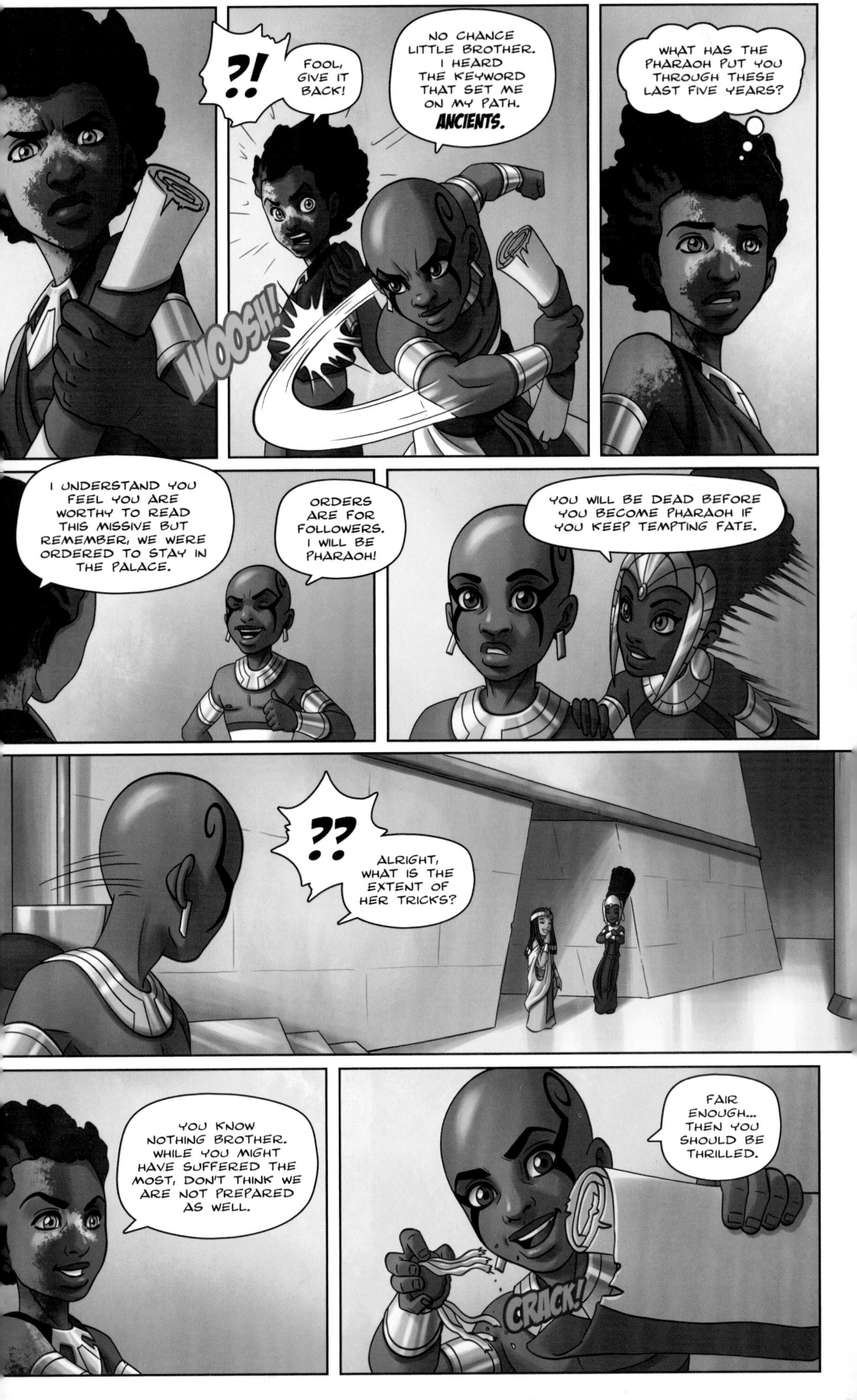
?!
FOOL, GIVE IT BACK!
NO CHANCE LITTLE BROTHER. I HEARD THE KEYWORD THAT SET ME ON MY PATH. ANCIENTS.
WOOSH!
WHAT HAS THE PHARAOH PUT YOU THROUGH THESE LAST FIVE YEARS?
I UNDERSTAND YOU FEEL YOU ARE WORTHY TO READ THIS MISSIVE BUT REMEMBER, WE WERE ORDERED TO STAY IN THE PALACE.
ORDERS ARE FOR FOLLOWERS. I WILL BE PHARAOH!
YOU WILL BE DEAD BEFORE YOU BECOME PHARAOH IF YOU KEEP TEMPTING FATE.
??
ALRIGHT, WHAT IS THE EXTENT OF HER TRICKS?
YOU KNOW NOTHING BROTHER. WHILE YOU MIGHT HAVE SUFFERED THE MOST, DON'T THINK WE ARE NOT PREPARED AS WELL.
FAIR ENOUGH... THEN YOU SHOULD BE THRILLED.
CRACK!

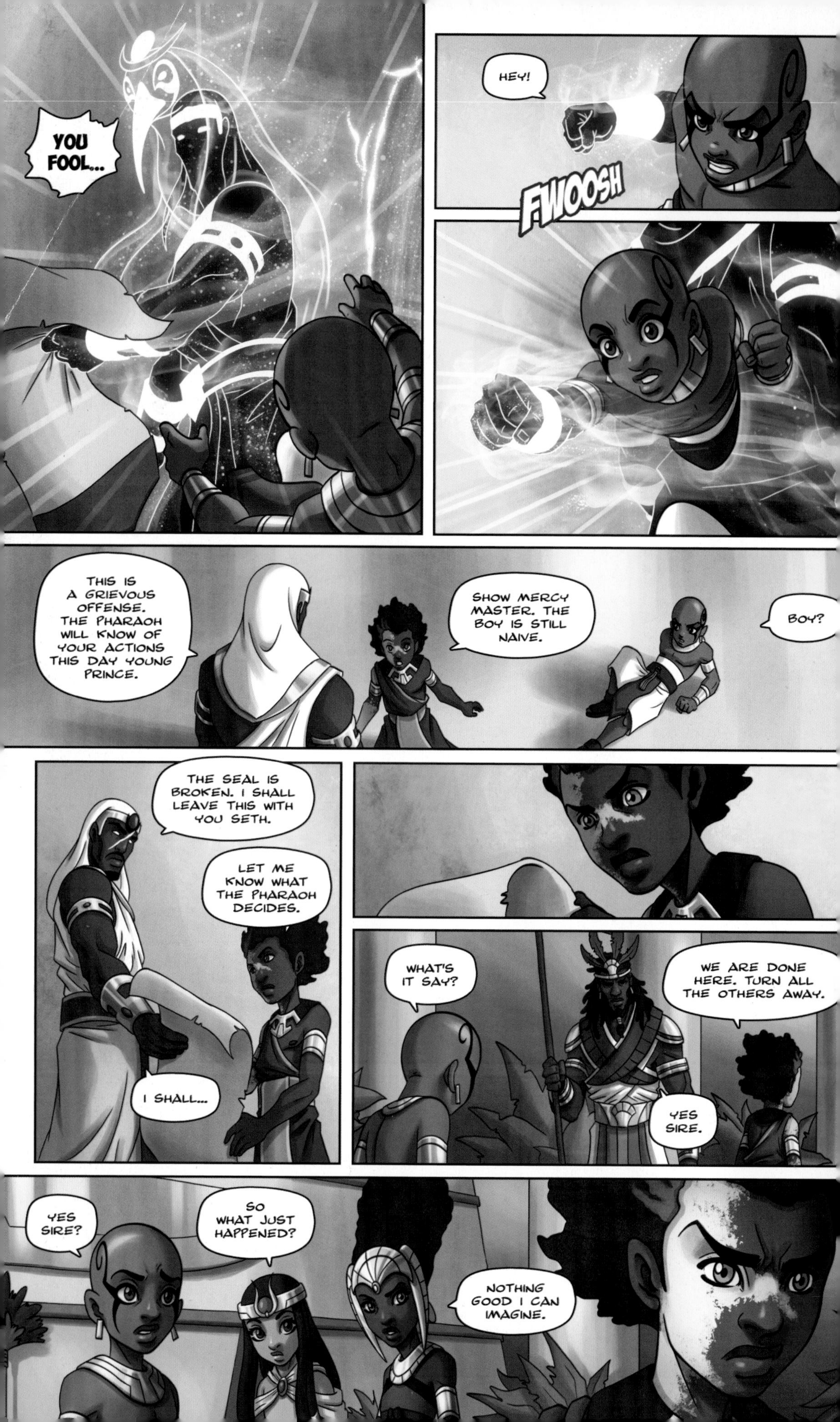
YOU FOOL...
HEY!
FWOOSH
THIS IS A GRIEVOUS OFFENSE. THE PHARAOH WILL KNOW OF YOUR ACTIONS THIS DAY YOUNG PRINCE.
SHOW MERCY MASTER. THE BOY IS STILL NAIVE.
BOY?
THE SEAL IS BROKEN. I SHALL LEAVE THIS WITH YOU SETH.
LET ME KNOW WHAT THE PHARAOH DECIDES.
I SHALL...
WHAT'S IT SAY?
WE ARE DONE HERE. TURN ALL THE OTHERS AWAY.
YES SIRE.
YES SIRE?
SO WHAT JUST HAPPENED?
NOTHING GOOD I CAN IMAGINE.

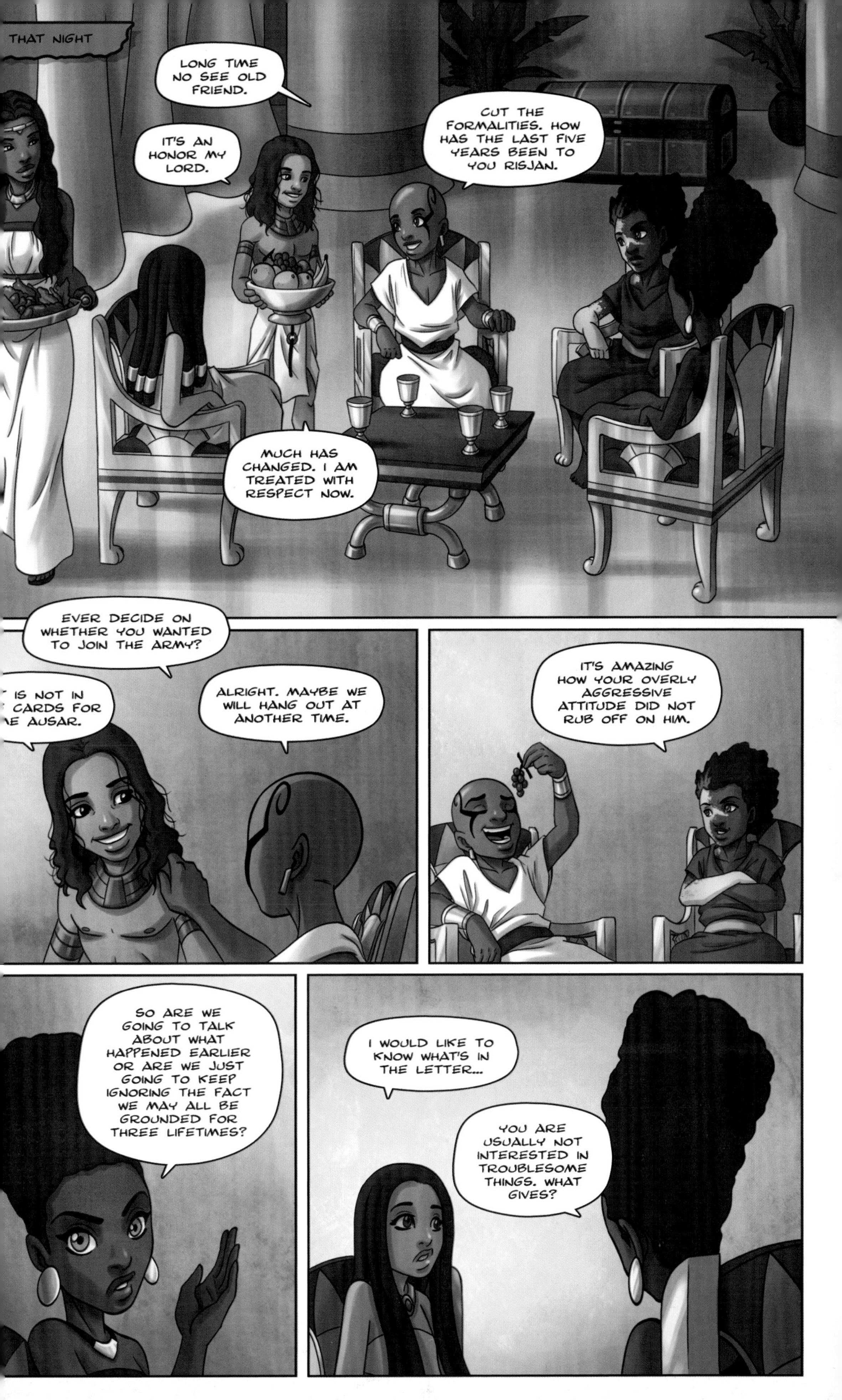
THAT NIGHT
LONG TIME NO SEE OLD FRIEND.
IT'S AN HONOR MY LORD.
CUT THE FORMALITIES. HOW HAS THE LAST FIVE YEARS BEEN TO YOU RISJAN.
MUCH HAS CHANGED. I AM TREATED WITH RESPECT NOW.
EVER DECIDE ON WHETHER YOU WANTED TO JOIN THE ARMY?
IS NOT IN CARDS FOR AUSAR.
ALRIGHT. MAYBE WE WILL HANG OUT AT ANOTHER TIME.
IT'S AMAZING HOW YOUR OVERLY AGGRESSIVE ATTITUDE DID NOT RUB OFF ON HIM.
SO ARE WE GOING TO TALK ABOUT WHAT HAPPENED EARLIER OR ARE WE JUST GOING TO KEEP IGNORING THE FACT WE MAY ALL BE GROUNDED FOR THREE LIFETIMES?
I WOULD LIKE TO KNOW WHAT'S IN THE LETTER...
YOU ARE USUALLY NOT INTERESTED IN TROUBLESOME THINGS. WHAT GIVES?

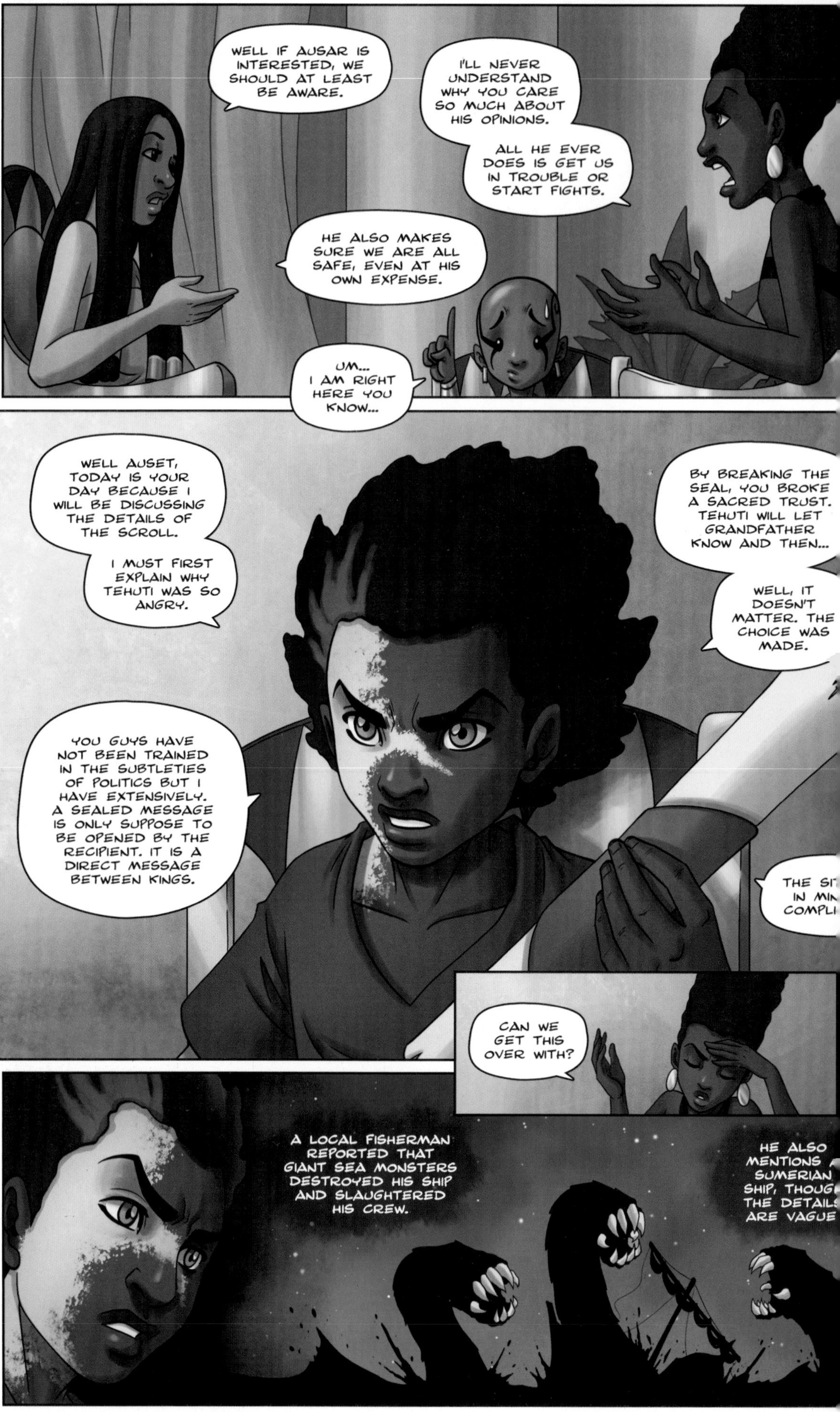
WELL IF AUSAR IS INTERESTED, WE SHOULD AT LEAST BE AWARE.
I'LL NEVER UNDERSTAND WHY YOU CARE SO MUCH ABOUT HIS OPINIONS.
ALL HE EVER DOES IS GET US IN TROUBLE OR START FIGHTS.
HE ALSO MAKES SURE WE ARE ALL SAFE, EVEN AT HIS OWN EXPENSE.
UM... I AM RIGHT HERE YOU KNOW...
WELL AUSET, TODAY IS YOUR DAY BECAUSE I WILL BE DISCUSSING THE DETAILS OF THE SCROLL.
I MUST FIRST EXPLAIN WHY TEHUTI WAS SO ANGRY.
BY BREAKING THE SEAL, YOU BROKE A SACRED TRUST. TEHUTI WILL LET GRANDFATHER KNOW AND THEN...
WELL, IT DOESN'T MATTER. THE CHOICE WAS MADE.
YOU GUYS HAVE NOT BEEN TRAINED IN THE SUBTLETIES OF POLITICS BUT I HAVE EXTENSIVELY. A SEALED MESSAGE IS ONLY SUPPOSE TO BE OPENED BY THE RECIPIENT. IT IS A DIRECT MESSAGE BETWEEN KINGS.
THE SI IN MIN COMPLI
CAN WE GET THIS OVER WITH?
A LOCAL FISHERMAN REPORTED THAT GIANT SEA MONSTERS DESTROYED HIS SHIP AND SLAUGHTERED HIS CREW.
HE ALSO MENTIONS A SUMERIAN SHIP, THOUG THE DETAILS ARE VAGUE

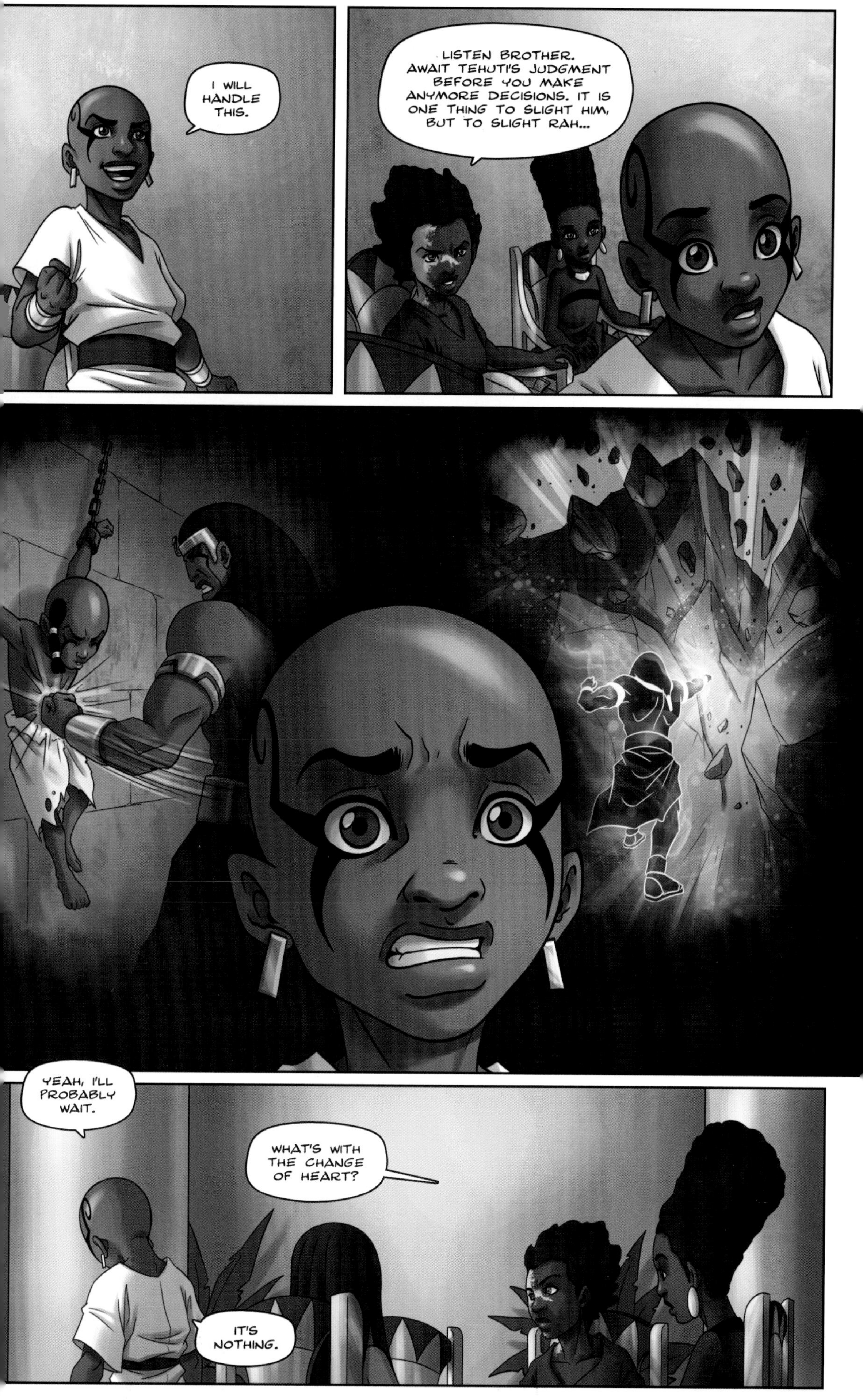
I WILL HANDLE THIS.
LISTEN BROTHER. AWAIT TEHUTI'S JUDGMENT BEFORE YOU MAKE ANYMORE DECISIONS. IT IS ONE THING TO SLIGHT HIM, BUT TO SLIGHT RAH...
YEAH, I'LL PROBABLY WAIT.
WHAT'S WITH THE CHANGE OF HEART?
IT'S NOTHING.

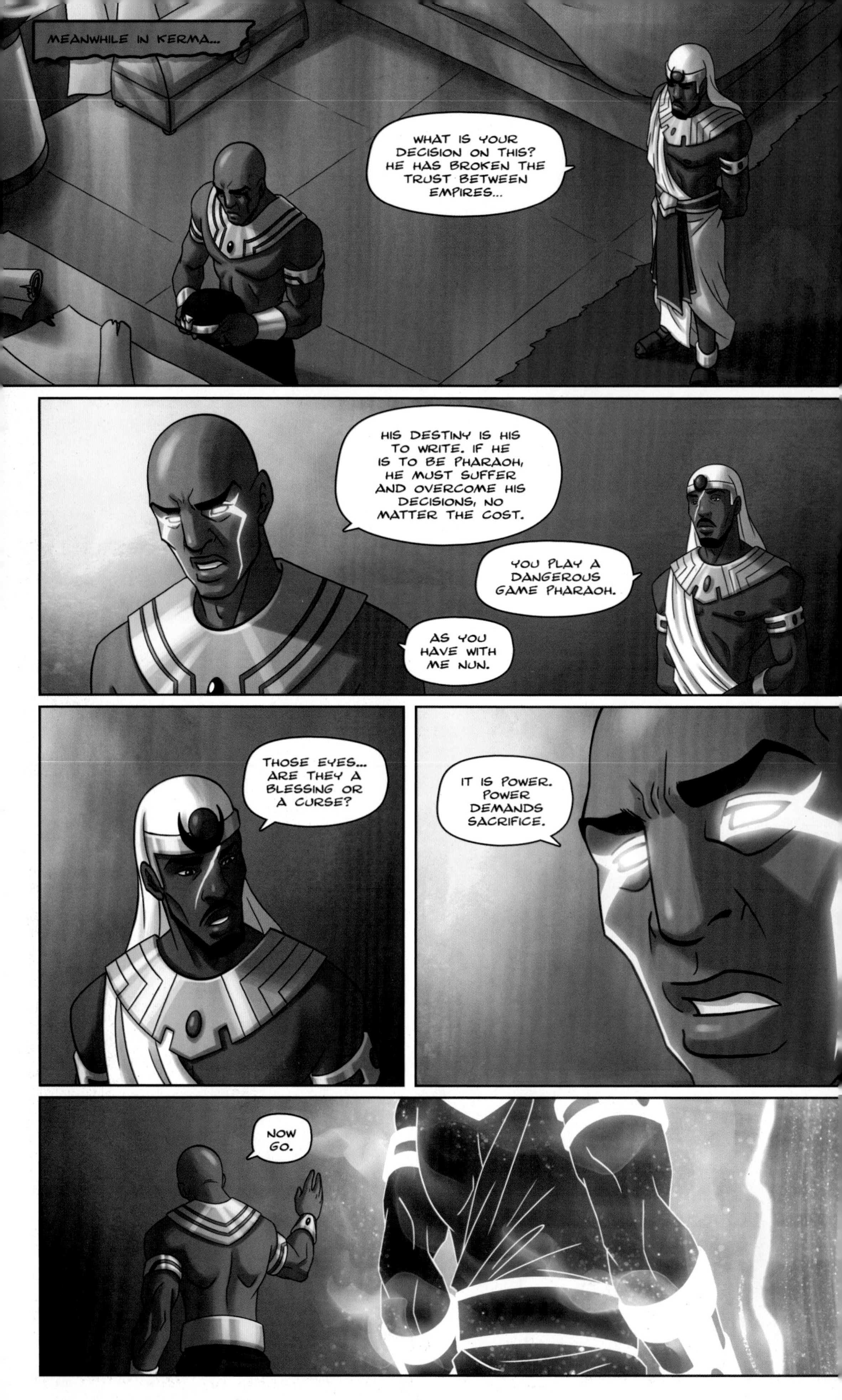
MEANWHILE IN KERMA...
WHAT IS YOUR DECISION ON THIS? HE HAS BROKEN THE TRUST BETWEEN EMPIRES...
HIS DESTINY IS HIS TO WRITE. IF HE IS TO BE PHARAOH, HE MUST SUFFER AND OVERCOME HIS DECISIONS, NO MATTER THE COST.
YOU PLAY A DANGEROUS GAME PHARAOH.
AS YOU HAVE WITH ME NUN.
THOSE EYES... ARE THEY A BLESSING OR A CURSE?
IT IS POWER. POWER DEMANDS SACRIFICE.
NOW GO.

TEHUTI!

YOU HAVE DISSAPOINTED ME CHILD BUT IT IS NOT MY PLACE TO PASS JUDGMENT.

YOU ARE AS STUBBORN AS THE PHARAOH.

YOU ARE FREE TO DO WHAT YOU FEEL IS NECESSARY. RAH PERMITS ALL YOUR FUTURE ACTIONS...

THEN I AM TO GO?

REMEMBER CHILD. THE FATE OF YOUR KIN IS ALSO IN YOUR HANDS. YOUR HEADSTRONG ACTIONS MAY LEAD TO THEIR END.

I PRAY THAT YOU WILL ACT WISE AND WITH CAUTION.

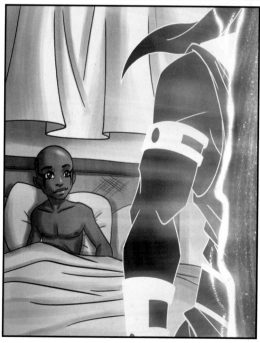

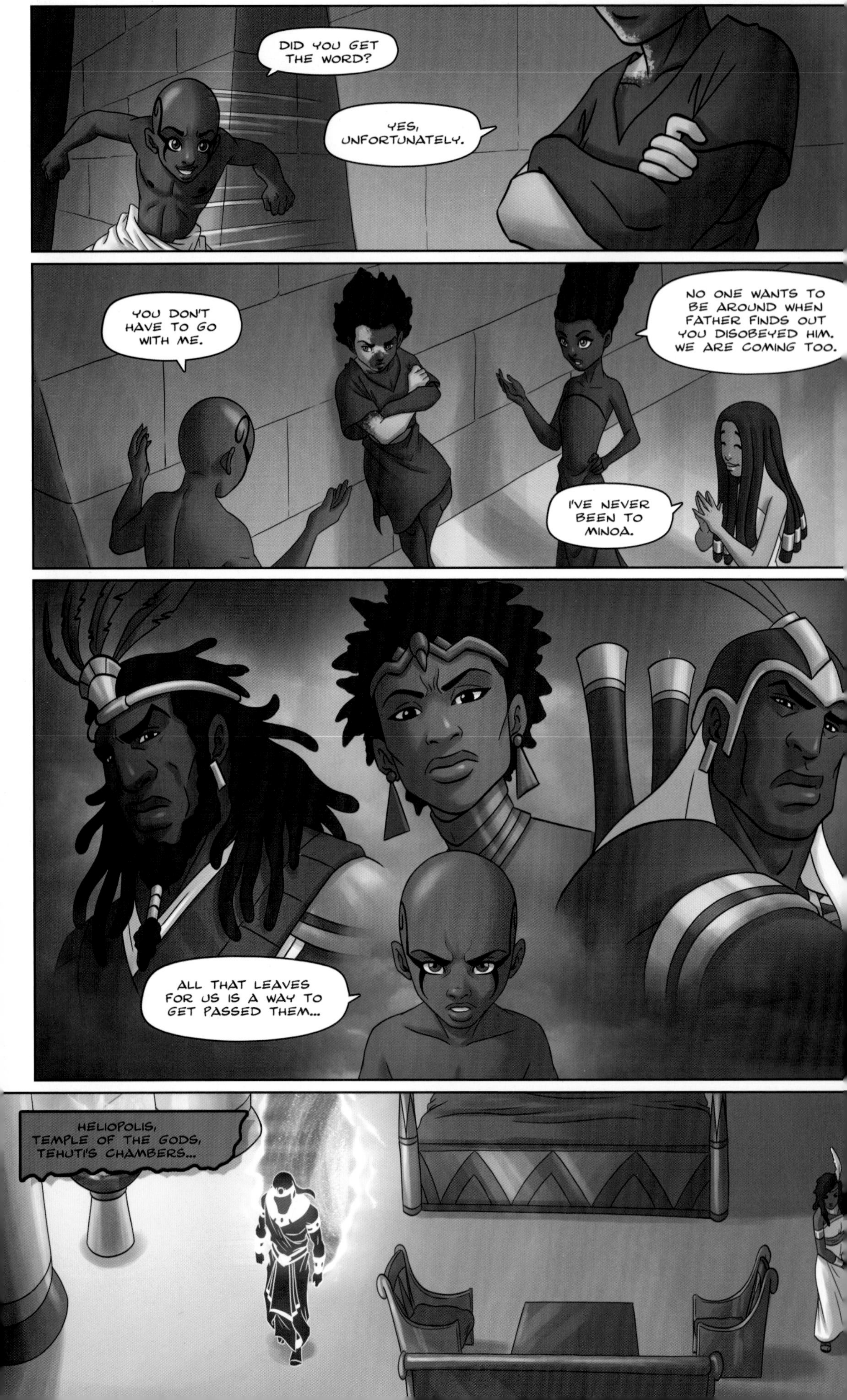
DID YOU GET THE WORD?
YES, UNFORTUNATELY.
YOU DON'T HAVE TO GO WITH ME.
NO ONE WANTS TO BE AROUND WHEN FATHER FINDS OUT YOU DISOBEYED HIM. WE ARE COMING TOO.
I'VE NEVER BEEN TO MINOA.
ALL THAT LEAVES FOR US IS A WAY TO GET PASSED THEM...
HELIOPOLIS, TEMPLE OF THE GODS, TEHUTI'S CHAMBERS...

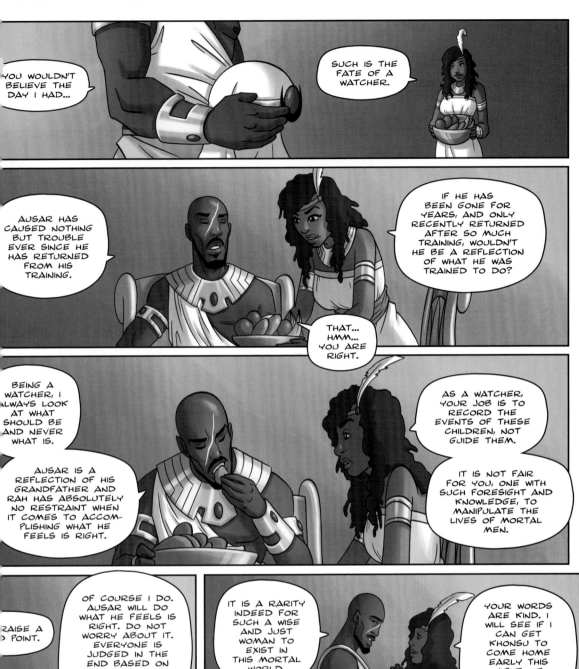

YOU WOULDN'T BELIEVE THE DAY I HAD...

SUCH IS THE FATE OF A WATCHER.

AUSAR HAS CAUSED NOTHING BUT TROUBLE EVER SINCE HE HAS RETURNED FROM HIS TRAINING.

IF HE HAS BEEN GONE FOR YEARS, AND ONLY RECENTLY RETURNED AFTER SO MUCH TRAINING, WOULDN'T HE BE A REFLECTION OF WHAT HE WAS TRAINED TO DO?

THAT... HMM... YOU ARE RIGHT.

BEING A WATCHER, I ALWAYS LOOK AT WHAT SHOULD BE AND NEVER WHAT IS.

AUSAR IS A REFLECTION OF HIS GRANDFATHER AND RAH HAS ABSOLUTELY NO RESTRAINT WHEN IT COMES TO ACCOM-PLISHING WHAT HE FEELS IS RIGHT.

AS A WATCHER, YOUR JOB IS TO RECORD THE EVENTS OF THESE CHILDREN, NOT GUIDE THEM.

IT IS NOT FAIR FOR YOU, ONE WITH SUCH FORESIGHT AND KNOWLEDGE, TO MANIPULATE THE LIVES OF MORTAL MEN.

OF COURSE I DO. AUSAR WILL DO WHAT HE FEELS IS RIGHT. DO NOT WORRY ABOUT IT. EVERYONE IS JUDGED IN THE END BASED ON THE WAY THEY LIVED THEIR LIVES, NOT THE WAY THEY WERE GUIDED TO LIVE.

IT IS A RARITY INDEED FOR SUCH A WISE AND JUST WOMAN TO EXIST IN THIS MORTAL WORLD.

YOUR WORDS ARE KIND. I WILL SEE IF I CAN GET KHONSU TO COME HOME EARLY THIS NIGHT. HE HASN'T SPENT MUCH TIME WITH YOU LATELY.

...RAISE A ...D POINT.

YOU ARE RIGHT. LET'S RELAX FOR A FEW DAYS. I'LL TELL RAH I AM TAKING A VACATION.

REALLY?

YEAH.

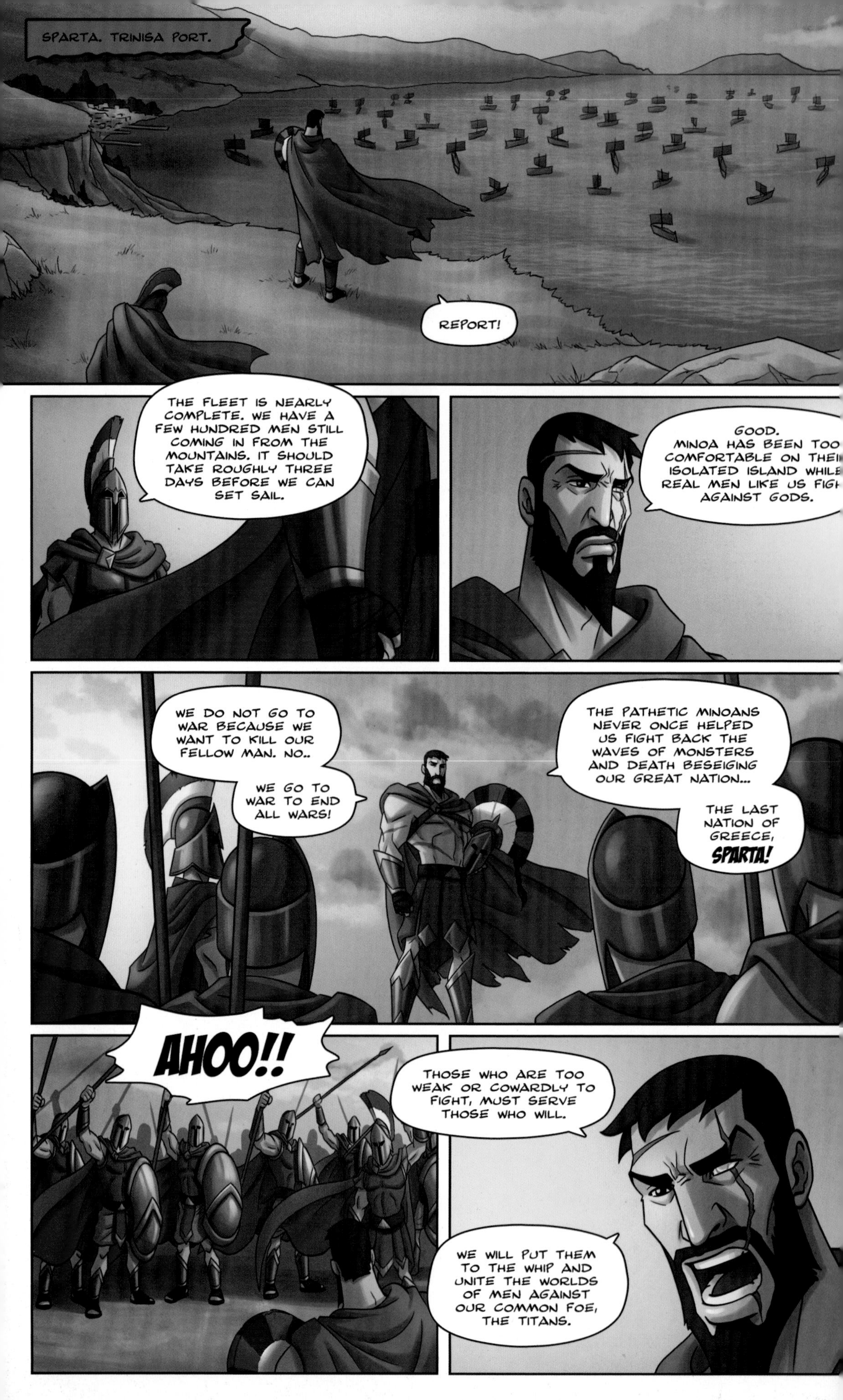
SPARTA. TRINISA PORT.
REPORT!
THE FLEET IS NEARLY COMPLETE. WE HAVE A FEW HUNDRED MEN STILL COMING IN FROM THE MOUNTAINS. IT SHOULD TAKE ROUGHLY THREE DAYS BEFORE WE CAN SET SAIL.
GOOD. MINOA HAS BEEN TOO COMFORTABLE ON THEI ISOLATED ISLAND WHILE REAL MEN LIKE US FIGH AGAINST GODS.
WE DO NOT GO TO WAR BECAUSE WE WANT TO KILL OUR FELLOW MAN. NO..
WE GO TO WAR TO END ALL WARS!
THE PATHETIC MINOANS NEVER ONCE HELPED US FIGHT BACK THE WAVES OF MONSTERS AND DEATH BESEIGING OUR GREAT NATION...
THE LAST NATION OF GREECE, SPARTA!
AHOO!!
THOSE WHO ARE TOO WEAK OR COWARDLY TO FIGHT, MUST SERVE THOSE WHO WILL.
WE WILL PUT THEM TO THE WHIP AND UNITE THE WORLDS OF MEN AGAINST OUR COMMON FOE, THE TITANS.

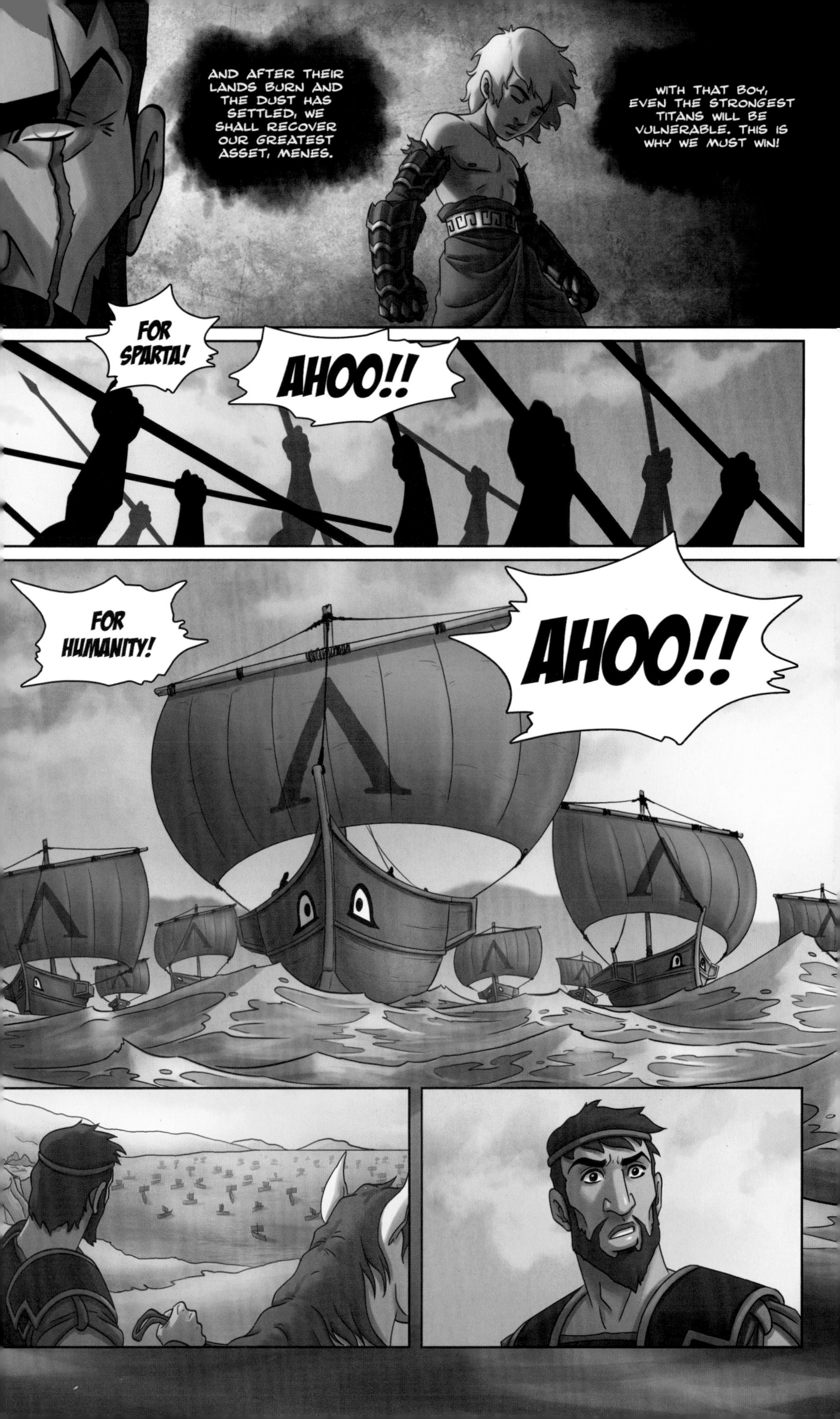
AND AFTER THEIR LANDS BURN AND THE DUST HAS SETTLED, WE SHALL RECOVER OUR GREATEST ASSET, MENES.
WITH THAT BOY, EVEN THE STRONGEST TITANS WILL BE VULNERABLE. THIS IS WHY WE MUST WIN!
FOR SPARTA!
AHOO!!
FOR HUMANITY!
AHOO!!

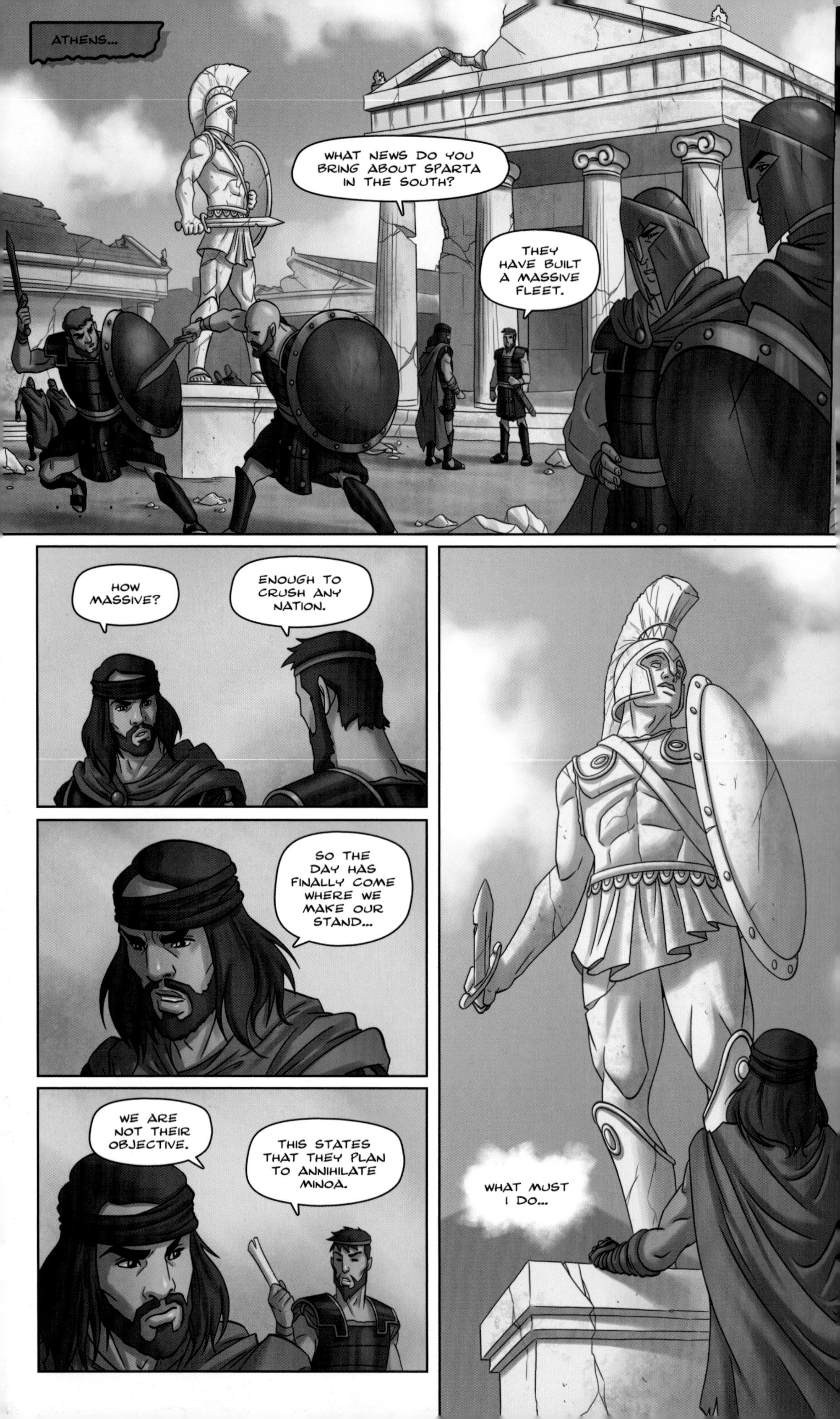
ATHENS...
WHAT NEWS DO YOU BRING ABOUT SPARTA IN THE SOUTH?
THEY HAVE BUILT A MASSIVE FLEET.
HOW MASSIVE?
ENOUGH TO CRUSH ANY NATION.
SO THE DAY HAS FINALLY COME WHERE WE MAKE OUR STAND...
WE ARE NOT THEIR OBJECTIVE.
THIS STATES THAT THEY PLAN TO ANNIHILATE MINOA.
WHAT MUST I DO...

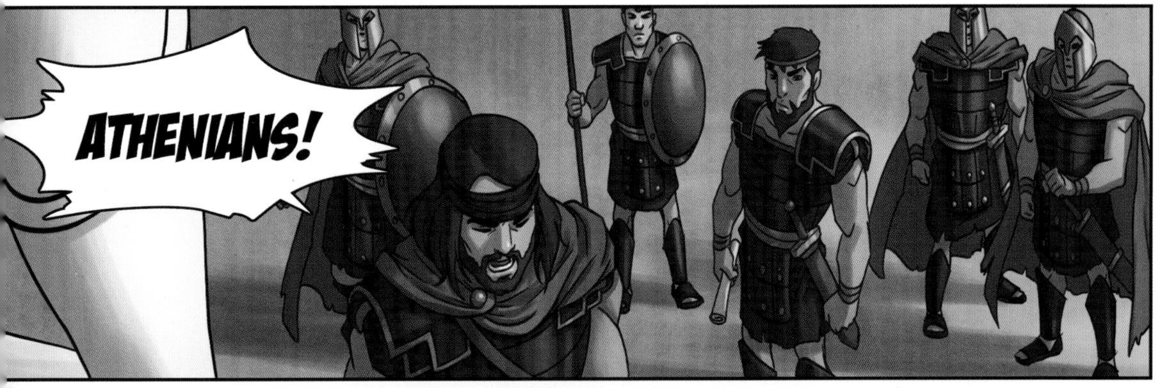
ATHENIANS!

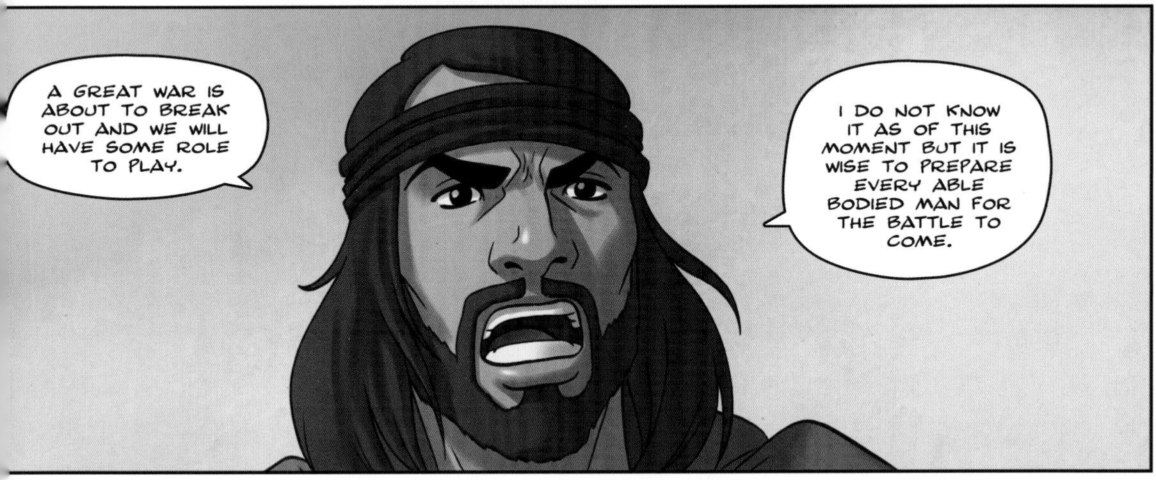
A GREAT WAR IS ABOUT TO BREAK OUT AND WE WILL HAVE SOME ROLE TO PLAY.
I DO NOT KNOW IT AS OF THIS MOMENT BUT IT IS WISE TO PREPARE EVERY ABLE BODIED MAN FOR THE BATTLE TO COME.

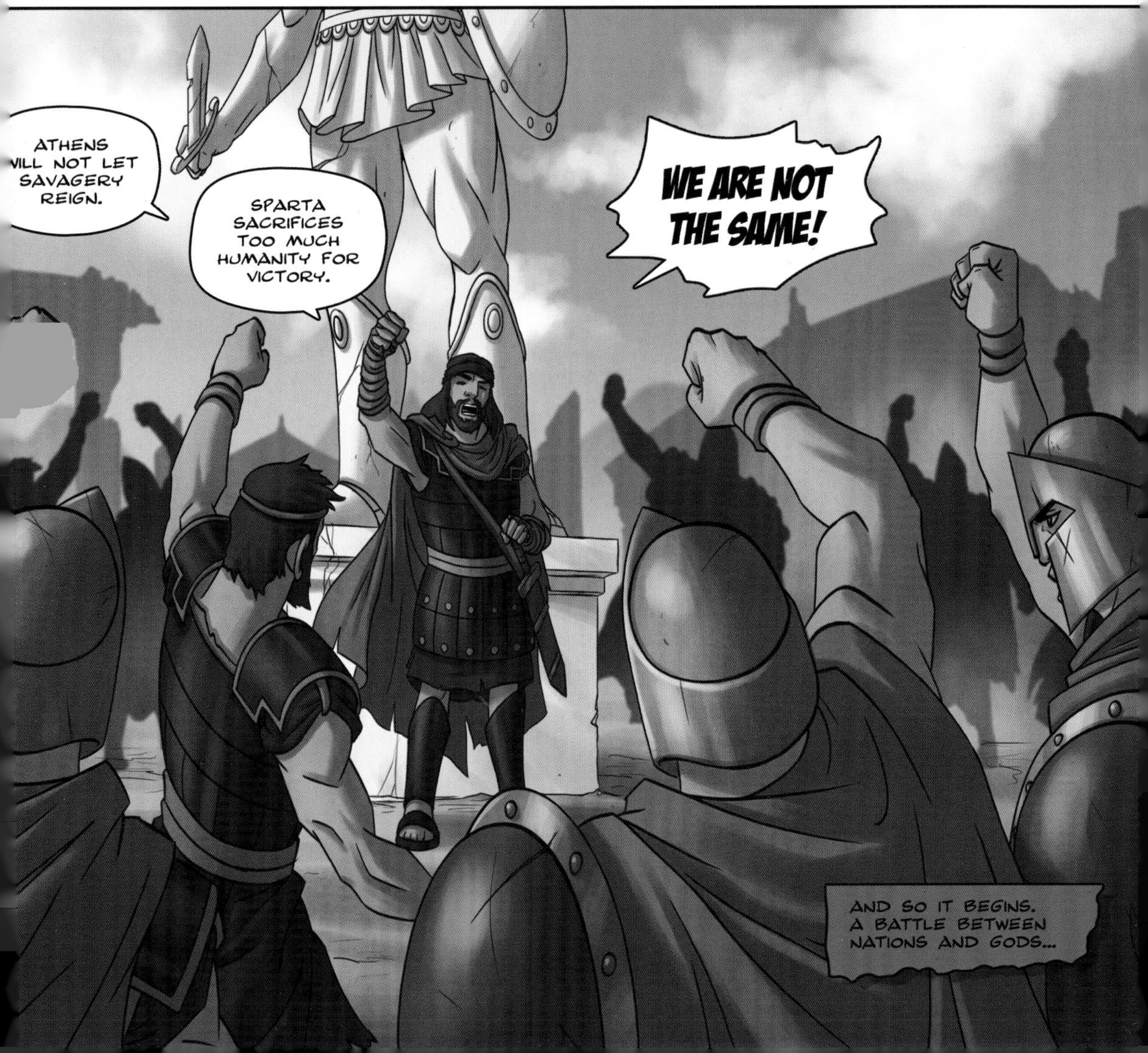
ATHENS WILL NOT LET SAVAGERY REIGN.
SPARTA SACRIFICES TOO MUCH HUMANITY FOR VICTORY.
WE ARE NOT THE SAME!
AND SO IT BEGINS. A BATTLE BETWEEN NATIONS AND GODS...

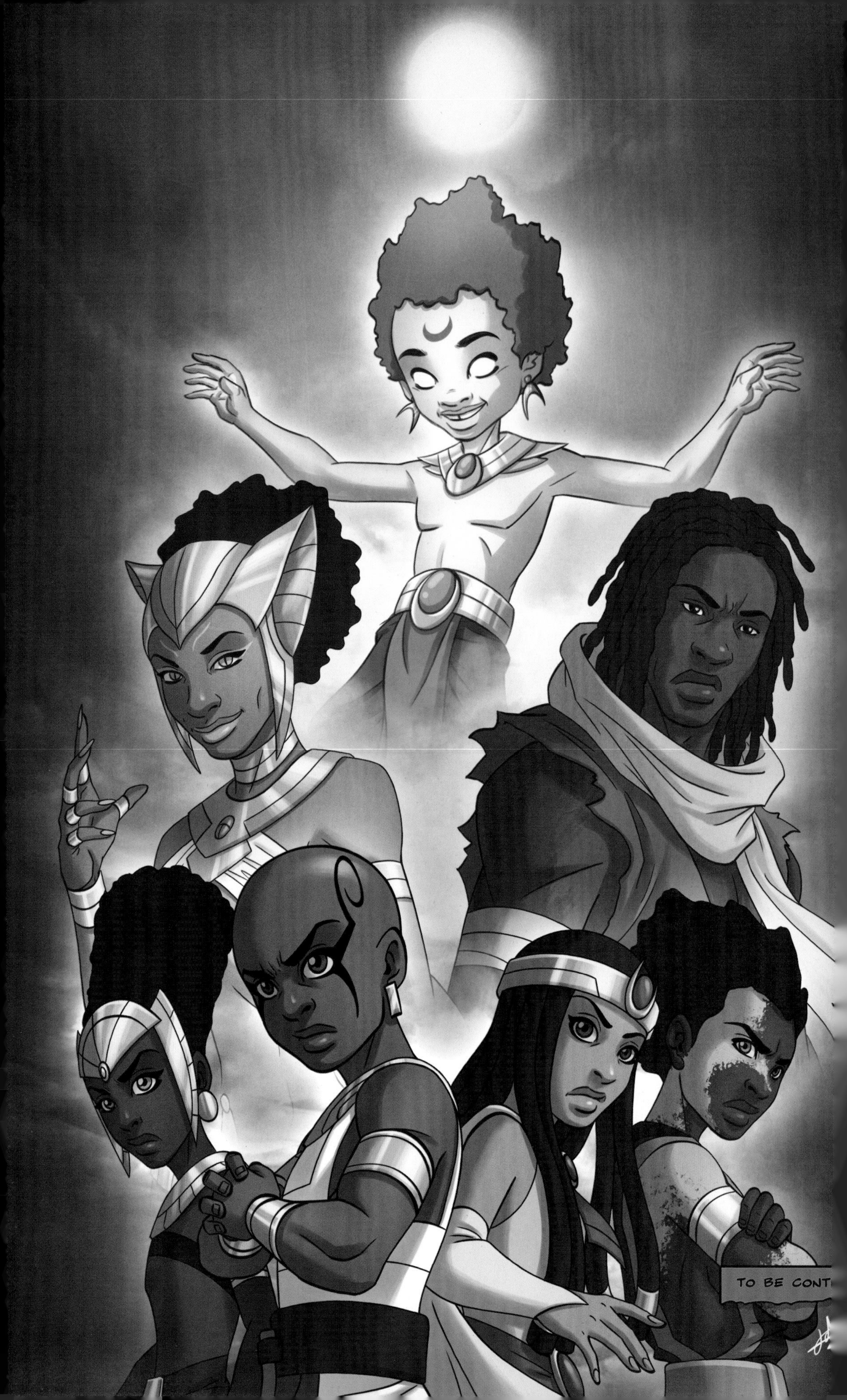
TO BE CONT

he Island of Minoa

ancient times, the people of noa were regarded as an remely advanced matriarch :iety. Their trade with oenicians and Kemetic people re extensive but their religious ictices annoyed their neighbors the north in Greece. Many wars ke out between Greece and noa but for centuries, Minoa l the upper hand. That all anged when a volcanic eruption stroyed most of the island and ced the original inhabitants to e or die, causing a major shift in power structure of the editerranean Sea.

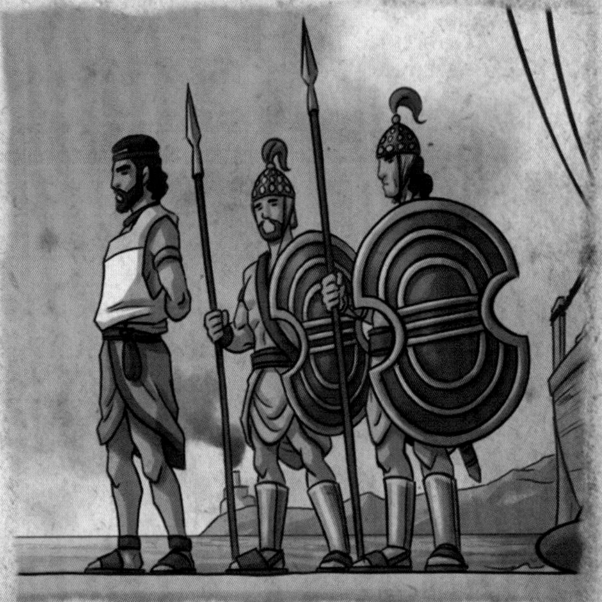

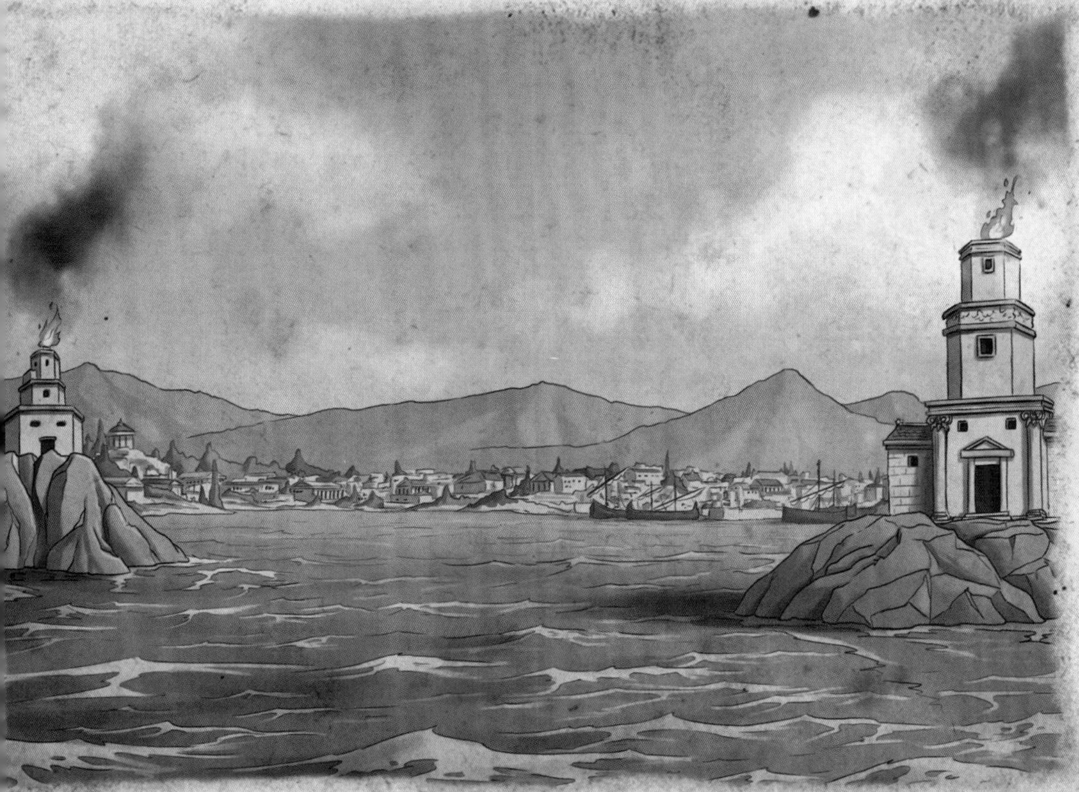

Titans

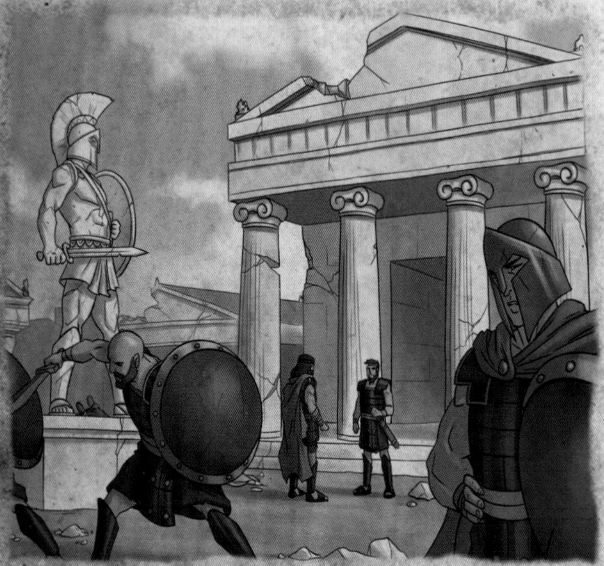

Known as the founding gods in Greek mythology, the Titans wer otherworldly beings with unbelieva destructive power. Humanity did n pray to Titans. Instead, they fear them. In Black Sands, the Titans destroyed most of Greece,and th Olympians do not exist yet. It cou be said that thiswas a real-world retelling of the myths when the w was at risk of destruction by the chaotic powers of the Titans.
In mythology, some Titans survive the war with the Olympians but w bound to an eternity of service th many would deem as punishment.

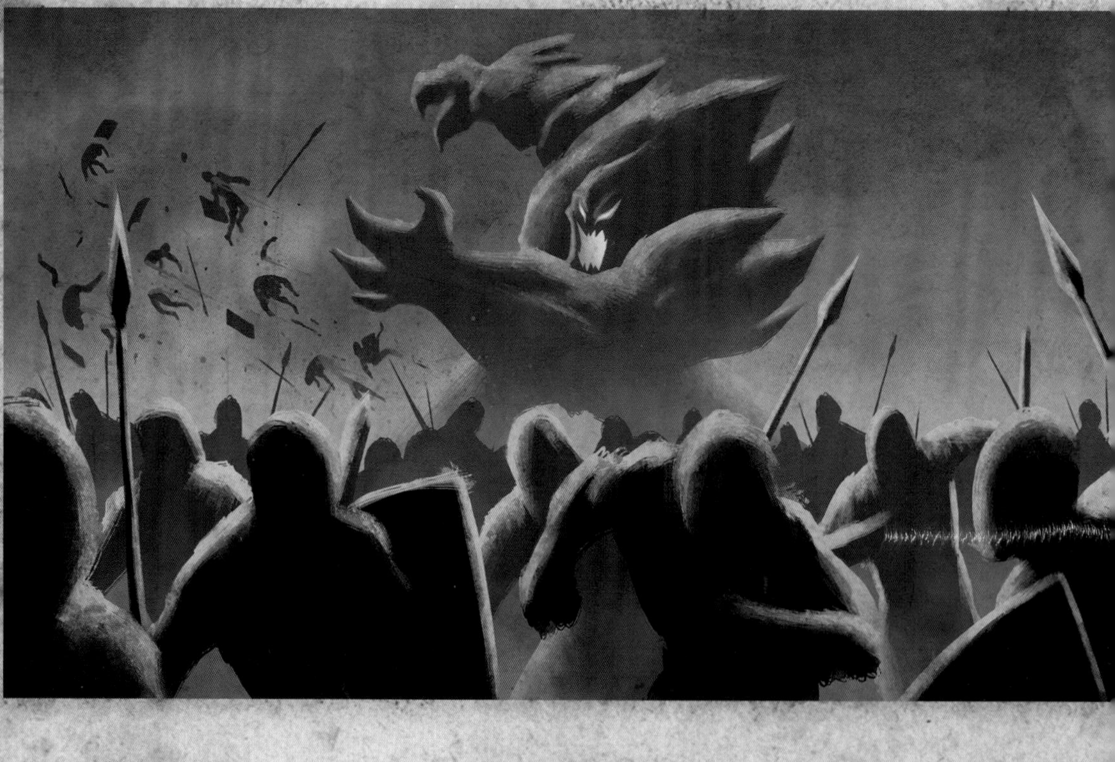

Memphis

Memphis was the capital city of the Kemetic Empire in the Old Kingdom. Located at the beginning of the Nile Delta, Memphis served as the gateway to the Mediterranean Sea and was within range to defend Kemet from any foreign invaders from Canaan. By being in such a strategic location, Kemet dominated regional trade and had easy access to the lush lands of the Delta, becoming a superpower as the world's food exporter. Many religious cults formed over the years in Kemet and power was structured and predictable, resulting in little internal strife for thousands of years.

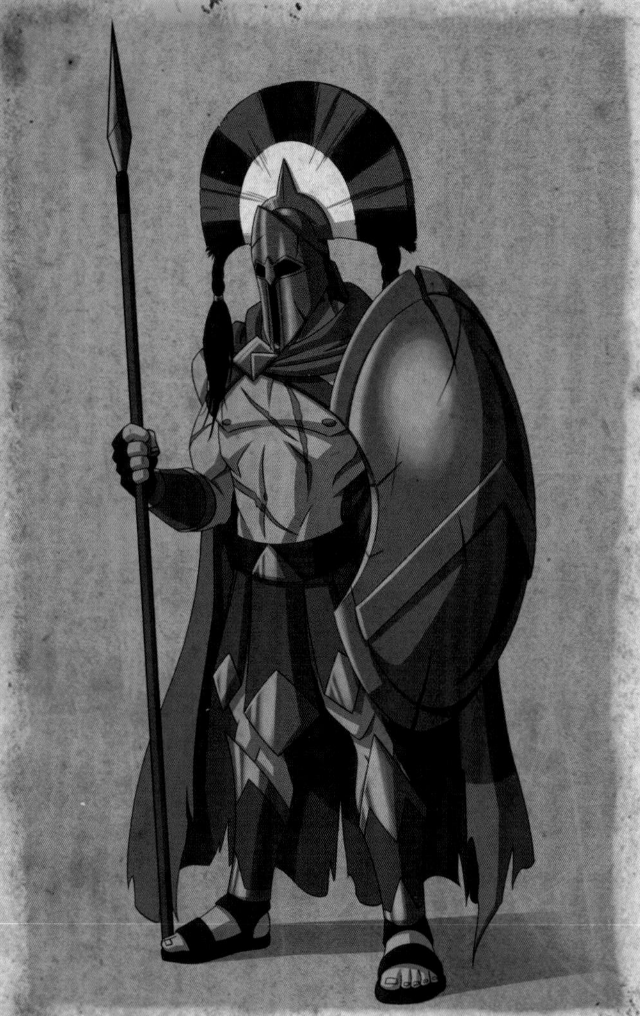

Spartan Society

Spartan society had an unusual caste system dating back to antiquity. All of the male citizenr trained exclusively for war while women handled the regular work society. In Spartan life, there we huge populations of slaves who all the manual labor the city-state needed to survive, and they wer treated quite harshly.

In Black Sands, we give an origi to this social practice by having Spartans be the only Greeks lef standing against the Titans. The Spartans also have great rage f their neighbors for not helping in the fight and put them to the wh for this reason.

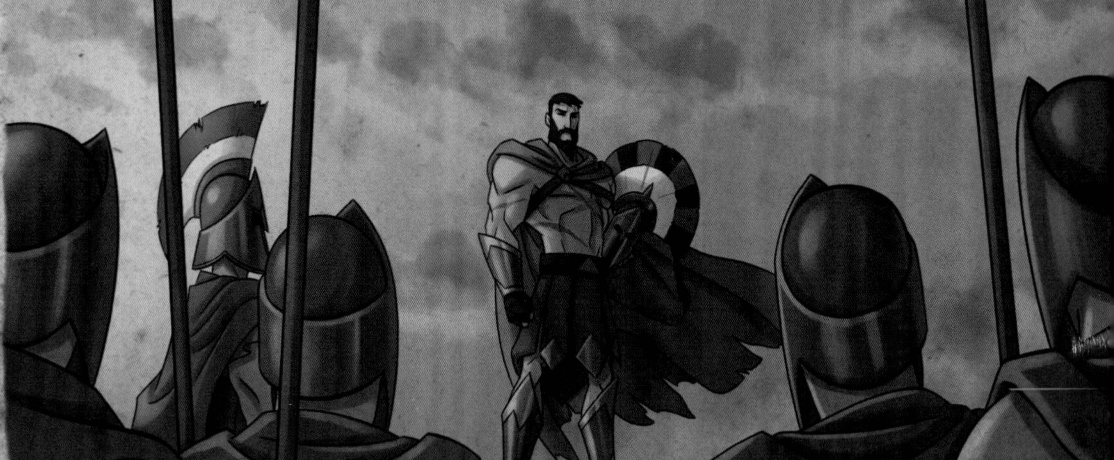